ALiBi
CREEK

A novel by

Bev Magennis

TORREY HOUSE PRESS

SALT LAKE CITY • TORREY

ALiBi
CREEK

This is a work of fiction. All names, characters, places, and incidents are either the products of the author's imagination or are used fictitiously. No reference to any real person is intended or should be inferred.

First Torrey House Press Edition, March 2016
Copyright © 2016 by Bev Magennis

Published by Torrey House Press
Salt Lake City, Utah
www.torreyhouse.com

International Standard Book Number: 978-1-937226-55-8
E-book ISBN: 978-1-937226-56-5
Library of Congress Control Number: 2015930136
Author photo by Erin Magennis
Cover design by Rick Whipple, Sky Island Studio
Interior design by Russel Davis, Gray Dog Press

For my daughter, Erin

"You take what you're given, whether it's the cornfields of the Midwest or the coal mines of West Virginia, and you make your fiction out of it. It's all you have. And somehow, wherever you are, it always seems to be enough."

—Larry Brown

ALiBi CREEK

PART ONE

1

THE TWINGE CAUSED BY A drop in barometric pressure shot from Lee Ann's shoulder up her neck into her left eye. Rain, the most cherished commodity in the southwest, made her sick. She turned from the bedroom window, fell back against her pillow, and shut her eyes against black-bottomed clouds stalled over the east mesa, multiplying, hanging there, heavy and close. Of course, she would not curse such benevolence, for across the range wildflowers, grasses, and trees had extended their delicate arms, embracing the recent moisture after cringing in defense of a hot, dry summer. But enough rain had soaked the land, and the plains, mesas, and mountains were plump and green from downpours that passed through quickly, dumping inches all at once.

She sat up and hugged her legs and lowered her head between her knees. Eugene laid his hand on the base of her spine and they breathed in unison. She needn't remind him that even gently rubbing her back increased her suffering. His hand rested where it was, its weight and warmth a comfort, if not a cure, and when he removed his hand the place he'd touched cooled as if a hot compress had been lifted.

At the courthouse, she struggled through work on migraine pills that had little effect, gathered her untouched lunch and sweater an hour early, and stumbled to the

3

Blazer, parked between the sheriff's cruiser and county treasurer's Subaru, her spot for over twenty years. Shielding her eyes, she reached inside her purse for the key (always in the outside compartment with comb, nail clippers, and yet-to-be-filed receipts) and drove past Walt's Mercantile and Art's bar, across the San Carlos River onto Highway 14, the smell of co-workers' perfume on her clothes and the sum of $346,000.00 wedged next to her eye, hovered over by three over-fed county commissioners. Her index finger found a hangnail on her thumb and she worried the thing the entire thirty miles to the family ranch—hills dark under low clouds, cattle facing west, no birds in flight. A shaft of light escaped through a crack in the gray ceiling and struck Solitaire Peak. Clouds bunched together patching the gap, and as if the lights went out, the land fell under shadow.

At the junction of Highways 34 and 14, she stopped to pick up the mail from one of fourteen battered mailboxes nailed to a rotting pine plank in front of the Alibi Creek Store. Normally, the contents of 477-C could be retrieved from the Blazer's window, but a Budweiser truck with its motor running blocked access to the boxes. She massaged her temples and forehead, twenty paces through the exhaust an impossible distance. Holding her breath, she leaned her shoulder against the door and pushed her way out.

Phone bill, electric bill, Vermont Country Store catalog, junk mail, and a letter in a regular white envelope with the stamp stuck on crooked. Return address: *Central New Mexico Correctional Facility, Los Lunas, NM.* Two *W*'s had been scribbled together, like a child's drawing of mountains, creating a jagged line under *Adult Prison Division.*

Wind twisted her skirt around her knees and one by one, fat raindrops pelted her head, becoming a deluge in seconds. She ran for the car. Inside, the windows fogged as great sheets of rain lashed at the hood and pummeled the roof.

Peace. In the last two years, she'd obtained some in good measure. And for that, gratitude, for contentment depended on a predictable routine with an attentive, capable husband who managed the ranch, and two grown sons, one a cattleman, the other college bound—a trio that for the most part worked in harmony, as if each member had mastered a specific instrument, their combined effort producing a light tune played at a steady tempo.

Trembling fingers tore at the envelope. Large, loose script paid no attention to lines or margins, climbed hills and descended into valleys without punctuation, one long scrawl that ran out when the page ended, the last crunched sentence ending with *Sept 29th*. Already an inch of water had accumulated on the gravel lot, pooling under the mailboxes and filling the bar ditches. Directly overhead lightning cracked a cloud and thunder shook loose its contents, blurring everything beyond fifteen feet. More lightning zapped the northern sky, the east, and west. The Budweiser truck flickered through the glittering haze, flashing for a moment as the great ark packed with creatures, she a dove with her mate among them, to be swept away to nameless and unchartered land.

In half an hour Alibi Creek, which ran through the Walker Ranch, would flood, leaving her stranded on the highway for hours until the water receded and she could cross to her house. Dinner needed fixing. Mother needed tending. The ranch's entrance was two miles north of the store, a familiar route driven as easily through sleet, dust, and rain as on clear days. She could make it.

The letter fell on her lap like an anchor, preventing her from driving on. Lee Ann clasped her hands under her chin.

"Lord, he'll be home in just over two weeks. Make this time different."

Could Jesus make out her words above the screaming wind and beating rain? Surely.

Five-thirty—time for Mother's medication. She inched the Blazer up the highway, windshield wipers swatting on high speed, and slid onto the turnoff, skidding down the dirt incline to the ranch. At the crossing she got out. The lazy creek had swollen into a fast-moving, muddy river with tree limbs and branches rolling in the current. Headlights beamed from the other side and Eugene's white diesel pickup moved steadily through the water.

She grabbed the handle above the door and pulled her body into the cab, dripping letter in hand. He touched her thigh, stretched his arm across the seat and looked over his shoulder, backing the truck a quarter-mile up the slick road.

Two houses stood an acre apart.

"Drop me at Mother's," she said.

"Get into some dry clothes first."

"Walker's coming back on the 29th."

He maneuvered out of a rut.

"A letter came today," she said, louder.

He stopped outside the mudroom. "I'll wait here while you change."

She opened the door. He didn't want to hear. No one in the family would want to hear, except Mother.

2

W ALKER WINKED AT THE SECURITY guard, pushed his hip against the metal bar on the EXIT door and pranced out of a two-year stint at the Central New Mexico Low Security Correction Facility, head back, yipping, imagining folks in Dax County reacting to his release. They'd grin, hands reaching inside their back pockets to confirm the location of their wallets.

First thing, after Edgar came to collect him, they stopped at Palms Trading Post in Albuquerque where Walker picked out a silver bracelet inlaid with turquoise and coral for his big sister, Lee Ann. Next stop Walmart, for a Coleman cooler and bag of ice. At Save-on Floral he had the girl cut the stems on a long bouquet of glads (Mother's favorite) to fit that cooler without crimping a single bloom, leaving enough room for a six-pack of Corona. He ordered Edgar to spread his legs and set another six-pack between the old ranch hand's boots, caressed the hood of the '84 pickup, beat it like a bongo drum, and climbed into the driver's seat. Destination: Alibi Creek.

Whooee! Blue September sky. BIG sky. Bigger than the ocean, 'cause even though the ocean was deep, it had a bottom. Using snorkeling gear, a man might study sea life spawning beneath the water's surface, but a space ship hadn't been invented that could scope out the heavens. The sky owned the sun, stars, and clouds. Its moon pulled tides, its winds churned up waves. Every single person's hopes and dreams flew up there and the sky held them all, with still room for more. God lived there.

Speaking of God, he was sorry. At this moment, he truly was. He did "borrow" that jewelry from Harry Simmons' wife to cover the debt on some land he'd bought. And although he'd needed the money in a hurry, he'd been a fool to take the stuff to Gallup, hockshop capitol of the United States of America. No sooner had he got Chase Cummings off his back over the late real estate payments, state police had come a-knockin', asking about the origin of the turquoise rings, bracelets, and necklaces at Big Boy Pawn. He explained he had every intention of buying back each item as soon as he raised the money. That didn't go over with the cops.

But, hey, he was out. He'd lost the Cummings place, but he might get his hands on Ross Plank's piece, a prize two sections not far from Mother's ranch, and turn it over to a prospective buyer in Arizona, the name given to him by Pat Merker, his cellmate.

Man, look at those harmless, cotton-ball clouds scattering shadows over the Plains of San Agustin. Sunflowers bowing and waving on each side of the black highway. Bordering Arizona and encompassing the west central mountains and high plains, Dax County happened to be the most isolated region in New Mexico—seven thousand square miles of wilderness, three thousand people, ten thousand elk, and not one traffic light or fast food restaurant. In the last several years, retirees from Arizona and California had started creeping into the area around Brand, the county seat, voicing their opinions at commissioners' meetings, organizing a Health Council, and instructing folks on how to conduct local events, their ideas on "improvement" upsetting old timers. Tucked in a fold of the Mariposa Mountains, Brand had been overrun by unfamiliar faces, the locals showing their disapproval by shunning greetings, refusing to indulge in small talk, and forgetting names. Walker, however, saw this small, steady influx of newcomers as Opportunity for Lucrative Creativity. He'd have a close look at Ross Plank's 1,280 acres, figure an angle to get him to part with it. The old skinflint had moved to Sierra Vista, Arizona, twelve years ago. What did he want with it, anyway?

Skinny as a pencil line, flexible as a wet strand of spaghetti, Walker seated his hat so far back a sneeze might knock it off. He never strolled, but scampered, took steps two at a time, three if he wasn't hung-over, swung around porch posts, jumped off fence railings and landed easy, lips sculpted in a permanent smile, no matter what the circumstances. *Modus operandi*: never allow a lady to open a door or struggle with a bag of groceries. Never let a man finish a sentence without topping his story.

At birth, his parents called him Gaylan, after his maternal grandfather, the name originating from ancient Greek, meaning "calm." After six months, they admitted their mistake, for he never kept still. Green eyes darted. He scooted across the floor like a wind-up toy, pulling himself up on any object within reach. At eight months he took his first steps and never stopped going, into the next room, onto the porch, across the yard, around the barn, and down to the creek. Edgar, watching his father chase him around the place, tipped his whiskey glass and said, "Well, you got half his name right," and dubbed him Walker the Walker, then just Walker Walker. Now a man of forty-two with ropey limbs, cantaloupe head, big ears, and long nose, Walker wore two-inch heels to add to his height (5' 10" *with* the boots). Extra tall hats, straw in summer, felt in winter, shaded silky hair the color of caramel candy. His presence seemed innocuous until he moved, then folks watched out. He jerked, leapt, hopped and sprinted, stirring up a mini dust devil all his own.

After three hours heading southwest, Walker turned the pickup north onto Highway 34, past a row of empty chairs on the Alibi Creek Store porch. Ahead, lumpy Bruja Mountain rose behind the west mesa, the Randall Range sprawled to the east. He checked the sun's position—one o'clock, too late for the morning coffee crew, too early for the mail. Taking the corner, he leaned on the horn and waved anyway.

"Ain't nobody there but Shelley and she's probably out back," Edgar said.

"When they hear I'm home, they'll be hanging around all day tomorrow until I show up."

A mile north he swung left onto the dirt road leading to the Walker Ranch. The pickup splashed across Alibi Creek, low after the seasonal monsoons, cottonwood roots like straws sucking up moisture, the water a silver thread looping through rugged mesas covered with piñon, scrub oak, and pine. Cattle grazed on strips of lush bottomland. An eighty-year-old weeping willow draped its limbs over the dark cedar-sided house he shared with his mother, partially concealing a black walnut loaded with nuts just outside the back door. Directly south, the chalk-white stucco walls of Lee Ann's place bounced off the landscape, assaulted by early afternoon light.

3

LEE ANN PULLED ASIDE THE maroon living room drapes and opened the sliding glass window. Below her, along the length of the house, red hot pokers and beds of annuals had suffered from the first frost. Yesterday, she'd crushed a few precious remnants of summer, letting the petals and leaves sift through her fingers. God had His plan for rest and renewal, for flora and fauna, for beginnings and endings, bounty and famine, floods and drought. And God had His plan for people, for mothers and children, husbands and wives. Brothers and sisters.

The dark blue pickup crept its way up to Mother's, the dogs racing out to greet it. Walker lifted a bouquet from the back of the truck. Edgar, rumpled and weary as the hat he wore, limped off to the bunkhouse, shaking his head as Walker bowed to the trees, his words delivered by the breeze whether she wanted to hear them or not.

"Hello there, old willow and handsome cottonwoods. Well, howdy, you ugly mutts. How've you been? No, no, get away from them flowers. They're for Mother. I said, no. Go on, now. Git!"

But Patch and Blue, like all Lee Ann's pets since childhood, begged for his hand. Her loyal companions played aorund his legs as he danced up to Mother's house, flew up the steps and charged in without knocking.

"Never mind who feeds you," she mumbled, "hauls you to the vet for shots, and picks stickers from your ears. Go ahead, lie in front of Mother's door and wait. He'll come out when he's good and ready, maybe in five minutes, maybe tomorrow, some hair-brained notion on his mind, and not give you a second thought. It's me who cares. Me."

She ran her hand along the plaid sofa. A catalog order form blew off the windowsill and she stooped next to the front door to retrieve it. Everyone entered the house through the mudroom off the kitchen, so the door handle was as shiny as the day it had been installed. Other than that, the room was lived-in, with a threadbare rag rug, a pine coffee table stained with rings from forgotten coffee mugs, end tables stacked with Northern and Cabella catalogs, cream-colored light switches smudged with fingerprints, and molding dinged by work boots. Anasazi and Mimbres pottery discovered on the Walker Ranch and surrounding mesas lined a high shelf on the west wall, and bone tools and ancient rock implements covered the fireplace mantle. First husband, Wayne, who'd helped Dad build the house the year before they married, had mistakenly placed the big picture window sixteen inches off center. Despite Dad's horsing around and Mother's blueberry muffins, he hadn't smiled once during construction, or many times afterwards, hadn't ever apologized for this mistake, or anything else.

She frowned at the asymmetry. A naive girl with romantic dreams, she'd chosen a husband in haste, without consulting the Lord. At twenty, marriage had been expected—the white dress with lace bodice, party shoes, a rose bouquet (bought at the Safeway in Round Valley and kept fresh in a Styrofoam cooler)—as were the babies she longed to birth and nurse.

Wayne used silence, which at first seemed like a clean slate on which to write the future, as a weapon. Comfortable alone, he avoided family occasions, tolerated affection, seldom returned it. A fire lookout position on Solitaire Peak came up and without consulting her, he took the job, leaving for four months every summer. When he returned, attempts to draw him out were met with indifference. Come for a walk along the creek. *Not today.* Let's treat Mother and Dad to dinner at the café for their anniversary. *You take them.* The kids need help building a fort. *I'm busy.* Normal household activities, games, and roughhousing drove him outside. A portrait of Dad covered the patched wall where, during an argument over disciplining the boys, he'd thrown an Anasazi stone axe, missing her head by inches.

She'd tried, for herself and for God, for forever and ever, whenever, however, whatever the circumstances. When Eugene stepped in, as if he'd been Lee Ann's intended partner all along, as if Wayne's sole purpose had been to participate in conceiving the boys, the eight-year marriage ended.

She closed the window and straightened the drapes. They were faded and shabby, in need of washing. The color had once seemed elegant—a joke in the country. She stood on a dining room chair and unhooked the curtain rod and let everything fall to the floor. Time for something light and colorful. The window frame filled with knee-deep golden grass, almost concealing the narrow path to Mother's. The sky to the north was cloudless and brilliant above willows crowding each other along the creek where it swung west and east again. More than once, Eugene had offered to center the window. It would take only a day or two, but it seemed more important to live with the irritation—a nudge, reminding her to appreciate Eugene all the more.

For two years, with the help of visiting nurses from Socorro and the daily care of Grace Delgado, Mother's health had held steady. Eugene and the boys had managed the livestock and run the place without distractions, two calves dying last winter the only catastrophes. But now Walker's truck was parked at Mother's, the bumper dented from drunken accidents, the doors scratched from swerving into the corral, the windshield cracked straight across.

She'd been a mild-tempered two year old when Dad brought Mother home with an adorable bundle of trouble and all eyes turned away from her brown hair and soft brown eyes, as if captivated by a brilliant star dimming all others in the heavens. She'd coped with Walker by faking amusement, imitating her parents' adoration of this towheaded marvel. Oh, they'd loved her, no question of that—Mother, with that sure hand and no-nonsense voice, had taught her to bake, sew, and garden. Dad, at once ornery and kind, had set her in the saddle, held her waist as they practiced the two-step, and let her tag along to the cattle auction. But even as a toddler, Walker dazzled, and each year his exaggerations doubled, tripled, his voice grew louder, his arms waved, his body bowed forward, bent back, mouth blabbing as he played the room, everyone exclaiming, "Oh, no, impossible!" while laughing, enrapt.

He'd follow anyone, especially her—get so close she'd shiver at his breath on her neck as he yapped at her back, blurting a stream of nonsense. She'd raise her eyebrows, lips frozen in a smile, for indifference led to yammering, pestering, pleading, until she responded with put-on enthusiasm. Arguing was pointless. He out-talked, out-convinced, and out-smarted the most rational line of reasoning. She'd sneak off to walk the dogs up the canyon, or tiptoe onto the back porch with a glass of lemonade and her Bible, identify and mimic bird songs down by the creek, or snuggle up under the bedcovers with a Nancy Drew mystery. Walker couldn't be alone. An empty room held no challenge, an open field little interest. He thrived on the manipulation of people and events.

Shortly after her eleventh birthday, he'd stolen money from Mother's bureau and placed one of her barrettes on the floor. She'd been questioned and punished. Crying, she pointed her finger at him and retrieved her jewelry box to prove the contents amounted to nothing more than her allowance. Sent to her room, responsible for all the chores for two weeks and ordered to stay home from the 4-H dance, she hid behind the bathroom door and jumped him, pulled his hair, punched his stomach, and kicked his legs. He absorbed the assault without a peep and went limp, his mouth curling into a grin as he left her whimpering with sore knuckles, runny nose, and red cheeks.

With no one to turn to, she hiked up the canyon and fell on her knees asking Jesus how to handle hatred of a wily sinner who could appear innocent as an angel, who displayed affection, but would as likely throw her into the pigpen. A hand reached down and lightly touched the top of her head and Jesus answered, saying He understood, that reading and heeding scripture would instruct how to approach Walker and all troublesome situations with love and compassion. Pastor Fletcher had preached those words, but coming directly from the Lord, they took on deeper significance. *Love* meant more than *feeling gushy about*. *Love* implied deep appreciation, devotion, and acceptance. And *compassion* meant more than *feeling sorry for*. *Compassion* called for sympathizing with the suffering and struggles of all creatures. In her bedroom, she propped her pillows, kicked off her boots, and tucked her toes under the folded pink and white gingham quilt at the foot of the bed. Delicate fingers turned the Bible's pages, thin as tissue paper. Words written in old-fashioned language transported her to the *beginning*, when people wore loose clothes belted with ropes and lived in tents without toilets or running water. The stories were complex—full of intrigue, twists, and turns, woven from intricate family histories, tales of betrayal and loyalty, good and evil, feuds, and acts of forgiveness. She named her sheep and rabbits Samson, Delilah, Esther, Rachel, Moses, Sarah, and Solomon and would sit among them in the barn dressed up as Queen Esther, reading aloud Ruth's story, plopping one of her rabbits, David, before the milk cow, Goliath. "How will you, a mere bunny, gain enough power to destroy this giant? With God's help, of course, with Him on your side!"

The kitchen door burst open and boot heels clattered down the hall. He waved his hat and swooped her off her feet, set her down like a precious object and holding her shoulders, peered into her eyes.

"Welcome home," she said, patting her hair in place.

"Lannie, you don't know how good it feels. *This* good." He spread his arms as if to embrace the entire world and everything in it, twirled around and hunkered over, dug into the pocket of his jeans and slipped the Zuni bracelet over her wrist. "Got a beer?"

How he got anything done with one hand permanently around a beer can, she never knew. Later in the day it would be a tumbler of Jack Daniels. Her body leaned slightly to the right, in need of Eugene in his sweat-stained denim shirt, hat shielding blue eyes outlined in deep purple, the iris just like an iris. When Eugene was around, rules were obeyed, the truth was spoken, equipment was maintained, and property respected. But Eugene was out among the cattle, repairing fence, or checking the stock tanks. She adjusted her weight evenly on both legs and called on Jesus and He appeared in a crimson robe with gold trim, haloed, semi-opaque, and stood behind her as a guide.

"In the fridge," she said, running her thumb over turquoise and coral, the inlay smooth as polished river rock. "Then we'll go out to the barn. I want to show you what the boys have been up to before they come in."

She heard the pop, waited while he took the first gulp off the top, and they set off across the field.

"Jesus, man alive! Look at the color of those leaves! Yellow as egg yolk. Prettiest fall I ever seen. Guess those trees heard I was coming home. Guess they're putting on a show just for me. Mother cried like I'd been gone twenty years."

"You must have found her improved."

"About the same. No better, anyway. I thought she'd be talking by now."

"Our routine is so regular, I can pretty much read her thoughts." And yours, too. You think you're going to liven up the house, bring joy to an afflicted old woman.

"You want to be careful," she said. "Or you'll not ease her condition, but make it worse. The light you've put in her eyes will turn dull if your shenanigans confuse her." Not to mention the liquor on your breath, your quick step, and fast talk.

"Don't you worry."

Worry she must, for he flung a stick high in the air, catching it like a boomerang, as if he hadn't a care, as if Mother, disabled and mute due to a stroke, would be thrilled to witness anything he did, from burning his breakfast toast to playing cards to resting his feet on the coffee table switching TV channels fast as he blinked. Had she, just once, commanded the same attention, she might have become gregarious, even daring, whooped and hollered at the rodeo, allowed the boys to lead her around the dance floor at the Volunteer Fire Station Bar-b-que, shared the thrill of her first kiss with girlfriends, plotted tricks on Halloween.

They climbed the slight incline to the barn, feral cats jumping into hiding as they passed the open doors. He took a deep breath.

"Oh, yeah! Hay, manure, and mouse shit!" he said, detouring inside to run a circle around the old lime green Yanmar tractor.

She plodded on around the corner.

"Well, look-ee here," he said, catching up.

A sow sprawled in damp earth, six piglets snuggled up to her belly.

"Yes, ma'am!" Walker said. "I see honey glazed ham with raisin sauce and mashed potatoes." He ran his hand along the pipe fence. "You done your research, I suppose. Remember when Dad brought home those half-dozen baby turkeys? Christ. They trailed after me like I was their mother. I'd hear them pecking at the door while I ate lunch, sending a message in code: 'Hurry up! What are we going to do next?' If Dad and I drove off, I'd glance out the rear window and I swear, they'd be staring at the pickup through the dust, lost as orphans." He leaned back and gave Lee Ann the once-over. "You're getting some gray in your widow's peak, but you know, it becomes you. Makes you look sort of dignified. Wise. Of course, you're still damn good looking, in a quiet sort of way. If I compared you to an animal, it'd be a doe." He jumped the fence. "Don't be alarmed, Mama. I ain't going to steal your babies. Just want to hold one of these darlins. Hey there," he said, raising a piglet to his face. "You're going to make a mighty fine dinner."

"Pastor Fletcher and Harley McKenna are each taking one," she said.

"Harley looks like a sow. He doesn't need but the skinniest. The fattest goes to Fletcher. It's beyond understanding how he keeps on a pair of pants."

He oughtn't talk. Prison food hadn't done him much good. His chest sunk slightly, as if his stomach muscles had been tied in knots that wouldn't come loose. His Adam's apple poked out of a scrawny neck too skinny to support a head with a nose that size. Still, he looked younger than his forty-two years.

"I'll give you a haircut," she said.

"All right then. Only no buzz cut. I'll go bald naturally, thank you. And make it quick. I'm meeting Jo at Art's."

"I thought you'd join us for supper."

"Tomorrow. That's a promise."

Tomorrow. The distant future. Twenty minutes from now any plan would be forgotten. He didn't waste a second of today thinking about what might happen after the sun went to bed, got a good night's sleep, and topped the mesa in the morning. She started back toward the house, weary of his behavior. Hers as well, for accepting that the bar crowd was more important than family, for forever taking second place, for trying too hard to maintain a pleasant attitude. Her two-year reprieve had ended. But wait, she must make the best of an inevitable situation. Give him a chance. Forget the shame resulting from his past schemes, believe those escapades were over. Trust the boys were mature enough to resist farfetched, ill-fated temptations. Forgive. Forgive again, and again... *put on tender mercies, kindness, humility, meekness, longsuffering; bearing with one another, and forgiving one another, if anyone has a complaint against another; even as Christ forgave you, so you also must do.* Colossians 3:12-13.

All right. Let's get the haircut over with, get him out the door and off to town to hypnotize the Saturday night crowd, and end up Joanne's concern for the night.

In bed, she sought the arm she'd needed that afternoon. Eugene's muscles were hard, his skin soft, excepting his calloused palms, and she pressed his hand, its touch as sensitive as its texture was coarse, to her breast and brushed her lips against his neck.

He lay quietly, his breathing even, staring at the ceiling.

She pulled away.

"Tired, that's all," he said.

She stroked his brow, wide beneath wavy, dark hair cut at a respectable length. Most often, a finger hooking a finger, a certain word or chuckle, or a discussion about buying a new tractor led to kisses, and more. Last Saturday he'd acted the rogue preying upon an innocent victim, making her laugh as she played at resisting, until, helpless against his charm, she swooned and submitted. Now his arms rested at his sides, his head tilted toward the wall.

When it seemed he'd fallen asleep and she'd turned on her light and opened her book, he reached for her hand. Her finger traced the vein that ran from his wrist up the inside of his arm, the one that bulged when unloading hay or handling building materials. His voice was tender, even when quoting mundane information from a price list and his expression was intriguing when frowning over a bill incorrectly tallied. He carried a lame hen so she didn't squawk and scooped up a kitten so its belly rested in his palm, its four legs sprawled, and before long that kitten purred as if it had found heaven. She moved his beautiful, able hands onto her hips and whispered his name, enticing him to linger over parts of her body and devour others. And he obeyed.

But when she unfolded her arms from around his neck and held his face, his eyes remained closed. Coyotes howled up the canyon and he aimed his ear toward the window.

She put on a nightgown—flannel, now that the weather had changed—and lay on her side facing him, her arm tucked under her head.

"I'd like to buy Scott a laptop," she said.

"The more he studies, the less interest he'll have in the ranch."

"He'll need one for college. I've been setting something aside each week."

"We'll need to hire a hand."

"He's so smart. And lonely here, not at all interested in raising pigs."

"He's never complained."

"I know," she said. "That worries me."

He kissed her forehead and rolled over.

"You worry too much."

She switched off the lamp and extended her leg, inviting his to rest alongside, or over it.

The boys were different.

"I want my own room!" Dee had demanded when he was nine. "I'm sick of living with snakes and bugs and lizards. They belong *outside*."

"Scaredy-cat," Scott said.

"He lets them out of the box. It's creepy!"

"The snakes I keep are harmless," Scott insisted. "Nature is interesting."

"Nature is *outside*!"

Scott cut out pictures from *National Geographic* of country houses in Austria where families lived in open lofts above their animals. Down the road, he said, Iris Herrington nursed motherless lambs in her pantry for months. Lee

Ann agreed to accept the lizards, mice, and horny toads that Scott invited to share his bedroom, and raised no objection when he housed injured birds and slept across from snakes.

Dee threw a fit.

And so, Eugene had added an extra bedroom onto the east end of the house.

Scott wandered the hills collecting rocks and scat, then measured, sorted, and filed his findings. He couldn't walk from here to there without stopping to inspect a leaf or insect, turning some newly discovered specimen this way and that under a magnifying glass slipped from his back pocket. Pottery sherds were carefully arranged on his dresser next to a snake box with glass sides in which he rotated living creatures. In bed, under the beam of a flashlight, he entered data in a notebook.

Last month Lee Ann had picked a common flower and asked Scott its name. Retrieving a binder with fine drawings of plants that grew along the creek and in the fields, he identified this one as *blue vervain* or *Simpler's joy/verbena hastate/verbanacea family*, an herb used to cure respiratory ailments, depression, nervous disorders, and bladder infections. She'd held the book to her chest like a newly found treasure and turned each page, studying medicinal benefits of familiar "weeds" she'd brazenly stomped over.

Dee, a natural cowboy, was as easy on a horse as in a pickup. He would insist on herding cattle long after it was declared a failing proposition in the southwest, and protect his inheritance from falling into developers' hands. When asked why he didn't study, he said, "The only historical facts worth remembering are the owners of every acre of land back to when Hispanics first settled this county." From the start, he hammered forts and go-carts, tore the rototiller apart and rebuilt it, roped the porch post, handled guns, tools, and equipment as if they'd sprouted from his fingers in the womb. He danced, competed in rodeos, played guitar, and brazenly chased Ginny Alcott, the girl he'd fancied since sixth grade.

Dee looked at the stars, awed by their brilliance. Scott named the constellations.

Pastor Fletcher warned that knowledge was a dangerous thing. An inquiring mind led to more questions, which in turn spurred discontent. One had only to put their faith in God and He would provide. On this point, Lee Ann disagreed. When boiled, *yerba negrita* could be applied as a hair rinse. Early Native Americans layered *mullein* leaves for diapers and used the *yucca* root for shampoo and its leaves to make fine paintbrushes. Brewed *cota* made a fragrant, relaxing tea. She adjusted the covers. Scott would have his computer.

4

THE SAME HEAPS WERE PARKED in the same spots in front of Art's Bar. Only difference, a headache rack had been welded onto Perry's dented Ford. Carl rode for years on tires with no tread, just aired 'em up daily. Those who crossed the creek had mud-splattered bumpers, those who lived in town had spotless hubcaps. Plush dice hung from Terry Lyn's rearview mirror. Seemed like Moni was still hauling the same two years' worth of trash in the back of his pickup, his brain or his vehicle incapable of following directions to the dump. And there at the end, Owen Plank's spiffy Toyota Tundra, so clean you'd never guess he drove it every day over all sorts of terrain for a living.

Art's gathered a collection of down-and-outs, five o'clock happy hour patrons, rowdy ranch hands, well-behaved alcoholics drinking to maintain and women who went for one or all of the above. In a town of 396 residents, this meant about a dozen regulars and a fluctuating flow of customers, depending on the season. In the fall, hunters packed the place. During the winter, the odd truck driver took a lonely seat at the bar. Spring attracted those itching to get out of the house and summers were steady, with tourists adding a touch of awkward sophistication to the scene. Once a month, Art shoved the chairs and tables against the walls and couples scooted across the worn wood floor to the No Name Band's rendition of classic country, the evening incomplete without at least a couple of brawls interrupting the two-stepping, women fighting as hard as the men.

Walker snuck in with downcast eyes, ready to burst into laughter and shake hands, squeeze the old boys' shoulders and pat the ladies' bottoms.

"You all watch yourselves," Art yelled. "Don't turn your back. A hardened criminal has entered our midst."

Walker made the rounds, some happy to see him, others turning away, and found Jo at the far end of the bar, face partially hidden by a puff of frizzy red hair, a half-full Manhattan in front of her. Expensive date.

"Get off that chair, gorgeous, so I can swing you around."

She cocked her head.

"And risk you tripping over a chair? I got osteoporosis."

"Nice welcome," he said.

She traced the rim of her cocktail glass with her finger and broke into a big smile that wrinkled her face.

"Shit, Walker, you know I'm damn glad to see you. I'm so happy I'll buy the first round."

"No way, darlin'. It's against my principles to have a woman buy me a drink."

"You don't have principles."

"Speaking of which," he leaned close and breathed in her ear. "Let's get out of here for half an hour, if you know what I mean."

She stubbed out her cigarette and rested her hand on his wrist.

"Oh, I hear you," she said. "But you don't hardly rate a D in the lovemaking department. That little pecker of yours is broke, or asleep, or dead, and you know it. Let's not embarrass ourselves."

He straightened and shoved his shoulders back.

"It worked good enough to produce two kids."

"Twenty years ago. With a hot, young wife."

Danielle.

"I guess Lee Ann told you she's back," Jo continued. "Living in a trailer on Ross Plank's ranch."

"Shit. No." The very land he aimed to turn.

"Maybe she didn't want to be around for your reaction."

"I'd have found out sooner or later," he said.

"Later's always better."

He took the stool next to her, signaling two fingers to Art.

"Fill me in," he said, lighting a cigarette, taking a drag, and placing it between her lips.

But a small crowd had migrated toward him, gathering behind his back, asking questions. He turned around and launched into tales of prison life, how minimum-security incarceration was just that, but jail nonetheless. Hell, no, he wouldn't have run the risk of walking away. Yeah, he'd made some good buddies, actually read a book about life in Mongolia. Nah, there were no riots. Lots of bitching, though. The food was about what you'd expect, maybe worse. Yeah, his cellmate, Pat, was pretty cool. Yeah, they got along. Did he repent? He'd have to think about that one.

5

SUNDAY
SEPTEMBER 30, 2007

HE CRACKED ONE EYE, THE tiny, square window carved out of cinderblock and Pat Merker's snoring and farting on the cot beneath him absent. The sun shone like a floodlight across his jeans and boots. He shifted his feet toward the edge of the bed and squinted at the ceiling and over to a map of the world on the west wall. Except for removing the pin-up posters, Mother hadn't changed his room since he was sixteen. Plastic horses posed atop the oak dresser with the loose drawers, awaiting riders, ready to trot off the edge seeking adventures. He rolled on his side, creasing cattle brands of Dax County ranches stitched onto a quilt by Aunt Stella, a Christmas present when he was eight. Dad's leather chaps, now brittle, hung from a peg next to a bookcase crammed with prehistoric Mogollon and Anasazi Indian pottery, the bottom shelf cluttered with arrowheads and tools discovered while hunting or hiking the surrounding territory. As soon as he could get up, he'd take down that number 37 purple and yellow football shirt tacked to the wall, a reminder of the one season he'd played. He detested sports. The only things you got after you'd won were cheers and a bruised body, no profit in terms of cold hard cash. Mother'd be upset if he threw that shirt out, but hell, the poor gal wasn't climbing out of that chair to dust his room ever again. Must be Lee Ann wielding a feather duster now.

He groaned and sat up, sending thanks to the benevolent soul who'd delivered him to this bed without a scratch and left him fully dressed. Jo must have driven him home. Or Owen Plank. He'd sidled up to Owen and inquired after his dad's health, saying what a shame Ross lived all the way over in Sierra Vista, far from his great grandkids and his home for over sixty years. Going into a nursing home! Now, that would take some money. The old man ought to consider selling his two sections.

"Admit it, Owen," he'd said. "Pack rats have been the only inhabitants of the house and barn for twelve years. Even if Ross eventually leaves you the land, wouldn't you rather have the money now? Don't you want to provide your Dad with the best care? Improve your own house in town? Renovating will take twice the work and double the cash if you wait until the old man dies. Man, it would be easy to sell a beautiful piece of property like that. As a matter of fact, a guy in Mesa, Arizona, has already expressed interest. For a small commission, I'll handle the sale."

He'd said, "Owen, you don't need a small ranch. You're a townie with a regular job. How long has Saul Gann's Construction kept you on as surveyor? Thirty-one years! Don't you get enough of the outdoors traipsing all over the county peeking through that transit-level? How old are you now? Fifty-nine! I hear your grandkids are pretty smart. Don't you want to send them to college? Maybe out of state? Time's running out on your opportunity to do all the things you dreamed of doing with your own life. Buy an RV, a flat-screen TV. Book that cruise to Alaska. Take Rita to Vegas."

Fortunately, he'd been drunk enough or had sense enough to back off when Owen said, "Walker, I'm going to stuff your head in the toilet bowl and drown you if you don't shut up."

He stumbled into the bathroom and threw cold water on his face and rinsed his mouth, ignoring his old toothbrush in the holder next to the matching soap dish. Mint toothpaste made him sneeze. A shot of whiskey was what he needed. In the dining room, he peeked through the china cabinet and opened the buffet, but with Lee Ann in charge, there wasn't a drop in the house. He latched the cabinet doors and walked into the living room, approaching Mother from the side.

"Good morning, beautiful," he said.

Her head turned a fraction, but not her eyes. The slightest crease crinkled her left temple.

"Cardboard," she said.

"Now, I know you said, 'cardboard,' but I think you mean, 'good morning, son, coffee's in the kitchen,' so I'll help myself to a cup. I think you want me to have a full breakfast, but my gut's in no shape to handle anything like that. Is Grace coming today, or does she still go to church regular? I imagine she and Lee Ann got a special deal with God for reserved seats. No need to answer—as a matter of fact, you don't need to do anything but sit there and look as pretty as the girl you were when you married Dad. Course, I don't remember that, but I've seen pictures. When you took me to school the first day of first grade, I was burstin' proud of my mother. I even remember the skirt you wore, tiered, like something an Indian woman would wear, and the pink blouse. Grady's mom was perky and Jessie's mom was sharp, but you were downright pretty. That's the only word to describe how you looked. And I see you that way today." He kissed her forehead.

Returning with a cup of black coffee, he scooted the ottoman and sat at her feet.

"This stuff tastes like hydraulic fluid," he said, making a face. "Lee Ann must have made it. Or Dee. When was it brewed? Last week? I swear we had better joe in the can. I'll tell you all about it one day, but this morning, or is it afternoon, I've got to locate my truck."

He got up and dumped the coffee in the sink.

"Mother, blink twice if you remember Owen bringing me home. Okay, blink twice if you heard Jo's voice." He bent over, peering at her face. "Well, what about waving your hand… that's okay, darlin'. You were probably asleep, lost in never-never land, dreaming of the days when the house smelled of fresh bread right out of the oven. You bet I remember when you used to bake. Everything you made came out golden brown, rose to the perfect shape and tasted better than the fanciest pastries from a French bakery. Not that I ever been to France, but I can't imagine anybody topping your cinnamon rolls or chocolate cake. And pies! I know you taught Lee Ann, but she doesn't have the magic. Never did."

He crept behind the barn to the pigpen and jumped into view, ran up to Dee and hugged his shoulder, grabbed Scott with his free hand.

"Mornin', boys."

Dee stepped back.

"It's time you quit calling us 'boys', like we're one unit," he said, setting his bucket down. Scott turned off the hose.

Walker cocked his head to the side, ran his eyes over each one, top to bottom. They were nineteen and twenty now, out of high school. Scott older and smarter, Dee taller and tougher. Scott lean, wearing glasses, a tee shirt, and baseball cap; Dee broad, in a denim shirt and weathered Milano cowboy hat.

"Well, okay. I can see you aren't boys anymore, but full-grown men with an exciting new enterprise."

"This is just something for now," Scott said. "I'm off to college in January."

Dee said, "I'm staying. School's not the only place to prove you're smart." He nodded at Scott. "He's promised to come back for butchering at fall break, perfumed in formaldehyde from dissecting frogs."

"Better 'n cow shit," Scott said.

"I admire you boys. Oops. *Excuse* me! I admire you, *Scott* and *Dee*. Pigs are a whole other trip. Myself, I'd rather travel with cows. But, a good pork chop is hard to beat." He leaned back and stuck out his stomach, drawing circles on it with his palm. "I can just about taste that chubby one on the end." He picked up the bucket and dumped the feed over the fence. "Let's finish up and I'll buy you a beer."

"Not me," Scott said. "I'm helping Mom clean out the flower bed this afternoon."

"I'm your man," Dee said.

"Good. We'll use your truck. Mine's at the bar."

"Always an angle," Dee said.

His pickup was right where he'd left it, key in the ignition. They drank a beer. Dee said as long as he was in town he might as well stop by Ginny's.

"Talk about an angle," Walker said.

He drank a couple more. Art grumbled about Sundays being dead. Hell, Sundays were always dead. Even drunks observed the Lord's Day, staying home to avoid Bible thumpers recognizing their vehicles parked outside the wrong places.

Driving back, he turned at the Alibi Creek Store and waved at the old geezers blistering their asses on rickety benches, whizzing by too fast to notice that they didn't raise an eyebrow, stop mid-sentence, or wave back.

The sign used to read "Plank's Plot." Now it looked something like "P n 's ot." Walker mouthed the words and bumped down the dirt road, turned north along the creek, crossed over to where the land leveled out, and followed fresh tire ruts between two round hills. On the backside of the south rise, a white trailer snuggled up to Ross Plank's long abandoned ranch house. The Escondido Co-op would have hooked up her electric and some poor slob, trying to keep his eyes off her tits, had probably run a line to Ross's well and connected a pipe to the septic tank.

Some kind of insect seemed to be crawling inside his stomach, causing an itch he couldn't scratch. A red light spun like a strobe around his brain, flashing *warning…warning…* She'd screwed up his life more than once, or they'd screwed up each other's, and here she was squatting on property he intended to sell.

He didn't know what she drove now, but no vehicle poked its nose from behind any building, tree, or bush. Must be a couple of cats hiding out somewhere, no dogs. He walked around the trailer, tried the door, and stepped inside. The same ratty brown throw she'd knitted twenty years ago lay in a heap at the end of a beige couch. Christ, Danielle, throw the damn throw out. Though winter hadn't announced its arrival, she'd be pulling the blankie over her ever-cold feet, stuffing her icy fingers between her thighs. On the fridge, cupcake magnets held pictures of their two daughters and their kids and he peered at each face, strangers to him now. That boy of Laurie's looked the spitting image of him when he was a toddler. My, my. He and Danielle, grandma and grandpa. Married at eighteen. Couldn't wait until they had sense, thought the party would never end. Two kids by the time they were twenty-one. Hands tucked inside his armpits, he bent forward. No men in the pictures.

She still drank Corona, still kept the opener on top of the fridge.

The trailer was a relic, built in the sixties, bedroom door missing, leaky bathroom faucet, peeling paint throughout, floor like a trampoline. Come November, she'd sure as hell need that ratty blanket against cold wind leaking through quarter-inch cracks around the windows. A longhaired black cat stared at him from the double bed, the covers drawn up haphazardly, pillows bunched together.

"Meow," Walker said.

The top dresser drawer was open, some underwear and socks bunched together. This was shelter to a person without possessions, a person getting by, a person come home because every other option had been exhausted. He wished he could muster up some pity.

A car door slammed and he walked down the hall to meet whoever it was climbing the steps.

"I should have known," she said, dropping a bag of cat food by the door.

He sucked in a deep breath. She was even better looking than the woman who'd spit at his feet, taken each of the girls by the hand, revved the engine of her dinky, yellow Nissan and taken off fifteen years ago.

Familiar, yet strange. Husky voice. Tall body shedding her purse, flinging her jacket on the couch. Graceful, though. He hadn't remembered that, or maybe she hadn't yet developed grace at twenty-seven. Her touch had always been light, a caress. When working animals and doing chores, the palms and backs of her hands had stayed soft, her slender fingers tipped with manicured nails. She'd been one to linger in the tub, pamper her body with lotions and scented soaps, color her fine hair platinum blond. Ranch women seldom bothered with cosmetics. Danielle outfitted the bathroom with a magnifying mirror rimmed with little lights. Tweezers, eyelash curler, liner, mascara, rouge, and lipstick littered the counter around the sink. Colorful ribbons, earrings, and necklaces dangled from hooks. Barrettes and rings filled the medicine cabinet. When she left, the bathroom was what changed most, swept clean of feminine indulgence.

Maybe it had been worth it, maybe all that plucking, dabbing, and soaking had preserved her youth.

"You look good," he said.

"You don't."

He winked.

"Still got the charm, though."

"Depends on your definition of charm. I see you've helped yourself to my fridge."

"Just one."

"I can't wait to hear what you're doing here."

He was about to say, "I was thinking of asking you the same question," when it hit him. He smacked his hand against his forehead. She was letting Owen Plank *plunk* her in exchange for a place to stay.

"Let's catch up," he said. "Tell me what you been doing all these years, give me details about the girls, what the grandkids are named, their ages."

"It's a little late to be caring," she said.

"People change," he said. "Where I been the last two years, a man does a lot of thinking."

"Walker, you're a liar. I don't believe a word you say."

"Well, you might be right. But then again, you might be wrong. I won't say I missed you all this time, but I sure as hell ain't lyin' when I say I'm glad to see you right now." He hung his head and shuffled his feet.

"Don't act pathetic."

She handed him another beer and he followed her outside. No cattle had grazed this land for twelve years and the bleached grass arched high. Scrub oak, brush, and piñon circled the base of the hill, like a fringe of hair on a bald man. The place seemed to whisper, its tranquility a secret only they shared. Halfway to the old barn they each grabbed an end of a toppled picnic bench, set it upright, and sat with their backs to the sun.

"We did have some good times," she said. "Long ago."

"Look here," he said. "I have a proposition for you."

"You were such an asshole, though."

"I'd make a lot of folks happy if I changed my name to Asshole Walker."

"You should. From what I hear, most call you that, anyway."

"Now, listen. If you cooperate with my plans for this place, you'll be sitting pretty for a long time." He rested both elbows on his knees and glanced at her sideways, shaking his head. "I don't know if I can trust you."

"You probably can't." She threw him that look, the one that said she was ready to jump on an unbroken horse blindfolded and risk the consequences for the thrill of the ride. "Unless there's a hell of a lot of money to be had."

6

Her Bible rested beside a portrait of Jesus on a small round table in the corner of the dining room. The table was covered with Grandma Edna's tatted, floral and honeycomb patterned tablecloth with scalloped edging. A bookmark with praying hands and the words *Do Justice/ Love Mercy/Walk Humbly* remembered the section currently under study. Lee Ann smoothed the embossed leather and carried The Book out to the truck where Dee, in pressed jeans, plaid shirt and vest, sat behind the wheel and Scott, in one of his cleaner baseball caps, held the door.

Vines covering the wire fence that enclosed the small churchyard had been nipped by frost, the leaves shriveled and brown. At one time the fence had supported Cora Russnell's wild roses, and after Cora died, church members tried to maintain the garden, but over the years everything but the roses thrived, weaving unruly tendrils through the open mesh. Each spring new growth sprouted over old vines, creating a thick wall of weeds no longer in need of an armature. Lee Ann led Scott and Dee through the gate, frozen in place by untended growth. Something ought to be done about it.

Folding chairs, eight on each side of a narrow aisle, made up nine rows. Grace, always early, had saved their seats. Lee Ann remarked, as she did every week, how tall Grace's great grandson had grown. She nodded at the sheriff and his wife, slipped by the county commissioners and their wives and sat down, a son on each side. Pastor Fletcher stepped in front of the pulpit and reached for the heavens, calling on the congregation of seventy souls to rise for the first hymn. Lee Ann sang, and as her voice blended with the rest, the song grew from timid to exuberant, lifting her on her toes. The pastor's tall, skinny form faded. Scott and Dee fell from her sides. Parishioners dissolved and the beam of skylight expanded and spread throughout the room. Her chest swelled and the cross hanging behind the pulpit glowed and the piano's notes rang pure and clear. The magic spot on top of her head opened, connected to certain eternity, from where she and all living things originated and would return.

And she sang:

> *My opening eyes with rapture see*
> *The dawn of this returning day;*
> *My thoughts, Oh God, ascend to Thee*
> *While thus my early vows I pray...*

And God selected her voice from the melody all around, from the harmony of millions of worshippers in distant cities and other lands, calling upon her singular devotion, asking specifically for her requests, reassuring her to place all problems in His hands. And she prayed, Lord, guide me. Silence my tongue so that You may do Your work. Increase Eugene's patience for Walker. Lead Walker to meaningful, honest work. Generate peace between them. Instill the glory of Your kingdom. Assure Mother that she will continue to be cared for. Ease her suffering. Edgar's, too—winters are so hard on him. Provide the means for Scott to attend college in January. Clear my conscience while performing my duties at work. Correct my superiors' misdeeds. Amen.

Pastor Fletcher's sermon went on and on, endlessly on, drawing sighs from various parts of the room, ending when all hope of a conclusion had been abandoned. As a reward for their endurance, the congregation filed into the adjoining kitchen for coffee, tea, and cake. Ginny Alcott sidled up to Dee with a flirtatious smile that broke into a loud laugh at something he said. She wore black jeans and a frilly white blouse with too many open buttons, her hair swept to one side and held in place with a red plastic clip. Hard and soft, boisterous and subtle all at once. Lee Ann turned to Eileen and Jim Raines and congratulated them on their new grandbaby. Scott disappeared with a couple of teenage boys and would remain outside until it was time to leave. Agnostic, he called himself, skeptical about God and religion. He was wrong. Logic and science could never explain the miracle of creation.

At five o'clock, she carried a Corningware casserole to the back of Mother's house, swooshing through a mess of leaves by the kitchen door. Autumn roused memories of chile roasting, Mother canning tomatoes and making jam, a favorite gray wool sweater scratchy against her skin, kicking stones across the highway while waiting for the school bus, Dad rising before dawn to go hunting, Edgar organizing the hired hands for roundups, butchering and branding, and with all the work done, the anticipation of a long winter's rest.

These days, after the chutes were closed and the lassos wound and hung, Eugene's longing to doze in a recliner by the woodstove lasted about three short weeks. He and Dee would fidget, exchange a private signal, and mosey out to the workshop, using any excuse to escape on horseback as soon as the sun stole the frost from the day, leaving Scott slouched on the couch researching the developmental stages of a certain beetle.

Lee Ann swung her leg from side to side clearing a path with her foot, the sound crisp as stuffing tissue paper into a box. The wind came up and corralled the leaves into a spiral before whisking them away to settle in the field. *This is the day the Lord has made. We will rejoice and be glad in it.* Psalms 118:24.

"It's me, Mother," she called.

On Mother's return from the hospital, the family had gathered for dinner in this kitchen. Lee Ann had served Eugene first. A man needs to feel special. She'd tied Mother's bib. A mother needs respect. Dee, pass Dad more potatoes. Here, Mother, let me get you some rice. Eugene, the rare meat is at this end. Mother, just one more spoonful of applesauce. Eugene, more iced tea?

She'd told Eugene, "Toss your work gloves on the counter. Put your elbows on the table. You can burp in front of Mother," but he ate in a hurry and after wishing Mother a good evening, excused himself. She wasn't his mother, after all. A week went by. Two. And when he wouldn't, or couldn't relax, Lee Ann began preparing an early dinner for Mother, and after feeding her, joined Eugene and the boys at home. An extra hour on her feet, when she could have contacted Perry about buying the right laptop for Scott, or shortened her black skirt to fit with the current style, or planted a cherry tree in the spot where the peach tree had died.

Whistling "The Farmer in the Dell," she set the dish on the old cook stove that served as decoration these days. Grace had cleaned up, down to the perfect fold of a dish-towel, tidy in the way of older women with time on their hands, who paid attention to dust on the telephone and mud on the welcome mat, crumbs on the counter, and spots on the windows. At the end of the day, her tea cup remained the only item in the dish rack. Although they'd grown up on ranches miles apart, Grace and Mother had remained best friends since childhood, tight as fingers locked in prayer. After marrying, they'd met most afternoons on horseback and synchronized shopping trips by car to the closest grocery store, two hours away in Round Valley, Arizona. When telephone service came, with the men cleared out and kids off to school, they'd found an hour to exchange recipes, gossip, and confide worries. Now, close to eighty and widowed, Grace visited every day to fix Mother's lunch and despite Lee Ann's protests, kept the house as neat as Mother would have wanted it.

Lee Ann envied their friendship. She didn't share secrets. She talked to God and asked for His help while planting the garden, driving to and from work, and hiking to her special place up the canyon. "Dear Lord, help me... Help me discipline the boys so they know I mean business, yet cherish them. Help curb my suspicion of two co-workers snickering on their break in the common room. Help me show respect to my superiors. You know I find them unworthy. Help me care for Mother tenderly. You know of my impatience. Help me sustain compassion for Walker. You know of my contempt and resentment and loathing."

Scott or Dee checked in on Granny at some point during the day, wiping their feet, sitting by her chair or bedside, Dee talking weather and livestock, Scott reading from a novel selected from the Bookmobile. The decision to bring Mother home, rather than install her in a nursing home, had taken only a moment. Lee Ann had told the boys, "If circumstances were reversed, Granny's top priority would be her children and grandchildren."

When Lee Ann's father had lost the race for county treasurer, Mother beamed as if he'd won. When the 1979 Archaeological Resources Protection Act prohibited digging

Indian artifacts on public lands, Dad got out his shovel, anyway, and Mother declared the pottery had been discovered on the Walker Ranch. And Walker... the trucks he'd wrecked, people he'd lied to, money he'd scammed, equipment he'd borrowed and "forgotten" to return—Mother supported every excuse and alibi, swore on the Bible in court in his defense, and allowed him to sell off large portions of the ranch to cover his debts. If she'd been well, the worst weather wouldn't have kept her from making weekly visits to the prison.

As for Wayne, Mother had run him off with a hoe, threatening to use a rifle if he showed his cheating face on the property again (the wretched recluse could have invited any number of women up to the lookout tower!). Truth was, Lee Ann had been the one to respond to Eugene's smile the morning they'd met by chance at the dentist's office in Round Valley. Her hair had been shoulder length at the time, and after her teeth cleaning she was headed to the hairdresser to have it cropped to ear length before going to the feed store.

Eugene said, "I'm curious to see how it turns out." A man couldn't possibly mean that, but Eugene did, and when he met her at the feed store, he cocked his head and grinned. He loaded the dog food, cat food, straw, and protein pellets and asked her to share a pizza at the new place down the street. He'd been sent from Wyoming to manage the 7 Bar Ranch, eighty sections owned by a wealthy Californian, and had been there about a year.

He said, "I'd love to show you the prettiest view in the whole world." And they'd gone to the red cliffs overlooking the gorge along the New Mexico/Arizona border. And from there... well, from there...

She hadn't asked, but begged the Lord's forgiveness for deceiving Wayne and worse, for abandoning to lust. She searched the Bible for examples of pardoned infidelity and finding none, appealed to God's mercy, all the while giving in to the churning in her pelvis at the sight of Eugene leaning against his white pickup, ankles crossed, waiting for her.

"It took only a second, Lord, for a friendly conversation to veer toward flirtation, for an innocent look to suggest something more, for that something more to turn into a rendezvous and for that rendezvous to develop into love. You judge the act, Lord, and make no exceptions. If You can't understand, I must forgive myself."

Mother's good hand rested in her lap, the right one curled into itself. Her wheelchair faced the TV, with Katharine Hepburn and Cary Grant bantering back and forth in *Bringing Up Baby*. Leaves dropped to the ground outside the window and black walnuts bonked against the roof. Lee Ann passed in front of the screen and removed the light blanket covering Mother's knees.

"I brought tuna casserole," she said, releasing the brake and turning the chair. "Remember the pale blue shirt with white fringe and pearl buttons you made on the treadle sewing machine for my first county fair competition? And the raspberries we collected in the Apache willow basket? How the bees loved those blossoms! Mother, I'll be honest. I've asked God to watch over Walker, because although Eugene thinks I can influence him, I can't. And although you believe he can do no wrong, he can. I've placed the future in the Lord's hands, as you have taught me, and trust He will increase Eugene's tolerance and curb Walker's unrestrained impulses."

She kissed Mother's cheek, smelled her hair, thin and wispy as a summer cloud. She'd need a shampoo this week. Grace had laid out the evening's pills in a neat line of various sizes and colors. Lee Ann tied a clean bib around

Mother's neck and spooned a portion of the casserole into a bowl, poured iced tea, added a packet of Splenda, inserted a straw, and stirred.

"Thirsty?" she said, holding up the glass.

Pale blue eyes gazed toward the cookie jar on the counter. Slip the straw between her lips. Place a fork in her good hand. Poke a noodle. Pick up the fork when it falls on her lap. Do not sigh. Do not show impatience. Mash the noodles, alternate with mouthfuls of pureed prunes. Please, hurry and finish. Eugene and the boys are hungry and the beans need to be heated.

With Mother's arm over her shoulder, she carefully, inch by inch, one baby step at a time, guided her onto the porch to feel the breeze. She eased her back in the chair, parked her in front of the TV, and changed channels. *Jeopardy* and *Wheel of Fortune* aired from six to seven p.m. She covered Mother's legs.

"I'll be back in an hour to get you ready for bed."

Only six o'clock and already the sun touched the top of the mesa. The weeping willow's shadow darkened the path. Tomorrow, she'd bring a flashlight. Pants and blouses for work lay in a heap in the dryer, needing ironing. Ham should be thawed for lunches during the week, the beans had to be heated. Walker might take over the morning routine, but he couldn't be depended upon to wake up on time, if he came home at all. He'd never leave a note, or call to say he'd be late. Expectation would lead to disappointment. Here it was Sunday night and it was anyone's guess where he was.

7

MONDAY
OCTOBER 1, 2007

L EE ANN ROLLED OVER, SHUT off the alarm and rested her arm across Eugene's pillow, his covers already pulled up. Wayne, first to share her bed, had started the night lying still, then like a great machine, sputtered and heaved, taking the blankets with him. Eugene slept quietly and soundly on his left side, facing the window, his leg in contact with hers throughout the night. Before bed, he emptied his pockets, placed his billfold, loose change, and keys on his night table, stepped out of his boots and set them together beside the closet, toes to the wall. He folded his jeans and put the day's shirt and underwear in the hamper.

From his hand, she accepted a cup of coffee made just right, a little milk, no sugar. The mornings were dark now, the sun waiting until after seven to send its rays over the mesa, the plaid bedspread lit by the lamp on her night-stand. One of the boys ought to rake the leaves around Mother's house and spread them on the vegetable garden and flowerbeds.

"Thanks," she said. "Today, will you remind Dee to…"

"Rake the leaves by Kay's back door." He stuffed his bill-fold in his back pocket and picked up his keys. "Everything's under control," he said. "Except your brother."

She wrapped her hands around the mug.

"Pretend he isn't here," she said, matter-of-factly—no problem, unless you choose to make one.

"That'll work for about a week."

She poked her feet out from the covers.

"Eugene, he's a fact of life. Even if he'd leave, which he won't, I have no right to kick him out. Mother would die. After she's gone she'll watch from heaven, heartbroken, when he sells his half of the ranch and squanders the money." She ran a hand through her hair. "Hopefully, she'll know I did all I could. She must know I'm doing all I can now."

"You can set rules. If he breaks them, out he goes."

She patted the mattress, please, sit down and talk this over.

He stood at the end of the bed, solid as a tree trunk, and as still.

"It isn't up to me to make rules," she said. "He and I are equal. You've disliked him from the first moment you saw him."

With the edge of his palm, he swept yesterday's loose change into a metal box. "As I remember it, at ten in the morning I could smell booze twenty yards away, upwind, while he sauntered around, assuming I'd fall for the B.S. he'd concocted to get out of doing a decent day's work."

"He's always been a drinker."

"A drunk."

"Call him what you want, he's here to stay."

"Until his next prison stint. He's one step away from a hard-core criminal."

She tucked her feet back under the covers and yanked the covers up around her chest.

"Please, a little compassion." Enough of this talk or she might cry.

"I'm not God, Lee Ann. I don't pity the weak, unless they make an effort. In my book, everyone does his share, drunks don't get special treatment, and rules aren't meant to be broken." He reached into the closet for his vest. "I'm off to Round Valley. I'll pick up any groceries you need."

Down the hall, the boys were getting breakfast, their morning talk muffled behind silverware and cereal bowls sliding across the table, the fridge door opening and closing.

"Some green beans, if they have any, and a sack of potatoes. He might want to help with roundup and branding."

"So long as he keeps a good distance from me."

She stood up, tipped her head forward, back, and around, stretching her neck. The simplest way to co-exist with Walker was to ignore him. The Lord taught *turn the other cheek, seek humility and forgive those who trespass against others.* Trouble was, Eugene didn't believe in the Lord. If pressed, he said nature was his god and when she explained that God created nature, he stepped back with a pleasant expression and cast his eyes somewhere near her elbow, a reluctant student receiving a lecture, counting the minutes before being released from class.

"Be safe," she said, straightening her side of the covers. The ranch still belonged to Mother. Lee Ann had power of attorney. Eugene and the boys ran things. Walker *helped.*

Eugene took a notepad from his vest pocket, added *green beans* and *potatoes* to his list.

"You be wary," he said.

She whistled "Moon River" while buttoning Mother in a yellow housedress with a Peter Pan collar and wheeled her into the kitchen.

"Monday mornings are so rushed," she said, heating water for instant oatmeal. "Today, I've got to organize the paperwork for Thursday's meeting. It's Tina Wiley's birthday and the girls are taking her to lunch at the café. I suppose I'll have to go. You know how I hate Vera's food—she's dipped into the same can of bacon grease for twenty years."

Walker's head poked around the corner.

Lee Ann's hand flew to her chest. "You scared us to death!"

Mother looked straight ahead.

"Yep, up early, alert as a jack rabbit, ready as a cocked pistol. What a day! I can give her breakfast, Lannie. You let me know. Of course, I can't do it as good as you, but I might make it a little more interesting, huh?" He pinched Mother's cheek, jumped in the air and turned a half circle before landing.

Lee Ann sat down and stirred the oatmeal.

"You should see the apples weighing down those trees at Plank's place," he said, rubbing his hands together. "I'm going to pick you ladies a couple of bushels today, before the birds get 'em. Apple crisp sounds good, doesn't it, Mother, with Cool Whip? Or vanilla ice cream?" He reached for the McCall's cookbook on the shelf above the stove, scanned the index and flipped the pages. "If there's cinnamon, pecans, flour, and oatmeal in the pantry and butter in the fridge, I'll bake us a batch this afternoon."

"That might be considered trespassing," Lee Ann said. "Or stealing."

It wouldn't matter. Now that apples had tempted his taste buds, he'd heave a ladder into his pickup and fill as many boxes as he saw fit.

"Danielle gave me the okay," he said.

Lee Ann cleaned Mother's chin with a damp paper towel, wheeled her into the living room and adjusted the volume on the TV. Judy Garland sang *Clang, clang, clang went the trolley…*

"You don't happen to have a couple of twenties on you..."

"Like always, there's cash in the cookie jar," Lee Ann said. She checked her watch. "I'm leaving. Grace comes between ten and eleven."

The pink stucco walls of the new, two-story courthouse were as out of place in Brand as a rose in a cactus patch. Lee Ann entered through glass doors in need of a shot of Windex and hurried across the terrazzo floor under a life-size portrait of Sheriff Woolie (1938–1946), arms folded across his plaid shirt above an elaborate silver belt buckle, cold blue eyes aimed at two men and a woman seated outside the Motor Vehicle Department. She turned left, toward the steps to the commissioners' office on the second floor, back straight, eyes straight ahead, prepared to offer nothing more than a pleasant "good morning" to anyone she met.

Harley McKenna, one of three Dax County commissioners, raised his head from the drinking fountain, early for a man who never waddled in before eleven. The girls in the office were right—he looked exactly like a mountain with a tennis ball on top.

"Lee Ann! Just the gal I was hoping to see." He snatched her arm and with a lopsided gait, swinging a black Naugahyde briefcase, pulled her into a corner at the foot of the stairs. Too fat to turn his neck, he pivoted a half circle and checked the hallway. A pudgy hand with a finger choked by a wedding ring withdrew a thick file containing fiscal allocations for various departments. He licked his finger, leafed through the papers, and thrust a stapled report titled "Federal Disbursement for Needy Women, Infants, and Children" at her waist.

"You look just like your mama did at your age," he said, every pore on his nose distinct as pencil dots. "She always reminded me of Deborah Kerr, and you do, too. Lovely, just lovely."

He squeezed her wrist. Words just above a whisper oozed out one side of his mouth.

"We've agreed $62,600.00 is an inappropriate designation for this department."

She smelled his breath, disguised with Scope, and turned her head and reached for the wall.

"We'd like you to re-distribute twenty percent to the County Highway Department."

We meant Harley, Ed Richter, and Saul Duran, the county's commissioners. *Agreed* meant once again, they'd met in closed session without her. The nerve of these men! Unwitnessed decisions were illegal. County law required that she, as county manager, be present at all meetings.

This time, confront him! Challenge Harley on altering state and federal funds and hatching corrupt county deals. All highway contracts are awarded to Saul's brother-in-law; construction projects, despite competitive bids, go to Harley's son; commissioners' relatives and friends fill any openings in county government. Lord, assure me I won't appear arrogant if I speak up. I am Your servant, not a slave to unethical men. Empower me with the courage to demand what's right. Give me a sign that You will protect my job, my benefits, and retirement.

Harley tightened his grip on her wrist. "Lee Ann, the papers."

"Sorry, Harley... yes, of course."

Her desk was situated in front of a window that didn't open, facing a large room with three workstations. She stowed her purse and sweater in the bottom drawer. The wall clock said 8:26. She put her lunch in the common room fridge, pulled a few files, and reread the minutes of last month's meeting, irritated with her subordinates who drifted in between 8:45 and 9:00. She lived farther out than any of them and managed to be prompt.

Her job required managing the courthouse according to the commissioners' wishes and years ago, after weighing the pros and cons of reprimanding tardiness, she opted in favor of preserving a pleasant atmosphere. In reality, twenty minutes made little difference in conducting county business, the letters "ASAP" about as effective as posting a "No Poaching" sign in the national forest.

The agenda for Thursday's meeting called for, a) the commissioners' written response to the U.S. Forest Service's refusal to allow the county to dump garbage on federal land without meeting the EPA requirements for the proper liner, b) consideration of Aaron Stark's request for county funds to run a small timber operation in the abandoned sawmill that had been shut down by the federal government fifteen years ago, and c) an address by the New Mexico State Engineer on water rights.

The same issues over and over. Although commissioners had come and gone over the years, she might have been dealing with the same three ranchers sitting poker-faced behind big bellies—facts and figures flying over their heads, procrastination their talent, private deals, secret budgets, and resistance to change their pact. Appointed when her uncle had served as commissioner, she'd held onto the position by obeying orders, storing facts, keeping secrets, and remaining impartial. But cutting funds for needy women, infants, and children—my God!

She opened the filing cabinet and began gathering data for the State Engineer and estimates for operating the saw-mill, miffed when the phone rang. Caroline hadn't arrived to answer it.

"It's me," Eugene said.

"I thought you were going to Round Valley."

"He's taken my truck."

She left the filing cabinet drawer open and walked to the window. Here we go. Nothing has changed. Still a brat. Still impossible. Doesn't try, doesn't care, can't focus, won't listen, selfish, selfish, selfish!

"There must be a reason," she said. Lord, I have begged You.

"He could have asked. Told me he was borrowing it. I've got to pick up that lumber today."

"Use Dee's truck."

"That's not the point," he said, and hung up.

8

"WHERE'D YOU GET THAT BIG, white diesel?" Danielle asked. "And what do you mean, I've got to move off this property?"

"I don't know which question to answer first."

"I'm due at the motel in half an hour."

"I don't guess anybody'll be checking in at nine on a Tuesday morning."

"They're not paying me to *guess* when folks check in or out. I've got to be there in case."

"I'll meet you back here tonight," Walker said.

"Owen's coming by."

Lord almighty. He tilted his head back, fluttered his hand over his heart and smirked, a snort bursting through his nostrils.

"To check the heater," she said.

"Right. Here's the deal. You aren't going to need a heater because you're going to be living in town instead of this crappy metal cage. I've got to haul it off so's I can sell this place."

"Does Owen know about this?"

"No. And if you want a cut, that piece of information will not escape your lips."

He kept his eyes on the dirt so he wouldn't get dizzy while she paced a circle around him, waving her coffee mug.

"Walker, I'm not giving up my home and moving, or getting mixed up in any deal with you unless you marry me."

Marry! Was she crazy? The word gave him the heaves. Why, they could barely exchange a sentence without driving each other's blood pressure to the point of busting an artery.

"Now wait a minute," he said. "We'll sign a simple contract."

"And stick me with hiring a lawyer to chase you around long after you've blown the money? I'd be a fool. Community property is the only way to insure I get what I'm owed."

"And all my debt, if things go bad."

"I'll take my chances. After I pocket my share, we'll get a quick, no-contest divorce."

She grabbed her jacket and swept past him, the scent of some flower floating off her, confusing the seasons.

"I'll think about it," he called after her, his words lost against her '96 red Jeep Cherokee rattling down the trail, license plate hanging on by one screw, tail pipe scraping the dirt.

He plucked a flask from his back pocket and sloshed whiskey between his teeth, licked his lips and wiped the corners of his mouth with the back of his hand. Those apples did look just right for picking. Okay, ladder and boxes. Right about here, under that low branch so laden it might snap any minute. He climbed four steps, reached out his arm and admired the rosy fruit in his hand. Might just take a bite. Mmm, mmm. He tossed the rest over his shoulder and shifted the box, making certain it sat firmly, and gently stacked the apples, careful not to bruise them. He paused for another swig, taking in the pasture rolling half a mile to the east fence line and beyond, all the way to the highway where

Danielle's jeep looked about the size of a ladybug. A red-tailed hawk patrolled the field and a slight breeze shifted the leaves, sunlight dancing a light step between the branches. For a stretch, Alibi Creek went underground, but still fed the cottonwoods and boxelder that blazed two yellow streaks along its route. Suppose a man saw the world from up here every day. Suppose the law required everyone walk on stilts. They'd have to raise ceilings and windows. Doors would be taller, way taller. The air'd be cleaner. You couldn't smell the earth. That might be better, but probably worse. Best take this box down before it gets too heavy. Marry Danielle again! Jesus. That would sure get her off this property, but right into his bed. Maybe they could work that out. Situate her down the hall in Lee Ann's old bedroom until they dissolved the marriage in a few weeks. He pulled the box toward him and swung it to the side, lowered his left foot to catch the rung and missed. He yelled "whoa!" and toppled sideways, apples pelting his face and arm, and did a quick somersault, landing on his feet as if he'd practiced the fall a hundred times.

"Christ almighty." Just thinking about Danielle threw him off balance.

"Here we are, Mother," he said, placing the first of the boxes on the kitchen table. "Grace, there's plenty. I put a box in your car."

"Scissors," Mother said.

"Why, thank you, Walker," Grace said. "I'm just getting ready to head home." She bent toward Mother's face. "See you tomorrow, Kay."

Walker opened the cookbook to the page he'd marked with a toothpick. While the oven pre-heated he got a beer, reached into his wallet, took out a crumpled piece of paper and dialed the number on it.

"Keith Lampert? My name is Walker Walker. Right, same name first and last... unusual, yes... I'm a friend of Pat Merker. I believe he told you I'd be calling... let's see, I think he's got a few more weeks. He said you were looking to invest in some property in southwestern New Mexico. We're in Alibi Creek...seventeen miles as the crow flies from the Arizona state line, about a two-hour drive through beautiful mountains from Round Valley. I do think it's about the best land for the best price you can find, an exceptional piece—two sections, 1,280 acres, house and barn. Well, we prefer to deal in cash...you would? Let's see, I'll check my calendar...Wednesday will be fine. Give me your email address and I'll have my wife send directions. All right then, Vera's Café in Brand at one o'clock."

He opened the pantry and took an apron off the hook. Yes indeed, the future looked promising. There was a little work to be done before Wednesday—a trip to Sierra Vista with a quitclaim deed, a marriage, lining up Dee and Scott to move Danielle's trailer up the canyon behind Mother's house. Good thing those boys have strong backs. Those cinder blocks by the barn will work for a foundation, provided that piece of junk can survive the move in one piece.

"Okay, Mother, here we go," he said, tying the apron behind his back and rolling up his sleeves. "First, peel, core and slice the apples...."

9

Lee Ann found Eugene and Dee down by the workshop unloading Dee's pickup.

"Excuse us for a moment," she said to Dee, looping her arm through Eugene's, guiding him toward the chicken house. Under the ancient, gnarled oak tree ground squirrels scurried about, scrounging acorns from under the leaves. The chickens came running and pecked the ground, expecting scraps.

"I see you got everything you need," she said, pointing to the workshop. "Please, don't make a scene about Walker taking the truck."

"Maybe if I wrung his scrawny neck just one time, he'd understand there are other people in the world with business to tend to."

"You know it won't make any difference. He won't even get angry, just shuffle his feet, slither off, and carry on as usual. You'll work yourself up for nothing."

Eugene stopped walking. "You got to quit defending him."

Take heed to yourselves. If thy brother sins, rebuke him; if he repent, forgive him. Luke 17:3. "Please, let's give him a chance. Let's see if prison has affected his behavior."

"Lee Ann, you're kidding yourself. You know it. I know it. It didn't even cross his mind that he might be screwing up my plans. You and I are playing some game where

Walker's concerned and I'm still going along. His disregard for everyone in the family is way out of line, for you, especially." He spit. "You tell him, if there's one more incident..."

She removed her arm. Eugene never spit.

The sound of the tailgate dropping and boards clapping came from the shop.

"Dee'll be needing my help," he said. "That lumber's green and heavy."

"I'd best get Mother's dinner," she said, starting back.

Normally, his eyes followed her and she'd swing her hips a little, or glance over her shoulder and shoot him a quick smile. Before meeting Eugene, she'd walked purposefully, taking big strides, arms swinging at her sides. But seeing herself from his perspective, she shortened her steps, turned her fingers outward, let them flutter just a bit, and reeled in her elbows, sometimes thrusting a shoulder forward in sync with the movement of her hips, like a movie star. Walking without enticing him would simply be a means of getting from one place to another. Of course, the Lord provided many things to admire when walking alone—grama grass seed heads curled into fuzzy commas, dried yarrow clusters on a plant she now knew, thanks to Scott, healed open wounds, and Solitaire Peak, a symbol of eternity formed eons ago and destined to be here eons from now. She turned to see if Eugene was watching. He carried a board into the shop, his back to her.

She heated a bowl of stew in the microwave, and whistling "Lara's Theme" from *Dr. Zhivago*, carried it to Mother's. The leaves had been raked from the back door. From the kitchen, the smell of baked apples drifted into the mudroom. By the sink, a colander of cores and peel overflowed onto the floor and a blanket of flour sprinkled with oatmeal covered the counter. A dishcloth and apron lay in a damp heap, rust-stained with cinnamon. Walker, a beer in his left hand, potholder in his right, tiptoed in front of Mother, whose eyes were fixed on some vague spot above the counter.

"I tell you, Mother, Plank's orchard is downright bountiful this year, perfect as the Garden of Eden. And there I was, Adam! I took a bite. From the forbidden fruit! I ate of it!" He clutched his stomach and laughed. "I should have stripped naked and hung a leaf over my privates." He dangled the potholder over his crotch, scooted around the table, bent over and peered underneath. "Shhhh…looking for the snake," he whispered.

"Really, Walker," Lee Ann said.

As if jerked by God Himself, he sprang up and twirled around.

"Ain't that perty?" he said, pointing to the baking dish. "I'm a darn good cook when I put my mind to it."

"How about putting your mind to cleaning up."

"Yes, ma'am. That's next on my list."

"You might have asked before taking Eugene's pickup."

He lowered his head.

"I will next time, Lannie. I just borrowed it for a couple of hours. Mine's low on gas."

"He needed it this morning. You didn't think. You never think."

"Christ, I know Eugene. Our Leader. Our Main Man." He patted his lips with his fingers and hooted a war cry. "Big Chief. You think I want to piss him off? No way."

"The chief has a limit." She reached into the drawer for a spoon and parked the wheelchair at the table. "Now, let's not argue. We don't want to upset Mother."

He made more of a mess cleaning up than he had while cooking, banging the colander and utensils against the porcelain sink. In the midst of splashing water all over the place he tossed the sponge on the counter, excused himself to go to the bathroom and never returned.

She went for the broom and dustpan. Duped again, stuck with the consequences after he's had his fun. And in front of Mother! The man has no shame. He needn't be hunting for the snake. He is one! We've been evicted from heaven because of the likes of him.

And the great dragon was cast out, that old serpent, called the Devil, and Satan, which deceiveth the whole world; he was cast out into the earth, and his angels were cast out with him. Revelation 12:9.

10

WALKER FUMBLED THROUGH THE RAGS behind the seat of his pickup and retrieved a crumpled road atlas, turned to Arizona, and located Sierra Vista. South of Benson, northwest of Bisbee. Population: 43,000. From Alibi Creek, about a five-hour drive. At the assessor's office, Eileen handed a quitclaim deed across the counter with a questioning glance, but he told her that baby blue sweater sure did bring out the roses in her cheeks. Was it angora, cashmere? She'd better watch it, he might have to touch it to find out, and it was obvious where *that* would lead. She turned away saying, "Get on with you," and he dashed out before the color of her neck toned down a notch.

He sprinted over to the motel. Danielle had the use of the computer and knew how to work it. She owned one of those digital cameras and he left her with orders to take pictures of the land behind Plank's house, views without the dilapidated outbuildings and rickety barn, scenes so pristine they swelled the throat and made the eyes water, and include a couple of shots in an email to Keith Lampert. From behind Walt's, he collected a bunch of cartons that smelled of oranges and bananas and drove out to Ross's property and tossed them inside Danielle's trailer with a note. *Get packing.*

At Mother's, he shook the manila envelope Lee Ann used to hold the month's receipts, dumped the contents onto the kitchen table, and inserted the quitclaim deed. The cookie jar contained $122.00 He took $80.00 and a box of apples, cut a bouquet from the last survivors of a clump of Maximilian daisies beside the front porch, and drove back to Brand. Jo would likely be in the back room of the county clerk's office. He hooked one arm around the doorframe and waved the daisies. When there was no response, he followed the flowers into the room.

"Don't be screwing up the records," he said.

"Says one who wishes he could screw anything."

"Honey, we can leave that topic alone and switch to a more pressing matter. Cash."

"I don't have any."

"Yes, you do. Let me fill this jar with water. I brought you the last of the flowers and a box of apples."

"So thoughtful. How much?"

"You're welcome. Three hundred. Don't shake your head. I'll give you half in a week and the rest, plus fifty, in two weeks."

She reached into her purse for her checkbook.

"Not a penny more until I get this back," she said, licking her finger and tearing off the slip. "Just looking at you means losing money. And don't think of paying me back *on* time so you can squeeze more out of me *next* time. I'm onto that one."

"*Oui, madame.* Your shrewdness, astuteness, and generosity are greatly appreciated."

"Your bullshit is not."

"Lighten up," he said. "It's only money."

"I'm the one working full-time for it."

He folded the check and put it in his shirt pocket. Taking her hand, he pulled her out of the chair and with his other hand behind his back, pressed his lips to the top of her wrist. With all the sincerity he could muster, he said, "Thank you."

"Christ," Jo said. "Get out of here."

He adored that woman. She put a smile on his face as he headed south out of town. Hell, he adored all women, but if asked to name a best friend, a loyal *compadre*, he wouldn't hesitate—Jo. Underneath all that grumbling and sarcasm, she understood his secret. He was born happy. Popped right into the world that way. Intended to spend every hour of every day that way and die that way. Inside her chest a big bleeding red heart beat to a melody they both sang, like a duet, she the bass, he the tenor. When they were kids, she'd been a silent partner in his schemes, egging him on for her own delight, taking great satisfaction in predicting the disastrous, or successful, outcomes of his pranks. He should have married her instead of Danielle, but that orange, cotton candy hair and all those freckles— couldn't do it. After Danielle split, God, he'd tried, but some things never change. Big fat rollers did nothing to calm the kinky helmet of curls, makeup couldn't conceal the brown splotches on her arms, and the NordicTrack in the middle of her living room didn't shrink the size of her thighs. The rest of her body was all right, but those thighs, white as cauliflower and the same texture, might never release his skinny hips if he got caught between them. Probably every man felt the same, because Jo never married. Come to think of it, she might have been so in love with him, no one else appealed to her. An image of a dart hitting the bulls-eye flashed across his mind. Yup. She'd loved him and only him, all along. He most certainly did have a way with women.

He opened a Tecate, lit a Winston. Other folks played CDs on a road trip. He liked quiet because music interfered with the consistently inconsistent brilliance of his own lyrics. Humming, he tapped a beat on the steering wheel.

> *Do all I can to find the old man, boom ka-cha-boom*
> *Take a look in a telephone book, boom ba-dee-boom*
> *Call each Elder Care, see if he's there, ooh pa-pa-shoo*
> *Direct this car to the closest bar, choo na-na do*
> *Make some connections, get directions, ooh la-la-shoo*
> *Find a notary, sign by four-thirty, oom ba-dee-boom*
> *Back home by ten. Good deal. Amen.*

He'd stop at a Burger King and order a Whopper with fries and a large Coke—food frowned upon in nursing homes. After spreading the meal on Ross's food tray, he'd dig into the paper sack and produce a dozen sugar packets. Old people stole them to prove they were thrifty, able to recognize an opportunity to save a few cents. "You'd better believe it," they'd say. "Every penny counts!"

The highway climbed through Sedillo Pass. Charred ground and black tree trunks told of a recent forest fire. He'd missed the event and no one had mentioned it. When he'd asked what had happened in his absence, folks had said, "Not a hell of a lot. Elmer Rodriguez got fired from his job at the high school for taking his Spanish class on a field trip to Chihuahua, buying them booze, and sleeping with two girls. At one time. Terra Thompson let her eight-year-old son offer a hot dog to a brown bear that had been curious about the contents of their garbage can and the kid got his hand chewed off. Alex Hampton couldn't get into the Volunteer Fire Department where he'd forgotten his glasses so he shot the lock off with his pistol. The bullet ricocheted and put a hole in his radiator." Really, seemed he never left.

Descending from the pass, prickly pear, bear grass, and yucca sprouted along the rocky mountainside. Ahead, the land spread flat as spilled paint through the rugged mountains of the Gila Wilderness. The trees were still green in the small town of Los Olmos. He continued south for another forty miles, turned west at Badger Creek and switch-backed down the tight curves into Arizona in second gear. No sense hurrying. Go slow or get killed.

Right away he felt trapped in strange surroundings, as though a twelve-foot-high concrete wall divided the two states, different as orange and purple. In Arizona, he'd have to abide by someone else's rules, look respectable, throw trash in a can, smoke outside. The fences said, "Do Not Trespass," instead of, "Jump Over Me," and the gates said, "Keep Out," instead of, "Please Close." He'd been to Colorado once and it was the same. Civilized. Already homesick, as if an invisible rope tugged him back to Dax County, he resisted the pull back to New Mexico and stayed on course. But man, he'd take a piñon-and-juniper-covered mesa over ocotillos and saguaros any day. This bleak desert was a long way from the Grand Canyon, the one appealing Arizona attraction. He'd love to hike to the bottom of that deep crack in the earth, but they wouldn't let you go without a guide. He'd never see it. Nobody was going to guide him, no way, no how.

He pushed through the glass doors of La Ventana Nursing Home. Holding his hat against his chest, he smiled meekly at the girl behind the reception desk, and signed in as "nephew" in the relationship column.

He found room 328 at the end of a long, wide corridor, the door ajar. Ross sat in a recliner holding a magnifying glass over the *Sierra Vista Herald*, the *Tucson Daily Star* scattered on the floor beside his chair. A wall-mounted TV, dresser, hospital bed, desk, and bedside table made up the furnishings. Pictures of Owen, Rita, and the grandkids faced the bed from the opposite wall. The place smelled like a mixture of antiseptic and grade school cafeteria. Through the window, wrought iron fencing enclosed manicured lawns. A grounds keeper drove by in a golf cart.

Walker cleared his throat. The old man barely moved, peering at the paper over a pair of thick glasses straddling the end of his nose.

"Hello, Ross," Walker said. "Didn't know if I'd find you asleep this time of day."

Ross raised his head and looked him over.

"Well, what a surprise. Pull that desk chair over and have a seat where I can get a good look at you."

"I brought you dinner," Walker said, holding up the Burger King bag.

"That's fine. Just fine."

Walker emptied the sack on the bedside table, itemizing the contents, and took a few sugar packets out, setting them beside the bag.

"I didn't pay for those," he said. "The way prices have gone up, I figure fast food joints owe us a few perks."

"I suppose you're right," Ross said.

Well, that went over like drawing Harley McKenna's two-ton bull at the rodeo.

Ross had lost maybe forty pounds, most of his hair, and almost all of his teeth. His ears looked twice their regular size and his cheeks seemed sucked into his mouth, leaving two round sockets, deep as pockets on a billiards table.

"They treating you good here?" Walker asked.

"Probably about the way you got treated in the last establishment you visited."

"Ross, I forgot all about it." Walker flipped the chair around, threw a leg over it and rested his arms across the back. "The day after I got home, the whole experience faded. Mother's about the same, no worse at any rate. Lee Ann and

Eugene got things runnin' smooth as a Broadway musical, all the legs kickin' at the same height. Dee and Scott help out real good. Go on. Have a few fries."

"No. Not right now. I never did develop a taste for that kind of food. Charlotte's chicken fried steak was all I asked for to celebrate any occasion. Her gravy and mashed potatoes went down easy, settled easy. She fixed stuffed peppers every Thursday, knowing that was my second favorite. She'd soak pinto beans and season them with pork fat. Her enchiladas beat anything they turned out at Vera's and her pot roast…"

"Ross, I'll come right to the point. Owen sent me down here to get your signature on a quitclaim deed to transfer the ranch." He reached into the manila envelope and unfolded the form. "He'd have come himself, but he had an important survey to complete this week."

"He never mentioned nothing about it when he called Sunday."

"I know. This came up sudden. Ted Bowles advised him to have you transfer the property directly to Owen before you passed on, to save having to go through probate. You know, Ted's the best lawyer in the county."

Ross folded his hands in his lap.

"I believe I'll wait until I talk to Owen."

"Ross, I drove all the way over here." He waved a woman into the room. "And I arranged for Miss Marlene Spencer here to meet with us in order to notarize this simple transaction. I'll tell you what. You sign and if Owen decides against it, he can toss the form out. But, see, he'll have the paper in case you both agree to follow Ted's advice."

"I'm sorry you took the trouble, ma'am," Ross said. He turned his attention to Walker. "I reckon you can stay one more day until I speak with Owen tonight."

"Well, now, that's not possible because I promised Eugene I'd be there to help get ready for roundup. Owen said he'd call you Sunday as usual."

He unwrapped the burger and tore it in two, laid a napkin across Ross's lap and wheeled the bedside table next to his chair, aiming the open bag of fries within easy reach of his right hand.

"Try one of them fries."

"I'm thinking."

Christ.

"Look, Ross. I hate to be so blunt, but you may not get up tomorrow. You might rest your head on that pillow tonight, count your blessings, and drift on up to heaven leaving a hell of a mess behind. Owen will have to deal with the courts all by himself. An only child gets stuck with the entire burden. He'll have to oversee the care of the ranch until probate is completed. Afterwards, he'll have to decide what to do with the property while bearing the sorrow of your death. Ross, I still feel sad over my dad's passing and it's been over sixteen years. The missing never goes away. The love never dies. Owen will be carrying you in his heart long after you've gone, the way you carry Charlotte. The least you can do is make the practical matters easy on him."

"I had no idea he considered it a burden."

"Well, Ross, Owen is a respectful son."

Ross adjusted his elbows on the armrests and shifted position.

"It's just he and I agreed to do it one way and now you're presenting me with another."

"A better way. An easier way. A way you can prove your love and kindness. Look at it like this—you're giving Owen a final gift."

He cleared the burger and fries off the table, laid out the paper and stepping aside, steered Marlene next to the old man.

"I'll need your social security number on this other piece of paper. You want your magnifying glass?"

"Just pass me a pen. Point to where I sign."

11

LEE ANN LEFT WORK AT noon to meet Mother's case-worker, Annette, for the quarterly documentation of the state agency's services. Working around rules that specified Do Not Tip Caregivers, she found other ways of showing appreciation for the women who drove the long miles to Alibi Creek. Today, a Mr. Coffee 12-cup coffee maker needed a home, if not with Annette, then some other staff member. She placed the box on the front seat and waved good-bye until her arm grew heavy and fell to her side.

The file on Mother's progress reported, "status unchanged." There'd come a time when that phrase would be replaced by "oxygen required," or "full time nursing care advised." Not only Mother, but Edgar, who'd been around since before Lee Ann was born, would be needing assistance soon enough. He'd taken to sleeping past nine, and although he never complained, his bad hip and twisted fingers prevented him from riding, or tying a knot. She'd taken to sending beans and chile over to the bunkhouse once a week and for a man who insisted on attending to all his own needs, his humble acceptance of the gesture signaled his decline. Within the year he'd quit driving, his eyesight failing as fast as his hearing.

She went inside for a sweater, called the dogs, and whistling the theme from *The Bridge on the River Kwai*, started off to the creek. Before taking thirty steps, the one-ton truck emerged from behind the workshop. She herded the dogs off to the side.

Dee pulled up and rolled down the window.

"I'm off to Plank's," he said. "Scott and Walker are already over there."

She brushed her hair back from her face, searching his eyes.

"You don't know," he said, shifting into neutral.

"I guess not."

"We're moving Danielle's trailer up the canyon behind Granny's. Walker told us to use the cinderblocks from beside the barn for supports. We've been working at Plank's all morning getting it loaded on the flatbed." He put the truck in gear and revved the engine. "See you later."

The dogs sat at her feet, tails wagging, waiting for the go-ahead. A scheme, this time involving Danielle. The only thing Danielle and Walker ever saw eye-to-eye on was a bottle of whiskey. If they couldn't find a party they'd make their own, which would invariably end in a fight they'd forget the next morning, then start all over again.

Along the creek bank, Patch and Blue picked up a scent in a pile of brush and began digging. Leaves landed like bits of paper on the water and swam downstream, catching on logs reaching out to snag them. She knelt and broke a twig in two, tossed one half in the water and followed its journey, the little stick incapable of turning back, powerless against the current. Tears filled her eyes, as if the twig was a living creature, robbed of free will, ignorant of rational thought or heart's desire.

"Lord, it seems we are helpless against an invisible current. This must be the great lesson we are meant to learn—to accept our fate with humility and grace. I trust You have a plan beyond my understanding, but I struggle to identify my purpose and determine when to assert myself. I question whether submission and resignation make me weak or strong. If we encounter an eddy drawing us to danger, free will allows us to decide whether to jump into the whirlpool or flee. I lack the drive, or courage, to go against the current when circumstances demand I should. I'm confused about when to take matters into my own hands. I submit to You out of fear of making a mistake. I dare not oppose Your wishes."

The twig floated downstream, undeterred.

"Walker rushes through life at a pace I can never match, driven by impulses I don't understand. Gone for whole days at a time, sharing details when it suits him, his pickup parked at Mother's when I leave for work, gone when I get home. Eugene insists I set limits, but You've created Walker untamable, uncontrollable, unteachable. I pray for him, for all things are solved through prayer. I try to forgive, as You advise."

The wind picked up and she wrapped her sweater around her chest and hugged her waist. During the first months of Walker's incarceration, she'd continued to hear his footsteps sneaking up from behind, until one afternoon, while planting petunias in the two oak barrels on either side of the front porch, she hummed while watering. Weeks went by, and she began moving easier, touching the fragile roots of the starts she set out, watching the clothes on the line dance in the wind, mimicking the crossbill finches on the garden fence, without worrying about what was behind her back. His return had tightened her stomach. Anxiety had raised her shoulders and stiffened her neck.

She dropped the other half of the twig into the creek and turned her back on its voyage. *Whatever one is, he has been named already, for it is known that he is man; And he cannot contend with Him who is mightier than he.* Ecclesiastes 6:10.

Back at the house, she traded her sweater for a jacket and drove the Blazer to the corral while Patch and Blue, still eager to play, raced alongside. Twisting the hair at the nape of her neck, in a steady voice she told Eugene about the plan to move Danielle's trailer up the canyon. He'd never met Danielle, but had heard plenty.

Eugene continued measuring the corral fence, jotting figures down on a legal pad.

"I'm sure she's different now," Lee Ann said. "She's got a job at the motel. I've bumped into her a couple of times in town and she's been pleasant enough."

Eugene tossed the tape measure and pad into the diesel and without a word took off, leaning across the seat, reaching into the glove box. Lee Ann released the curl at her neck and gripped her shoulder. Eugene always said hasty reactions made things worse. He always said, "I'll think about it," when Scott sought permission, "Give me a minute," when Dee asked a question, and "Let's consider all the options," before making decisions.

His truck splashed across the creek, climbed the incline, and stopped.

She drove back to the house and from the kitchen window, aimed the binoculars toward the highway. Eugene had retrieved a chain and padlock from the glove box and was locking the gate. That gate hadn't been locked in thirty years. She drove to the turn-around at the bottom of the incline and with a clear view of the road, Eugene, and the gate, eased her hands from the steering wheel and turned off the ignition.

A half hour later, the one-ton pulling Danielle's trailer stopped at the gate, Scott's pickup close behind. Walker jumped out of the one-ton and yanked on the lock. "What the hell…"

Eugene got out of the diesel. "Take that trailer back where you got it."

Walker slapped his hands against his thighs. "We're moving it up the canyon."

"No, you're not."

"We been workin' all day to get it over here."

Eugene stepped close enough to be clearly heard, far enough to keep out of trouble.

"I don't give a damn how long you've been working. It has no place anywhere on this property."

"Look, man," Walker said. "It's temporary. Just till I sell it." He jiggled the gate, did a little fast stepping, hands on his hips. "You know me. I can turn anything over in ten minutes flat, if not before. Soon as I hit the bar this item will be sold. Guaranteed."

"Then park it in Brand."

"I can't take it to town without you opening this here gate so I can get the blocks to set it on."

Eugene called to Scott and Dee. "You ought to know better."

"Open up, or I'll have to leave the damn thing out on the highway," Walker said.

"Do what you want, only don't set it on this property."

Walker beat his chest.

"It's my property, too."

"It's your mother's."

Lee Ann slammed the door of the Blazer and walked quickly to Eugene's side.

"Walker, you're overstepping the line. Had we discussed this, you'd know we do not want this trailer in the canyon. It's your business if you want to sell it or trade it, but you can't do it from here. It doesn't even belong to you."

Walker stuck his hands in his back pockets.

"Yes, it does," he said. "It's my wife's."

12

AT THE TIME, THAT WAS a lie. Five minutes with Carlos Barela, the municipal magistrate, would make it true. Walker left the trailer blocking the entrance to the ranch, borrowed Scott's pickup and drove to the Brand New Motel.

"Sweetheart, it's time to make our arrangement legal," he said, leaning over the counter.

Danielle said, "You got an email."

He zipped around the partition and rested his chin on her shoulder. Something about the mixture of body lotion and shampoo made him want to stick his nose in her platinum hair and leave it there for an entire day, maybe the rest of his life. Today, her long fingers had bright red tips and fake gold charms dangled off her wrist.

Keith would be arriving late. Could Walker book him a room at the motel and meet him the following morning for breakfast at eight o'clock?

"Sure," Walker said.

Danielle sent the reply and stood up.

"Let's make this quick," she said, jotting a note and taping it to the door.

Seemed he always took the lead, set the pace and dictated the action, except when it came to Danielle, and now he bounded after her across the paved parking lot onto a gravel strip strewn with trash. Catty-corner to the motel, a sign reading MAGISTRATE COURT tilted sideways in the window of a frame house painted red with white trim.

"We're here to get married," Walker said.

Rhonda looked up from her desk, folded her magazine, and took off her glasses.

"Fill this out," she said, reaching into a drawer and fitting a sheet of paper on a clipboard. "I'll get Carlos. You're going to need another witness."

"Jesus, Walker, I got to get back."

"Hold on just a minute. I'll get Walt."

When they all gathered in the office, Walker got the chills. Of all the mysteries on this great earth, attraction between the sexes was the most baffling. Life would be moving along just fine and some woman would cross a guy's path and drag him into her particular set of problems. And for what? A tussle in the sack. A teensy bit of s-e-x left men full and proud and complete. Stuffing their shirts in their pants, notching their belts, they'd walk around all puffed up, a man having done a man's job—satisfied a woman. Pffff. Problem was, the female half of the species could never be satisfied, no matter how hard the male half tried. They *always* wanted something else, something more, something different. Trying to provide that little something wore a man down until the allure that captured his interest in the first place turned him 180 degrees in the opposite direction. Love—men wanted it. When they got it, they could do without it. The best plan was to let women do the wanting. Stick with bourbon to ease the fall when reality sets in. Love = crazy. Love = danger. 1+1 = 2 fools spinning toward self-destruction. Yet, here he was at this very moment excited about the prospects of matrimony with the very woman proven to do him damage.

Carlos asked, "Do you take this woman to be your lawful wedded wife in sickness and health, until death do you part?" and Walker said, "I do."

Carlos asked, "Do you take this man to be your lawful wedded husband in sickness and health, until death do you part?" and Danielle said, "I guess."

Rhonda put on her glasses and applied her signature as witness. Walt wiped his hands on his grocer's apron and signed as second.

Carlos said, "Well," and shook Walker's hand, kissed Danielle's cheek.

Danielle said, "I'm outta here."

Rhonda took off her glasses.

Walt went back to work.

Walker tripped after Danielle, heart somersaulting like a new penny flipped in a coin toss, landing heads up, you win—the prize, prettiest gal in Dax County, not counting those gorgeous black-haired beauties. Course, comparing blonds to brunettes was as meaningless as analyzing the difference between tequila and bourbon. Hey now, this called for a celebration! He dashed over to the bar and bought a bottle of Jose Cuervo, stopped at Walt's for limes and continued down the street to Vera's. He snatched a saltshaker off the nearest table and waved his fist, promising to return it tomorrow. At the motel he spread everything out on the reception desk, flicked open his pocketknife and sliced the limes on the laminated list of daily rates. This was their wedding night. They might get a room.

"Are you kidding?" she said.

Walker poured them each a shot in cups from the water dispenser.

"To marriage," he said.

Danielle raised her cup.

"To the divorce settlement."

He rested his elbows on the counter like a customer and tried to get Danielle reminiscing about the old days. Damn, she was knockout gorgeous, silky smooth. The longer he talked, the more his body stretched over the partition, until he was half hanging, toes barely touching the floor, nearly drooling when she occasionally deigned to look at him with half closed eyelids. Hell, darlin', lighten up, this ain't all that serious. Might as well lap up the moment as well as the tequila. He wasn't about to take advantage of her body, or anything else. Actually, she didn't have anything else. Probably down to her last matching lace bra and pantie set, the pizzazz of the old days buried under a stack of credit card debt. He piled on the compliments and jokes, coaxing the dimple in her left cheek to crease, overlooking her distinct distaste of his antics. Questions about the girls and grandkids softened her some and he kept on, pretending to care about the exact date Billy got potty trained and how many teeth Jessica had (upper and lower) and what they did to celebrate Tamara's last birthday. In the end, he forgot what kid belonged to which daughter, the ratio of girls to boys, their ages, and where they lived.

They'd finished over half the bottle when Suzette showed up for the evening shift. Danielle collected her purse and Walker guided her by the elbow to her Jeep.

"Follow me," he said, pointing to Scott's pickup.

She hiccupped.

No way to count the times he'd driven home drunk, crooning away with a smiling moon above. Hit an elk only once, a young bull that leapt out of the bar ditch and knocked off the passenger side mirror with his antlers. That was the only time—the best view of the road, and the way to keep a vehicle going sort of straight, was to drive on the centerline.

After what seemed like no time at all, a white shape glared like a giant TV screen in the headlights. He stopped on the side of the highway in front of the trailer, right where he'd left it, and stumbled to the gate. Still locked.

He helped Danielle out of the Jeep.

"Honey, we'll have to stay out here tonight," he said. "Look at it this way—a minor inconvenience on the way to your fortune, a sweeper in the river, a worm in the apple, a bruise on the arm, all of it temporary. Tomorrow, I'll have this baby moved."

"I'll be cold."

"We'll snuggle up together under every blanket, towel, and coat we can find. Besides, you got me to keep you warm. Now, don't go cryin'. This is only one night out of your whole life, one little discomfort."

"You've got it wrong," she said. "It's the final blow."

13

Lee Ann sat quietly while Eugene drove her out to the highway. She pressed against his arm as he unlocked the gate. A wink, pat, or kiss would be nice. Have a good day would be nice. A smile, a bump on the hip. He unlocked the gate. She slipped through and he locked it again.

"Call me if Lyle can't bring you home," he said.

She straightened her skirt and adjusted her purse over her sweater. Across the road, the sun broke through Red Bull Canyon, splashing yellow on the pines along the south slope, the trees' roots firmly planted, their limbs bathed in warmth. She shivered in the shade, the Lord standing with her, His glow radiating into her body, filling her up. Unfortunately, He emanated light rather than heat. She should have worn a jacket.

Danielle's and Scott's vehicles were parked on the wrong shoulder, leaning into the ditch, the Cherokee's door hanging open. She walked away from the trailer where the newlyweds were likely passed out or hung over. The curtains were open, but nothing moved inside. Lord, do not tempt Walker's imagination with opportunities that will distract him today. Please, provide a home for the trailer. Weaken Eugene's resolve to keep the gate locked.

A red-winged blackbird screeched from somewhere nearby and she imitated its call. The bird answered and she scanned the mesa and sky for red and yellow swatches on a black wing, perhaps the last sighting before winter. The bird flew from a cottonwood branch and headed south. To the north, she saw Lyle's patrol car curve through the valley, long before she heard it.

The trailer was ugly. No matter how poor, Mother and Dad would never have stooped to living in a trailer, even a doublewide. And Eugene felt the same. The ability to build and maintain a home on a solid foundation set them apart from the riff-raff who hadn't the energy or skills to afford more than a down payment on a pre-fab home. Danielle fit that category. Worse, she probably rented.

Walker wouldn't leave the trailer there in spite, but in thoughtlessness. He understood the difference between borrowing and stealing, honesty and deceit, but the difference didn't mean anything, nor did the consequences. With a baffled expression, he'd exclaim, "Why, I'm just going about my business. Really, I had no idea I'd inconvenienced you. Sorry you're upset. Okey-dokey, I'll get to it right away," as if apologizing excused the damage, as if the insult hadn't hurt, as if passing out passed as a good night's sleep. At least he'd never done drugs. Jesus had always been her best friend, the bottle his. And Jesus, forgiver of all, would not discriminate against, or fault the weak.

Lyle pulled over and she opened the cruiser door with so much force her arm about left its socket. Yes, chilly morning. The trailer? It belongs to Danielle. Oh, one of the tires blew on the flatbed and it's temporarily out of commission. Walker has plans to haul it to Los Olmos. Of course, it'll be moved today. He's doing fine, helping Eugene and the boys rebuild the corral before roundup, glad to be part of things, a real member of the team. *Lord, how often shall my brother sin against me, and I forgive him? Up to seven times?" Jesus said to him: "I do not say to you, up to seven times, but up to seventy times seven."* Matthew 18:21-22. Yes, it seems prison has calmed him down, and yes, he intends to stay out of trouble this time.

The meeting convened at eleven, late enough for ranchers to have completed their chores and close enough to lunch for the commissioners' stomachs to call for closure before noon. Lee Ann placed copies of the agenda on the long Formica tabletop and set out Styrofoam cups, Coffee-mate, sugar, and plastic spoons beside the thirty-cup percolator. More knowledgeable about county law, federal regulations, and the business at hand than any of the commissioners, her presence would be required. They would lean back with expressionless faces and defer to her, and she'd pretend all three had done their homework and act as their spokesperson.

She scooped coffee into the basket, forgot the count and started again. She hadn't slept well. Before bed, Eugene had said he and the boys were almost finished rebuilding the corral, changing the shape from rectangular to oval. The work had required tearing down the old fence and chutes, pulling posts, cutting new ones, and repositioning them. The gates had yet to be completed and attached. With roundup a few days away, they could use an extra hand.

"Damn it," he said. "He's worse than useless. Not only does he not help, he undermines our efforts."

She went to the bathroom and brushed her teeth, got into bed. He'd always rehash the day's events, discuss plans for tomorrow, affirm the wonderful job she was doing with Mother, reassure her that he wouldn't overwork Edgar, but would assign him the task of overseeing supplies and equipment. Usually he predicted the weather, praised the lasagna, or agreed with her list of their many blessings. He sat on the edge of the mattress, half-turned toward her.

"He's got the boys thinking it's smart to mouth off about anything that bugs them. They got into it today over cutting wood."

"They always go together," she said.

"Dee blamed Scott for slowing them down, getting distracted by bug patterns in the bark, something like that. Scott shot back that Dee had a three-track mind—cows, cows, and Ginny Alcott. Smart-ass talk they've learned from their uncle."

She said, "The boys will not succumb to Walker's ways." They would not.

He lay down with his back exposed. His neck was sunburnt above the collar line, the rest of his skin smooth and white. Two small moles huddled close to his spine. Her finger touched them, and when he stayed on his side and his back muscles tightened, her eyes filled and overflowed onto her pillow. Throughout the night his leg hadn't touched hers. She woke early and tiptoed to her private corner of the dining room. Yesterday morning's coffee mug had been left on the Bible, a dribble having run a straight line from the rim down to the cover. She wet a sponge and scrubbed the spot, which left a discolored streak through the *B* in *Holy Bible*.

With just enough time to deposit last week's revenue, she returned to the office, removed an envelope from the safe and hurried across the street to the bank. A truck screeched to a halt behind her.

"Peek-a-boo." Walker grinned.

"The trailer," she said.

"I'm on it. As we speak."

14

"MY DAD DOESN'T WANT ANYTHING to do with you," Jo said. "He isn't going to let you dump a trailer out at his place."

"Well, I'll park it behind your house then," Walker said.

"No."

"Just until I find a buyer."

"N. O."

"No" seemed to be the word of the day. Walt said no, even though he owned thirty-six square miles of useless range over-run with chamisa and tumbleweed. Conrad, chairman of the County Fair board, said no, even though they needed extra storage space for fold-up tables and signage. At the bar, Art said no, even though the garbage-strewn, vacant lot out back provided a home to nothing but a rusted '64 Dodge.

"I don't see what it would hurt," Walker said. "Give me another Corona. I'll have it sold in two days."

"It's a piece of shit," Art said.

"Exactly. Goes right along with every other piece of shit in this town. I promise you, within two days someone will think they've lucked out on the bargain of a lifetime."

"Trouble with bargains is, there's always a reason. And whoever figures out the reason for this one will be coming after you. And where will you be? Here. I don't want trouble."

"Jeez, talk about putting a downspin on a venture. There's nothin' wrong with that trailer. Danielle's been living in it for months. Toilet flushes. Thermostat kicks on. Water runs in the taps. A country palace, man!"

Art rested both hands on the bar and leaned forward. N.O.

At the motel, he found Danielle turning a swivel chair to the right and left with her big toe, reading a fashion magazine.

"Listen, darlin'," he said, pushing two twenties with two fingers across the counter. "Plans for the trailer haven't quite solidified yet. I want you to be comfortable tonight, so book yourself a room." She kept her head lowered and raised her eyes without closing the magazine. He got the message—a creep was ruining her day spewing a load of bullshit. He understood without a doubt that number 16 would be hers alone, no visitors, no guests, and no roommates.

"I'll stay in the trailer," he said.

What to do with the damned thing. Driving out Forest Road 47 in search of an out-of-the-way spot with easy access to stash it, clouds popped up over the mesa in puffy, puppy-like formations. Woof. Here comes an elephant. Galoomp. Galoomp. Man, don't let it rain. There ain't one thing in life guaranteed, but whoever directs the weather, let that sun break through for the next few days. Let it shine and shine and shine, elevate the spirits, make the world sparkle!

The road climbed and leveled out high above the valley. He got out to take a leak, wilderness around and below; in the distance the two round hills on Plank's place and the parallel tree lines along the creek, their gold leaves beginning to fade from brilliant to bronze. He opened the glove box and took out the quitclaim deed and held it over his heart, ran his tongue over his lips and kissed it. Smack.

Tomorrow evening Keith Lampert would arrive. The following morning they'd meet, come up here and sniff the air, bask in the silence, spot some wildlife, sigh with the splendor of the vista and descend to where the big, blazing cottonwood marked Ross Plank's homestead, right there.

15

"You said he was on it," Eugene said. "Not staying in it."

Lee Ann pulled the wool blanket over Mother, tucked the satin edge around her shoulders and pecked her forehead goodnight.

"Shhhhhh…we can discuss this after she's settled."

"I'm no longer your taxi service to the gate. Drive yourself and leave your car in the turn-around."

"Maybe you can talk to him."

"It'll result in a fist fight and you know who'll come out on top. You want that? You want him beaten to a heap of slop? Believe me, there's nothing I'd like better than to bounce his scrawny hide off the walls of that trailer." He nodded at Mother. "For her sake, it's best I keep my distance."

In the kitchen, Lee Ann collected Mother's supper dishes off the table and ran the water.

Eugene said, "Can't burn that trailer, bury it or sink it. What I'd like to do is plow into it, but I'd wreck my pickup. Moving it to a repo lot would take time and effort and you can be damn sure I'm not about to do his dirty work for him."

"You don't need to swear. And please, keep your voice down."

He slammed his hand on the counter, rattling the plates.

She turned off the water and sat down. The air buzzed with a high, nerve-shattering frequency sending vibrations from her scalp to her toes.

"I'll ask Lyle to have the road crew move it to the county yard," she said.

"They'll have to slap a warning on it first, give him three days."

"In that case, I'm sure Walker will have moved it by then."

"You're always sure. One thing *I'm* sure of is that nothing you're sure of with Walker ever comes to pass. Your certainty is a means of avoiding the inevitable."

"Eugene, sit down. I'm not trying to make things worse."

He stayed put. "Well, you do. When the happy carpenter whistles, he's estimated wrong. That's you, whistling away, ignoring a nightmare about to happen, denying how much you hate Walker, refusing to take a stand. You're stuck in your faith, thinking it makes you strong, but it's like quicksand, pulling you under."

The clock said 8:20. Saul Duran had tampered with a paving bid for the road to second mesa. This week she'd obeyed Harley's request and "adjusted" the budget for the Supplemental Food Program for Needy Women, Infants, and Children. Her job might well be re-titled Commissioners' Flunky.

She scraped a dab of crusty lasagna off the edge of the table, scratching the spot after it flaked off. Lord, Eugene doesn't understand the power of prayer. Faulting my faith is unfair! He doesn't see that forgiveness is the way, that changing Walker is Your job.

She rose to take his hand, but he shook her off and left. Years ago, they'd taken a picnic lunch to San Marcos Lake. After lunch, she'd fallen asleep and woke to find herself alone. The day was warm and she set up a camping chair and passed the afternoon reading *No Life For a Lady*, recommended by Scott, about a woman's country life in the last century. Eugene returned in the late afternoon with a bouquet of wild asters, his first of many gifts from nature. During the winter months the gifts continued—mistletoe, a pine bough for the fireplace, a heart-shaped rock, arrowheads, and turquoise beads he discovered when cutting wood. When asked what inspired such offerings, he said, "Pops always treated Mama that way." She kept a dried flower from each arrangement in a glass bowl on her bureau and the smaller tokens in a cookie tin on her night table, close to her dreams, first reminder of his affection each morning.

There would be no such offering tonight. She rose and walked to the sink, turned on the tap and moved the sponge over a plate's surface, round and around, the water getting hotter and hotter. I do feel mired down, Lord.

16

THE DUDE STOOD 6' 4", weighed maybe 220. Walker shook Keith Lampert's hand, asked if he'd spent a pleasant night, and without waiting for an answer, waved him to a table, apologizing for the lumpy upholstery and Vera's décor—chicken salt and peppershakers on soiled tablecloths printed with Barred Rocks strutting around fairytale barnyards. Walker faced him away from the Rhode Island Red plaque above the order window that read, "What is Superman's real identity? Cluck Kent," and the ticket holder plastered with chicken decals that twirled next to shelves of poultry bric-a-brac.

Walker studied Keith's face. If he covered the left side with the menu, the right side would look like a cartoon of the Handsome Man with chiseled lips, smooth skin and a direct, open gaze. Covering that side, the left half would appear tight and mean, as though a cord ran through Keith's lip and nostril, pulling them up, cutting deep lines across his cheek and over his cheekbone. A heavy brow pressed down over a squinted eye. The right side suggested he might be fifty-five, the left maybe sixty-five. Smiles seemed to be missing from his repertoire of expressions.

Walker asked for *chorizo* and eggs smothered in green chile. Keith ordered *huevos*, scrambled, red on the side.

"I got a big mouth," Walker said. "And lots to say. I'll

dominate this conversation in two minutes if I don't give you a chance to tell me about yourself. Go ahead."

Keith picked up a knife, ran his thumb along the serrated edge.

"Not much to tell," he said. "My dad and I operated a slaughterhouse on the outskirts of Phoenix. When he died last year, I sold the business and a piece of adjacent property." He raised his eyes. "I'm wanting out of Phoenix. Too many people. Too much traffic."

"A butcher! Man, you'll make a killing around here come hunting season. The county has no regulations on game processing. Anybody can do it. With your skills and reputation, you'll have all the business you can handle. Work a few months a year, bring in a bundle. As for getting out of Phoenix, I'm hearing that more and more. We're trying to keep this part of the world a secret, but some of you Arizonans have discovered the cheap prices and low taxes in the spectacular state to your east."

Vera set their plates down.

"I'm not sure about continuing that line of work," Keith said. He reached for the salt.

"Sure, you want to retire. Throw your feet up. Get a few chickens, plant some tomatoes and cucumbers, a dozen rows of corn. Once you experience the P and Q, there'll be no turning back. This is hidden treasure, man. I'm going to drive you around today, introduce you to the country and let me tell you, you're going to feel privileged to get a piece of it. Because, to tell the truth, there's not much land available. Less than twenty-five percent of Dax County is privately owned. The rest is public land, managed by the BLM and US Forest Service." He picked up his fork. Shut. Up. The guy's stingy with words. Give him an opportunity to relax, ease up, and spill a few details.

Vera poured more coffee.

Walker shoved his eggs around his plate, stifling the urge for a cigarette in case Keith agreed with the rest of the world that smoking in restaurants was offensive.

"I've lived here all my life," Walker said. "A *ranchero* for all of it. Tried to enlist in my twenties but they wouldn't take me. Got thrown off a bull when I was sixteen and busted my right eardrum. I guess my left ear is super sharp, 'cause I hear the slightest sounds, even some I'm not supposed to, like two gals whispering about a man's talents, a mouse in the cat food, thunder a county away." He shoved his plate aside. "I sure do admire any man that served."

Keith swallowed his eggs and gulped his coffee.

"Nam," he said.

So, that was it. The word dated the guy, implied life-altering experiences that worked on a man's face, forever changing it. The blunt way he stated the word, like a nut cracked against a tabletop, explained one side of his face battling the other. Walker watched him chew, the tight cheek doing the work, doubting the two halves ever lived in harmony.

They hiked up the mesa through cedar and ponderosa pine and stood above the valley on a flat ledge of granite. Walker pointed.

"To the south there, that's Solitaire Peak. Those are aspens setting fire to the eastern slope." He set his boot heel into the rock and turned a full circle, arms outstretched, palms up. "All this is your playground. That sandstone cliff's your slide. Your feet'll roll on fine gravel and you'll be flat on your ass in a split second, zooming down the slope fast as a rollercoaster with nothin' to grab onto to break the ride. In the spring, you can play hide and seek along that rim rock, searching for elk antlers disguised as fallen tree limbs. You can dress like Davy Crocket and cut you a stack of firewood, pretend you're sixteen and poke your girl in that open meadow over there, claim you're King of the World and hear your voice echo off the walls in Salida Canyon."

Keith locked his hands behind his back and inhaled.

"Yeah, take a breath. Nothing cleaner." Walker tore a small branch off a juniper tree, crushed it in his hand. "Now, that's perfume, man. Revlon can't bottle this. It's God's concoction. He ain't givin' out the formula, but you can sniff all you want for free all year round. And look down there, between the mesas. See the road crossing the creek as it curves west? That there's your property. Let's go."

Walker lit a Winston and let it dangle out the window. The wind blew through the cab and beside him Keith took in the land and sky. Lordy, the sun did shine, not a cloud in sight. He gave a few hits on the horn as they passed Shelley sweeping leaves off the store's porch. That open bottle of JD she kept under the register called out to him, but he whizzed right on by.

He drove across the creek at Plank's place super slow.

"You just missed the red Indian paintbrush, orange *yerba negrita*, and red and yellow *gaillardia* that color these fields all summer. Next year you'll be in for a treat. Sometimes, purple bee weed takes over unused pasture and every year sunflowers damn near blind a person."

They parked under the big cottonwood.

"Tomorrow I'll loan you my ATV and you can follow the creek, ride the arroyos, and cover most of the territory. If you're into hunting arrowheads, there's a big Indian ruin on the southern rim of the west mesa. Now, the house is solid. No one's lived here for twelve years, so you got to imagine the walls patched and painted. Ross stayed on quite a while after Charlotte died and let things slide. You know how it takes a woman's touch to warm a place, gingham curtains and the like. I been trapping skunks under the crawl space. That smell should disappear pretty quick. Me, I'd tear the place down and start from scratch, but some folks like the feel of an older home, take comfort in the evidence of family history."

The sun had climbed almost overhead. He took the flask from his back pocket. "Might be a little early for you," he said, unscrewing the lid and extending his hand.

"I usually wait until four," Keith said, but took it.

They walked around back, crunching weeds. The old fence had toppled and any semblance of a tended garden had long vanished. Walker's ladder leaned against an apple tree still laden with fruit.

"Pick yourself some."

"I'd like to stay on the land a couple of days, if you've got a tent I can borrow."

"No tent," Walker said, returning the flask to his pocket. He adjusted the ladder against the tree trunk. "But, I got just the trailer."

17

DEE DUSTED OFF THE CHOP SAW.
"We just moved it over here."

Scott removed the screw from between his lips and quit drilling.

"We can't help you. These gates have to be finished today."

Walker said, "What's more important? Moving the trailer or postponing roundup one more day? Them cows don't know the difference."

Dee sliced through a two-by-four.

"Dad'll throw a fit. Manuel and Rudy are already lined up for Sunday and Monday."

Walker picked up the sawed-off end and swung it like a baseball bat, raised his hand to shield his eyes as if he'd hit a home run so far out to right field he lost sight of it.

"He's going to blow up one way or the other," he said, tossing the wood on the scrap pile. "I believe he'll be more pissed off if that trailer's still here. But maybe that's my imagination. Maybe he'll think, gosh, it's just fine having that hunk o' junk blocking the road. Maybe every time he wants to get out of here, he'll think, well, that's okay, I'll wait until tomorrow. Maybe he doesn't mind the sight of the big ugly thing at all, just looks over it or around it. Hell, maybe he even *likes* it there, a reminder of how much unexpected joy I bring into his life. Come on. Won't take but a couple hours to reset the block and hook her back up. Then I'll help you slap these gates together."

Scott laid the drill on the table.

Dee unplugged the saw.

A couple of hours turned into five. Dinnertime came and went.

"Tell you what," Walker said, after completing the job. "You boys deserve a drink."

"No thanks," Scott said. "You going to help us now, or what?"

"Or what?" Walker whined. "Course I'm going to help. Said I would, didn't I?"

The evening star blinked in a deep purple sky as they pulled the vehicles to a stop in front of the workshop. They opened the doors to find Eugene beside the worktable, facing them.

Dee mumbled, "We were giving him a hand moving the trailer."

"I'm here to make up for lost time," Walker said. "These gates'll be ready to swing off their posts by midnight. Guaranteed."

The hit to his stomach came fast and hard. Walker buckled forward and another punch caught his jaw, jerking his head to the side. He heard his neck crack. Had no breath. Dropped to the floor. Eugene stood over him, his voice coming from far away.

"I'll break your neck next time. Now, get up and get outta here."

Walker rolled on his side and brought his knees to his chest.

"Pick him up and throw him out."

Scott and Dee lifted Walker by the armpits, draped his arms around their necks, dragged him to his truck, and propped him in the seat. Dee headed back to the shop. Scott searched for the Pleiades and greeted the sisters, huddled together in the sparkling universe, waiting for Orion, due in January. When Dee yelled his name, he floated down to earth, tossed Walker's hat on the seat and placed his dangling hand in his lap. He reached behind the seat and yanked out an old Mexican blanket, spread it over Walker's chest and tucked it behind his shoulders.

Ouch. And more ouch. A rib might have snapped like a cracker, his spleen might have ruptured. He slouched behind the wheel, uncertain whether he could steer, if bumping over the gravel road would hurt bad enough to knock him out, if a shot of liquor would cure him or kill him. Most likely cure him. He willed his hand to reach for the ignition. Get me to the bar, baby. His head rolled back and he closed his eyes. Short, quick breaths tickled his nostrils. From time to time he heard the saw tear through a piece of wood, the whir of power drills, the whack of a hammer, laughter and an occasional cough. Thirst drove him to lean forward and turn the key, the humming engine comforting as a lullaby. The blanket crumpled and he pushed it aside. Gingerly, his foot pressed the pedal. Roll on out of here. I-n-c-h across the creek. E-a-s-y does it, up the rise and onto the highway.

The Jeep was parked in front of number 16. His rat-a-tat went unanswered. He leaned against the wall until the pain in his stomach subsided and labored across the street. Inside the bar, Jo's red hair glowed like a lantern at the end of a line of unoccupied stools, cigarette smoke rising straight up from the ashtray next to her drink. Art stood across from her, talking low. The same hunters as last night moved between the tables.

Danielle was seated at a table for two next to the wall, leaning forward, gazing like a woman in a trance into Keith Lampert's dark eyes with adoring, mascara-caked ones of her own. Keith rested back, the Handsome Man profile semi-smiling.

Walker's feet stuck to the sticky floor. The onrush of heat could be jealousy, but he wasn't the jealous type—to each his own, and all that. If things didn't work out with one gal, on to the next. His rising temperature was due to the bitch operating on her own.

He managed a step, then another.

"I see you two have met," he said.

Danielle kept her eyes on Keith, who kept his on her.

Walker said, "I'll get a drink and join you."

He asked Art how long they'd been there. Over an hour, long before Jo came in.

Walker swallowed a shot and asked for another.

Jo said, "She's your wife. Go claim her."

Shit, it didn't work that way. Under the current circumstances, marriage meant nothing, had meant little even in their youth, when they'd imagined themselves in love. He carried his drink across the room. If Keith looked at Danielle close up, say at mid-day, he couldn't ignore the signs of wear that had been visible in the trailer that morning—lines around and between her eyes, gray circles under them, sagging skin on her upper arms, some problem in her right knee that caused her to get up like an old lady. Then again, Keith might not care that she couldn't stick with a job for more than six months. He might remain blind to the fact that her only aim in life was to dazzle any man who crossed her path and follow the poor sucker with no clear idea of where her latest conquest might lead her.

He rested a hand on the back of Danielle's chair.

"Honey, I guess Keith told you I showed him Plank's place today."

"He did," she purred, smiling at Keith.

The pain in his gut prevented dragging over a chair and lowering himself into it.

"You're all set, Keith," he said. "I've set up a trailer for you. You drive on out there and make yourself at home. I'll bring the ATV in the morning. Darlin', I need a word with you." He took her arm. "Step out back with me a moment."

Outside, Danielle shook off his hand.

"You said we had to get that trailer *off* Plank's property," she said.

"He wants to stay out there for a couple of days. You're going to make his visit extra special, so he falls in love with the place. I see the two of you, Miss Centerfold and Mister Tall, Dark and Sorta' Handsome, having a fling. You'll have him crooning love songs to the moon. Coyotes will answer. Mice will scatter. Your wide eyes and parted lips will suggest you want to be his slave. Shit, you hardly have to act. Watch out, though. The guy hasn't told us one thing about himself. He's locked tight as a garage door in suburbia and I ain't trusting what's inside." Her lower lip stuck out. Just hours ago that little pout had been cute. Amazing how the most exquisite woman looks kinda' ugly if there's no beauty inside, the façade as temporary as a coat of paint peeling with age. "You'll be fine. I been watching you. You already got it figured out." He pushed her inside. "Remember, we're married. You're doing this romancin' on the sly. You come home every night, like a good girl."

At the bar, he pulled the stool next to Jo under his butt. "That was quick," she said.

He squeezed Jo's knee, making her squeal.

"You're the only gal for me," he said, but his eyes drifted to the two-top by the wall and his foot jiggled up and down. Tonight, his bruised body would curl up alone in his single bed while those two snuggled up in number 16.

18

L EE ANN CAME IN FROM the chicken house with three eggs and put them in the fridge. The hens slowed production as the days shortened. She selected Marie Callender's Home Style Meatloaf Dinner from the freezer in the mudroom and balanced it on top of a Saran-wrapped bowl of cherry Jell-O. Mother frowned on frozen dinners. A woman's duties included serving homemade meals, preferably meat and at least one vegetable for supper, with dessert made from scratch. Planning ahead, making do with what was left in the pantry, using what was plentiful in the garden, and canning the rest were on Lee Ann's list of "should-do's." Sunday the men would gather for roundup. There simply wasn't time this week to be the perfect countrywoman.

Announcing her arrival with a sparrow's song, she left the food on the cook stove. Get her to the bathroom, dole out her evening pills, offer an explanation for the poor excuse for a meal, or not. Wonder if she hears or comprehends. Wonder if "roundup" tickles memories of Dad and Edgar on horseback working cattle. Wonder if she cares that Saul Duran ordered official documents shredded, along with memos re-apportioning funds for Head Start. Wonder if she understands the term "closed session," if she senses the pressure of covering up secret deals, or sympathizes with the guilt of cheating county residents.

Possibly, the commissioners' actions and Lee Ann's coercion fooled no one. While collecting files to be altered, the courthouse seemed hushed. Office doors closed. Clerks rushed down the hall, whispering, their eyes searching for double meaning in her requests.

When last consulted, the Bible had said, *Therefore, there is now no condemnation for those who are in Christ Jesus, who do not walk according to the flesh, but according to the spirits.* Romans 8:1. She'd shoved the passage aside and held up the portrait of Jesus with both hands, his face level with hers.

"Lord, in public the commissioners proclaim to 'walk with God, according to the spirits,' but pronouncements don't make it so." She shook the picture. "If they steal, they should be punished. Instead, You let them get away with it."

Her elbow knocked the Bible to the floor. She dropped the picture and snatched the Book up and wiped the front and the back with her apron and brought it to her lips. Sorry. So sorry. She propped His picture in place. A crack had split the glass across His forehead.

Tony Curtis and Jack Lemmon, clothed in women's dresses, wigs, and high heels, were chasing Marilyn Monroe down a busy street in *Some Like it Hot*. Boxes surrounded Mother's wheelchair, some stacked, one fallen on its side, spilling a hair dryer, alarm clock, and hand towels. Jackets and dresses draped the sofa and rocking chair. Two very upset cats cried from pet carriers on the front porch.

Mother's eyelids fluttered at a remarkable speed.

"Oh, Mother. Did we explain Walker remarried Danielle? These must be her things." She knelt beside the wheelchair. "You see, he's bringing her here to live. I know it will take some getting used to, but the company might do you good. Remember how lively she is. And she won't be here all the time—she works the day shift at the motel."

"Pebbles," Mother said.

"Don't worry, dear. I haven't forgotten you're allergic to cats."

Mother's eyelids settled down.

"Let's get you taken care of," Lee Ann said, shoving the hair dryer and clock aside with her foot. "Manuel and Rudy are taking time off to help with roundup Sunday. There will be leftovers after the men have eaten, but tonight I brought a frozen dinner. We'll make do. Claire Marsh was at the Extension Office today and asked about you, said to remind you of the time Alma Persons gave you both basket-weaving lessons and you made a tiny, misshapen pine needle basket with a narrow neck and acted silly, stuffing it with pine needles with their sharp ends sticking out the top. You tacked it to the living room wall, joking about your talent as an *artiste*. That must have been before I was born. I don't think I ever saw it."

The wheelchair nicked boxes on its way through the maze.

"Claire was reserving a space for the Democrats inside the exhibits building at the fair. She was huffy about it, complaining that last year they designated only one table, for Republicans. Claire warned that this year had better be different, with space allotted to *all* political parties. I pretended to sympathize." She steered Mother to the bathroom. "Mother, if God sees all and is just, I can't understand why some are favored and some are forgiven, some are lucky and others are cursed. Dishonest men are spared. Yes, I'm talking about the commissioners. I suppose they'll receive a fair verdict on judgment day, but in the meantime they're depriving low-income women and children of essential services. It's despicable."

Halfway down the dim hallway, she stopped short outside her old bedroom. Clothes covered the bed—sequined tee shirts and blue jeans, short skirts, and colorful blouses. Shoes and purses blocked the entrance. The room smelled like a hothouse overgrown with gardenias. Lee Ann had never dabbed scent behind an ear, sprayed her hair, or dusted with bath powder. As a teenager she'd tried lipstick, but at some point had read, *Do not let your adornment be merely outward—arranging the hair, wearing gold, or putting on fine apparel—rather, let it be the hidden person of the heart, with the incorruptible beauty of a gentle and quiet spirit, which is very precious in the sight of God.* 1 Peter 3:4. On the ranch she wore jeans, but always dressed in a skirt or pantsuit for work. A range of grays, tans, and dark blues filled her closet, no rainbows there. Bright colors conjured images of Indian powwows and native dances from south of the border. Swirling skirts and clicking heels accompanied by lively music aroused passion and excitement, emotions better kept under control. Donning a white blouse and gray suit brought things down to a calm level where the miracle of a mockingbird's song, a woodpecker's tap, and the hatching of a baby chick affirmed the glory of creation. In spring, pink apple blossoms burst open in the small orchard south of the house. All too soon their pastel beauty faded, their memory blotted out by the boisterous red and yellow red hot pokers Grace had given Mother thirty years ago. At the time, they'd formed a small clump by the porch steps. Now, they lined the entire front of the house, having multiplied to three feet deep. Although the garish, phallic flowers lived short lives and left a lush, green hedge that softened the chalk white stucco, as soon as Mother died, she'd have Scott dig them up.

She carried the two cat carriers to the workshop and set out a bowl of dry food and water, emptied a box of work gloves, filled it with dirt and set it in the corner. For years they had kept only barn cats, their feral population controlled by coyotes and bobcats. She unhooked the cat carrier doors and Danielle's two critters leapt to the floor, seeking shelter under the worktable. Eugene wouldn't be happy with these tenants. She fumbled through his toolbox for a pencil, tore a sheet from the legal pad on the table saw, scrawled a warning and tacked it to the door: *Cats inside. Enter quickly and shut the door.*

19

THE WIND DIED AND AS daylight faded the dogs began their anxious barking at real or imagined threats lurking on the mesa. Walker sat in the willow chair on Mother's porch, feet propped on the railing, smoking, and sipping whiskey on the rocks. Full darkness set in and the dogs shut up, scampering off to greet someone approaching from the workshop. Walker kept quiet as Lee Ann walked quickly to her house.

He'd give Keith some time to enjoy Plank's Plot, zero in and make the sale and haul ass out of here, cash in hand. Within a week every last one of them would be on his ass, teeth gnashing, CBs on, pistols loaded—Lyle, with deputies Jeremy and Lewis, Ralph Archuleta and a couple of officers from the state police, Owen, Danielle, and Eugene. You bet, Eugene. They'd call Ted Bowles at his law office in Socorro and check the legitimacy of the quitclaim deed, agree it was legal, and grumble about the stupidity (or senility) of the old man falling for the scam of a convicted criminal, a man Ross knew to be a con artist from the day he was born. They'd call Border Patrol, expecting him to head to Mexico, but he'd travel in the opposite direction, to Michigan's Upper Peninsula, where he and Pat Merker had plans to meet in a town called Paradise.

He lit another smoke and drank from the plastic cup that rolled around the floor of his pickup. Coming home after Mother went to bed and taking off in the morning before Grace arrived prevented getting trapped in matters of consideration—consideration of Mother's routine, feelings, and needs. Truth was, she was just a shell of her former self and probably didn't understand or give a damn about all the fuss over her wellbeing.

The full, white moon inched over the mesa and traveled its path over the northeast end of the house, shining in Mother's window. If she woke up, she'd be helpless, unable to call someone to close the curtain. Hell, in her shoes, he'd as soon give up food and water and be done with life in three short weeks. Poor Mother couldn't even tell her Christ-loving daughter to quit saving the dying, quit being a martyr, leave a worthless old woman's life alone, get on with her own.

Black walnuts hit the roof. Bonk. Bonk. Bonk. When Dad plucked that young tree from the forest and planted it out back, Mother had warned the nuts would become a problem—not a problem really, but something that might take getting used to. Dad had laughed, saying that'd be years away. When the nuts began to fall, they'd all grown used to the tree, welcomed its summer shade and by unanimous decision agreed to let it grow, although they half laughed, half grumbled about the concert every fall.

He poured another drink, and another. An owl hooted from the cluster of cottonwoods by the creek. Small rodents scratched under the porch. Past midnight, light hit the trees and Danielle's jeep slowed to a stop. He sat there until the last minute, and hop-skipped down the steps.

"Lady deserves an escort to her new home," he said, opening the car door. He sniffed for hints of sex on her, but liquor and cigarettes overpowered anything else. She wobbled against him and straightened.

"I'm fine."

"Sure you are," he said, clutching her upper arm. "Now we're going to tiptoe down the hall and tuck you into Lee Ann's bed."

Her tee shirt was inside out, lipstick gone, liner smeared into dark smudges under her eyes. Her feet dragged across the floor, and she held onto the wall as they made their way down the dark hallway.

He flipped on the light, shoved the pile of clothes to one side and turned down the covers. She dropped on the mattress like falling timber. He pulled off her boots and drew the quilt over her.

"I hope you got somewhere with the old boy," he said.

"Oh, we got somewhere," she said, as if in a trance.

"I'm talking about the land, the good deal we're going to offer him."

"He was interested in only one thing." She smiled. "You men are all alike."

"Christ, Danielle. You got to remember our purpose here."

Her tongue moved in and out like a turtle's, suggesting obscene, intimate acts and her eyelids closed over eyeballs rolling this way and that, dreaming about sex with a capital S. Her skin was pale, sort of the color of those piglets, and a spot of saliva collected in the corner of her mouth. Sober, she might hang onto their objective, steer every conversation with the vet toward the purchase of Plank's Plot, but drunk she'd throw a fortune away for Keith's prick inside her. She used to call Walker's cock Little Man. His ears turned red. The schemes he concocted and his own internal dialogue were way more interesting than sweaty encounters with women. Flirting served to sharpen his skills. He could do without the heavy breathing and wet stuff.

He checked the amount of cash in the cookie jar and carefully replaced the lid. The ceramic pig had sat beside the Folgers coffee can containing spatulas and wooden spoons as long as he could remember, hell, probably as long as Mother could remember, the glaze on its green bandana worn thin, only faint touches of pink still coloring the inner folds of his ears. Walker touched the pig's snout. Stay right there, Tubby. Hold onto what's inside you for a couple more days.

20

FRIDAY
OCTOBER 5, 2007

L EE ANN HEARD THE BATHTUB filling as she fed
Mother breakfast, could not remember indulging in
such luxury, did remember Harley's fat hand squeezing her
shoulder while asking her to change the second figure of
the lowest bid on an electrical contract from a three to an
eight. A slight swish of water sounded from the bathroom,
a body lolling, not rising. What must it be like, working at
the motel—checking them in, checking them out, telling
Carlinda which rooms to clean, showing up at nine, leaving
at four, reading magazines on the job, suggesting points of
interest to eager travelers, organizing the brochure rack and
driving home without budget details, altered documents,
and bothersome people to contend with, personnel who,
like herself, would never quit.

A copy of the Sunday *Albuquerque Journal* had been placed
on her desk with an article circled in red. Her purse fell
from her shoulder and still in her jacket, she sat down to
read.

*Several rural New Mexico counties have hit a jackpot—at
least temporarily—under a beefed-up federal program for those
with large tracts of federal forest.*

*The revenue stream known as County Payments swelled in
2007 as part of the $700 billion federal bailout program, with
New Mexico's share jumping from 2.3 million to 18.8 million.*

Forest payments in six counties increased as much as 1,000 percent, with about half going to county road projects and half to the school systems.

Dax County, according to the Associated Press, received the highest per-capita payment in the nation. Its federal payment grew from $733,422 in the 2006 fiscal year to $6.4 million a year later. Critics say the changes, originally intended to help logging communities hurt by the Endangered Species Act and battles over the Spotted Owl, have transformed the program into an entitlement.

Because four-fifths of Dax County acreage is federal or state trust land, economic development is greatly restricted.

The funds will likely rekindle a century-old debate about what rural counties should expect from the federal government in exchange for hosting public lands.

Her body bent toward the paper, fingers gripping her forearms. State reporters would likely show up at the courthouse within the next few days to ask just how Dax County planned to spend the windfall. The commissioners hadn't shared the news. She pictured Harley, Ed, and Saul standing side by side, collars choking thick necks, arms limp, shirts stretched tight, buttons threatening to pop their holes. Three little pigs. A padded wall of resistance. To her face, pleasantries. Behind her back, disrespect.

No doubt, within the next half hour one of the three would call to "chat." The room was cold. Saul Duran's brother-in-law, who constructed the building, had probably charged the county a bundle and scrimped on the insulation. Last winter the heat had gone out for four days and she'd had to call a plumber from Socorro. No one in town knew how to fix the furnace. She grabbed the closest folder to give the impression of impending business and went downstairs to the clerk's office to have them send a memo saying the heat would be turned on the following day.

In the hall she met the sheriff, a cup of coffee in his hand.

"Mornin', Lee Ann." He cleared his throat. "Ross Plank died last night, peacefully, in his sleep. The nursing home called Owen first thing this morning."

She hadn't been particularly fond of the man.

"I'm sorry," she said. "Let me know when they schedule the funeral. Tell Owen I'll contact the women's auxiliary and arrange for a potluck at the community center. He and Rita will have enough on their hands."

She opened the file in her hand and lifted her head, as if suddenly remembering an item needing attention, flashed a weak smile, and hurried down the corridor.

She could quit. Let them hire another patsy. Until now health insurance, retirement benefits, and a steady salary had justified sticking with the job. It hadn't mattered much if Saul Duran gave a construction contract to his broth-er-in-law. Things had always been that way. When federal funds specified for Head Start had been used to create a position for Ed Richter's niece in the treasurer's office, she'd looked the other way, like everyone else. But what she'd termed "misdemeanors" were indeed criminal acts, and passive acquiescence amounted to active participation.

In her dreams papers blew off her desk. Wind spewed data in all directions and her fingers reached for information beyond her grasp. The filing system was jumbled. Dates and titles made no sense. Numbers added up to incorrect totals, other pages were blank. Paper-clipped reports stamped Urgent and Top Priority had pages missing. Frantic, she leafed through them...1, 2, 3, 4...22...10, 11,...18, shuffling, re-counting.

The Jeep's squeaky brakes and bright headlights woke her at two a.m. The car door slammed and Walker muttered as he steered Danielle into Mother's house. Lee Ann got into her robe and pulled a chair up to the small round table in the corner of the dining room. Lamplight picked up her thumbprints on the glass covering Jesus and a smudge where she'd once pressed her lips to his image. She opened the Bible to Ecclesiastes, as it spoke to the meaninglessness of life's labors, the inability to change one's fate, and acceptance of the intrinsic nature of all God's creatures.

As she often did as a child, she selected a page at random. *One event happens to the righteous and the wicked; to the good, the clean, and the unclean. To him who sacrifices and to him who does not sacrifice. As is the good, so is the sinner; he who takes an oath as he who fears an oath.* Ecclesiastes 9:2. The passage implied all would suffer indiscriminately during catastrophic earthquakes, hurricanes, or floods. The good and faithful would not be selected, given preference, or be saved. However, the passage might also mean that even under ordinary conditions, kindness and faith do not determine a person's worth in the eyes of the Lord, that in light of all that may befall a person, to any degree, intention matters not a hoot, that God inflicts wrath or bounty indiscriminately, without preference for who will suffer and who will not. This couldn't be right, for the Bible instructs how to act, and that God will be pleased if His instructions are followed. There would be no point in living faithfully if there was no payoff. Good deeds *must* merit special treatment—if not in this life, then the next—or all efforts to live devoutly would be in vain. Tears fell onto the passage. She swiped her cheeks with the back of her hand, but the tears kept flowing, wetting the page clear through to the one underneath, and the one beneath that.

From the window, moonlight shone on Mother's house, all the windows dark. Walker home almost a week. Dad dead sixteen years. At some point Mother and Dad must have accepted that environmental influences had little to do with how Walker turned out. Like everyone else, Dad had been baffled at Walker's talent for getting into trouble, but played along, agreeing with Mother to bail him out of jams. Many were the nights Dad ordered Walker to sit on a stool, lecturing him on regard for others. As far as speaking the truth, Dad admitted no one did. From early on, Dax County folks learned to hide honest opinions under a façade of pleasantries and tuck condemning comments behind a neighborly smile. But damn it, the boy ought to have a sense of regard.

Mother and Dad argued behind their bedroom door. He means no harm. *He's got to learn.* This is a stage. *It's gone on too long.* He'll mature. *He ain't interested in being an adult.* A sigh. Another sigh. But most often Dad laughed at Walker's spunk and bravado, his daring, his defiance of authority, his confidence in being able to worm his way out of any scrape. What ingenuity! Such imagination! The two of them hung over the corral fence, Dad resting on his forearms, Walker letting go of the rail to imitate Pastor Fletcher slinking up the church aisle, his body concave as the hook on a coat hanger, or Ross Plank pushing his wife across the dance floor, rigid as a robot, or Grace following each sentence with her nose when she read up close, and Dad would roar. Pretty soon he'd grab Walker's neck, stick a shovel in his hand and shove him toward the barn. Walker would heave a few clumps of manure and the minute Dad disappeared, plant the shovel in the rest and mount Lucky, gallop across the field and up Salida Canyon. How she'd despised him! How she'd fought giving in to those contemptible emotions!

These days, folks sought explanations for reprehensible behavior—verbal or physical abuse during childhood the most common reason. Mother and Dad had their faults and idiosyncrasies, but they enjoyed their kids. They'd bicker over the date to plant the garden, how much household money to keep on hand, how rare to cook a steak, when to breed the heifers. Any subject would set them huffing and puffing, as if their particular point of view determined life or death, then one or the other would walk away or shrug their shoulders, the whole argument having amounted to nothing more than an exercise in who could banter better. Sunday morning, instead of dressing for church, Dad would be seized by an urge to organize the shop. Mother would dash about like a border collie herding the family together, fuming, in desperate need of a good sermon to settle her down.

If anything, Lee Ann and Walker had been spoiled as kids. Each rode their own horse, raised their own animals, wore new clothes, owned a personal vehicle at sixteen, had been allotted a generous allowance, and been given the freedom to arrange social activities, with one exception. Church attendance on Sunday was mandatory. From the start, the Bible's teachings from a God on high, delivered passionately by an emaciated pastor in a stark room, stuck to Lee Ann. Guided by the pastor's words, lifted by hymns sung in unison, greeted by a congregation decked out in their Sunday best, the church encouraged the best in her. If she forgot those qualities during the week, the Lord reminded her every Sunday. The same sermon delivered in the same environment by the same preacher passed straight through Walker's head, as if there were nothing in there for the message to latch onto.

She straightened the picture of Jesus and turned back to Ecclesiastes. The tear-soaked pages had begun to crinkle and curl. She closed the Bible and placed a high school atlas from the living room bookshelves on top of it.

Before breakfast, she set the iron on *delicates* and pressed a sheet of used wrapping paper. The creases disappeared. She opened the Bible and ran the iron over the corner of a wrinkled page. Faint lines showed and she increased the heat to *wool*.

The phone rang and she took the receiver from Dee's hand as he mouthed, "Harley."

"Lee Ann, sorry to bother you so early. Saul, Ed, and I would like to schedule a meeting with you today, as soon as possible."

"I assume this is regarding the windfall."

"Yes, we'll fill you in on the figures and discuss what we want you to say to reporters. We also need to go over the proposed bid for a youth center and some issues with the volunteer fire department."

"I'll meet you at ten o'clock in the conference room. I don't think there's anything scheduled at that..." She grabbed the iron. Where it had rested, the paper was scorched and hot to the touch, the page brittle and scarred.

21

PLANK DEAD. WHOOSH. GONE.

"It ain't fair, Mother. A sweet soul like yourself suffering day in day out, caught in limbo, and that old fart just closes his eyes and crosses the finish line easy as a racehorse."

"Bubble."

"Yeah, Danielle's somethin', huh? I see she's been watching TV with you this morning, munchin' chips and drinking Cokes. Probably switched channels to something you can't stand." He picked up the remote and found TCM. "And I bet you're pissed off she won't pick up after herself. Doesn't take much to carry a can to the trash and close a bag of Doritos. She never was one to pay attention to anything other than her body. Wait. Let me extend that to a man's body. She's got one now, but I can already predict the outcome. Our sly kitten will twist that guy into every possible contortion until he can't breathe, sneak every last dime out of his pockets, and spend it on junk 'cause she can't tell the difference between crap and quality. There'll be squabbles and resentments, lyin', cheatin', bric-a-brac flyin', until one of those weapons hits him on the head and he wakes up and pitches her out, far as he can, China maybe." He patted Mother's hand and turned up the volume. "Don't you worry. She'll be gone soon. There. Ray Milland in *Lost Weekend*. Never saw it. *Dial M For Murder* was one of Dad's favorites. Remember? He liked Grace Kelly, but she ditched every guy in America and married a prince. Every woman wants a prince. Women are too cowardly to take on the world alone and the richer a man is, the greater the opportunity of never having to face life. A woman can invent all sorts of reasons for wanting a man—soul mate, true heart, good in the sack, but in the end, it boils down to one fact—a man will allow a woman to slack off dealing with survival. Fill a pill with vitamins, you still got but one pill. Hell, I got to go."

Keith was off somewhere, the ATV's tires having flattened two strips of grassland toward the Randall Range. Walker tried the door to the trailer. The living room was empty, but for the couch and lounger, and of course, the brown throw. A shingle flapped on the roof and down the hall a branch scratched against one of the bedroom windows. The frills women collected mattered, and placemats and a few knickknacks might have cozied up the place, but Danielle obviously wasn't into decorating the same dump twice. Under grimy kitchen wall cabinets, Keith's red and black flannel shirt lay on the counter beside a leather wallet, loose change, and a checkbook. Walker shoved his hands into his pockets, hunched his shoulders, and stepped closer to the counter. Aside from Keith's driver's license, the wallet contained the usual credit cards and $643.00 in cash. He opened the checkbook. A balance of $1,266,000.57 written neatly in fine ballpoint pen popped off the page. He folded the checkbook and held it to his chest. Eyes closed, he rubbed the slick plastic cover, as if warming his hands, and slowly re-opened it. Yup. $1,266,000.57. Flipping back through the entries, he discovered $880,000.00 had been withdrawn just prior to Keith's visit. The vet was ready, and able, to buy. Walker rushed outside and hollered. "YEE-HAH!" A few grackles lit out from the trees. He threw his arms to the heavens, dashed the length of the trailer and back. Boy, he'd love to call Pat Merker, spill the news. Pat Merker. Merk the Jerk. The guy hadn't lied. All their jabbering and plotting and big ideas were about to pay off. Hot damn. Hot tamales. Hot stuff. Hot to trot. Hot spot. Good shot. Hit the spot. Thanks a lot.

Do not tell Jo. He drew an imaginary zipper with a silver tassel across his lips. Oh, but she'd get a kick out of this one. She'd be hurt that he hadn't let her in on the scheme, wonder for years what became of him, because this time he'd disappear for good. No sneaking back for a midnight visit to laugh at the havoc he'd created. Couldn't take the chance. This deal amounted to the grand finale, the culmination of forty-two years of practice.

A cloud passed in front of the sun, casting the dirt in even light. In prison he'd ached for sun on his skin. Lying on his cot at night, blinking into black stale air, he'd clear his mind and drift to a speck of ground out on the plains and stand in the sun he'd taken for granted, the horizon far off. The only thing to discover in any direction would be more space, the air so dry, sweat evaporated before it dropped. And he'd zoom like an aircraft, arms pressed against his sides, head directing his body west toward rolling hills, until he caught sight of the Rio Risa trickling out of the Mariposa Mountains. He'd follow the river to where it met Alibi Creek, where he could damn near smell ponderosa pine baking in the July heat, get a headache from juniper pollen, spit dust, and squint against snow that stayed dazzling white. He'd land and bow to lizards, gophers, rattlers, and bull snakes, his ears straining to pick up the low bleating of a cow, a baby elk squealing for its mama, or a coyote calling its mate, and drift off to sleep with the love of place, the missing of place and the longing for place. This place.

He reached into the bed of the pickup, took a beer out of the cooler and drove seven miles north, up through the rock cliffs onto the flats just this side of Arizona and parked between a couple of cedars and walked into the field. The final warmth of summer had put a hold on the season, refusing to let go. Flies and gnats buzzed lazily, about done with their frenzied dance until spring. His eyes fixed on a spot a hundred feet ahead and when he got there he tossed down his hat, lay on his back, arms tucked under his head. Pebbles poked his shoulders and rough clumps of grass tickled his neck, and a light breeze licked his cheek. He shut his eyes against the shocking blue sky and fell asleep.

He met Jo on her usual perch at 5:10 sharp and took the Manhattan from her hand before she took a second sip.

"Darlin', let's blow this joint, get some real food in a fine restaurant."

"Any restaurant classified as 'fine' is an hour and a half from here. I'm tired."

"C'mon. You don't need to do a thing. I'm driving." He poked the corners of her mouth into a smile. "That's better. Say, 'why Walker, I'd love to!' like a pleasant lady."

She removed his fingers and sucked in her cheeks.

"I'm no pleasant lady, and you know it."

"Sweetheart, I know just who you are and I appreciate every cell in your body. Tonight I aim to show you how much. This much." He pulled her off the stool and wrapped his arms around her and squeezed with all his might.

"I can't breathe."

"Don't sit down," he said, grabbing her purse, then her hand, and dragging her out the door. "Larry's Front Quarter, here we come!"

"Damn you, Walker. Maybe I got plans tonight."

"This is the plan. And I'm your man. The night belongs to us."

They drove west into the last of daylight and he hooked his pinkie around hers until she relaxed.

"Personally," she said, pulling her hand away and lighting a cigarette, "I've got nothing against your sister, but everyone else rolls their eyes. Running around with a clipboard clutched to her chest like a coat of armor, supporting all that crap those commissioners dole out. We're all waiting to hear the bullshit she hands to the press about the big federal handout. Nothing will change. Years from now, if we're lucky, we'll discover what the Three Stooges did with the money."

Walker drove in silence. He never spoke ill of Lee Ann, never defended her either. The favors she'd done him outweighed expressing personal feelings one way or the other. He had his opinions, though. Lee Ann wasted time trying to live up to Christian ideals that didn't exist. Any sane person would go nuts meeting those standards, even God Himself. Pious folks set the bar high to make sure there'd be a lot of room for failure and therefore, criticism, which meant a lot of room for improvement spelled out in the Bible. Lee Ann cared too much what others thought. There wasn't a person alive could please everyone. Trying to please everyone resulted in living carefully, self-consciously, and that amounted to keeping secrets about all sorts of ugly acts righteous people pretended not to have committed. Living carefully ruined spontaneity. Sure as a boot heel snuffed out a spark, the thrill of reacting in the moment couldn't thrive smothered with caution. Taking up with Eugene was probably the one time in her life lust drew Lee Ann into a whirlwind of emotion too powerful to resist. As if to repent, she loaded herself with a slew of duties. He'd caught her whispering, probably still begging for forgiveness for the sin of betraying Wayne, that clumsy, morose, first husband she couldn't stomach, a man with such a gray temperament folks skedaddled when they saw him coming. She should have dumped him the first week of their marriage, but oh, no. Lee Ann stood by her commitments.

"You listening?" Jo said. "I've only got a twenty."

"This is on me."

He'd sweet-talk Larry out of the bill once they'd eaten.

A lump the size of a wild plum, and growing, stuck in his throat and his tongue felt thick. Their last night together. Jo slipped her arms out of her jacket and opened the menu, candlelight flushing her chin and forehead, cheeks aglow. Why, her hair, which usually reminded him of a Brillo pad, looked soft as dandelion fluff. She'd dabbed her nose with makeup and swiped dusty rose lipstick across lips seldom bruised by kisses. Delicate, unadorned hands unwrapped the cloth napkin rolled around a steak knife and fork. Without missing a beat, she ordered a Royal Manhattan.

"Thanks, Walker. I didn't realize how much I needed a change from the same old grind."

When their drinks arrived, he cleared his throat, swallowed hard, and toasted their friendship, that damn thick tongue getting in the way of his words.

"Yeah, yeah, yeah," she said, smiling with her whole face, some of that candlelight dancing in her eyes. "I love you, too."

They recalled capers they'd pulled when they were kids. By the light of a full moon they'd raided Iris Herrington's garden, picked the corn, pulled up carrots, plucked tomatoes, peppers, cucumbers, and squash, and conned Art, who was old enough to use his dad's truck, into driving them to the farmers market in Show Low for a cut of the profits.

They'd convinced their classmates to invest in a group lottery ticket and kept the money. And what about the time he told everyone Jo was in the hospital and collected money to send flowers, plush slippers, and a terrycloth bathrobe when really, she'd skipped school to go to Phoenix with her mother. They'd shared the money and hitched a ride to Silver City and got stomachaches from an overdose of popcorn, Nibbs, and chocolate covered mints while watching *Indiana Jones and the Temple of Doom.* At some point Walker discovered the value of pre-historic Indian pottery—artifacts Dad had discovered atop the mesas along Alibi Creek, on the Walker Ranch, and in the national forest. Before Lee Ann found out, he and Jo sold half the family's collection to galleries in Santa Fe and dealers in Albuquerque. He'd put money down on land without clear title and resold the property indiscriminately, bought and sold crappy used cars and trucks. His first stint in jail had resulted from scamming folks into importing Mexican cattle with a make-believe partner in Chihuahua. He and the money disappeared. Six months later, broke and worn out, he reappeared having declared bankruptcy. Lyle showed up the next day and took him to jail, booked him on fraud.

Not only Jo forgave him. Folks blamed themselves, not Walker, for falling for his wild propositions. Sure, after losing money they'd get pissed off and upset, swear up and down and call him names saved for their worst enemy. In the end, however, they'd been entertained, beguiled, and enchanted by the thrill of believing in a dream. Deep in their hearts, they knew the unlikelihood of this "sure thing" paying off. But then again, maybe, just maybe it might. And when the scheme failed, and he looked so forlorn for disappointing them, saying no, there was no way to get the money back, most ended up feeling sorry for the guy. Of course, there were plenty who would never speak to Walker again, who spit at the mention of his name.

Jo dabbed sour cream on her baked potato and sprinkled chives and bacon on top, sipped her drink, and sighed before cutting into her steak, savoring each bite. She reached for a roll, broke off a piece, and slathered it with butter.

"Where's your wife?" she asked.

"Three guesses."

"I know you married her for a reason, and I won't pry, but I don't imagine her running off with Keith was part of the plan."

"Things couldn't have worked out better," he said. "I get to spend tonight with you."

He jumped from the pickup and escorted her to the door.

"That's not necessary," she said.

"I'm coming in."

"Walker, we've tried this. It doesn't work."

"You're killin' it by sayin' that."

She led the way up the flagstone walkway and he followed her inside. In the dark he held her shoulders and turned her to him.

"You're a married man."

"You're jealous."

"That's right."

"No need to be. I joke you're the only gal for me, but I mean it," he said. "All the others are either too young or too tall."

"That's not funny," she said.

He tipped her chin up and kissed her closed, baby soft lips.

"C'mon, relax," he whispered. "I got so much feelin' for you I'm about to bust."

He pressed her hand against his crotch.

"See."

Her hand rested where he placed it, as if deliberating whether his erection could hold up and deciding it just might, she led him into the bedroom. He unbuttoned her blouse and unzipped her skirt. She undid his belt and tugged at his shirt. One step dropped them beside each other in bed, one leg over another locked them together, one kiss led to lips against shoulder, breast, and belly. She smelled kind of like the courthouse, but he didn't mind. Those thighs, he welcomed their grip. She raised her arms above her head and moonlight caught the curve of her armpit and the swell of her breast. He looked down at her closed eyes and parted lips and his body moved as though he were singing to her, the rhythm carrying him along, her response spurring him on. She hugged his neck and moved with him and against him. In all his days, he never felt anything like it.

22

ROOT-BOUND HOUSEPLANTS HAD BEEN MOVED to the front porch. The ficus and jade trees desperately needed larger pots. Baby spider plants begged for freedom from their mother and the sansevieria cried to be divided. Lee Ann carried big planters from the garden shed and sliced open bags of potting soil, donned gardening gloves, and filled the watering can.

"There," she said, after placing the newly potted plants in the mudroom and sweeping up the mess. "If you aren't happy now, you will be by next week. I'll be in the kitchen if you need anything."

She had learned to cook from assisting Mother and watching Grace. Meat loaf, roasts, and pies from Mother. Mexican food from Grace, who claimed Lee Ann's flour tortillas looked like maps of Australia. Mexicans, Grace said, had the gene for rolling perfectly round tortillas, estimating how hot the griddle should be to receive them, and knowing the exact moment to flip them to freckle the surface.

Manuel and Rudy, the sheriff's ranch hands who would join Eugene and the boys for roundup, were raised in the Hispanic community of Alba and preferred New Mexican green chile stew, but Eugene and the boys preferred Texas-style chile and that's what Lee Ann planned to serve for the mid-day meal at tomorrow's roundup. In addition to tortillas, she'd add chopped green chile and cheddar cheese to a double batch of cornbread and bake a carrot cake with cream cheese icing for dessert.

From a sack in the pantry, she leveled off several cups of pinto beans into a big enamel pot and added enough water to soak them overnight. She'd already stopped by Walt's after work and picked up onions and a few of his famous withered bell peppers, lemons, and a cabbage for coleslaw.

In the old days, when they ran three times the cattle and needed three times the men, Mother would request volunteers to help in the kitchen, roundup the excuse for a social event that gathered folks from far-off ranches. The following weeks would bring the same crew and the same women to another ranch. But the cattle industry in the southwest had taken a beating. Five or six hands (depending if Walker participated or not) could handle the work these days. Edgar was too old and arthritic. The Walker Ranch acreage was puny, hardly looked upon as a ranch at all by some, lush bottomland and national forest grazing allotments the only advantages keeping them in business. The men would start early and bring the cattle in from the range, move them through the canyons, across the highway, and through the creek toward the chute, separate mothers from calves, inoculate, brand, and castrate, and pen those ready for sale. The following morning they'd move the herd to winter pasture.

Walker might ride along, or not. As a kid, he'd been too excited the night before roundup to sleep. As an adult, the events of the previous night determined the hour he'd wake and whether a hangover prevented participating. She preferred he not show. Save Eugene getting worked up.

After adjusting Mother's covers and whispering goodnight, she stopped in her old bedroom. Clothes still formed a mound at the foot of the bed and rhinestone jewelry, eye shadow, eyeliner, and every shade of lipstick covered the bureau. She opened a tube of Hot Stuff, raised the color to her nose and sniffed.

"There you are."

Lee Ann stiffened.

"Seems we're on opposite schedules," Danielle said, filling the doorframe, one hand on her hip, the other patting her thigh.

"I didn't mean to be snooping," Lee Ann said, replacing the top on the lipstick. "Just wanted to make sure you were settled. I've been meaning to stop by the motel and get re-acquainted…"

"I'm going out in an hour, just came home to change clothes."

Home. Lee Ann snatched the word, set it aside. Not yours. Mine. *My* kitchen waiting to be filled with men's chatter, casseroles bubbling in the oven, today's mail. Home. Mother waiting, clothes blowing on the line, elk passing through, birds nesting, dogs sleeping on the porch. *My* flowers, *my* orchard, *my* garden.

She said, "I'd like to sit down over a cup of coffee, catch up, and go over Mother's schedule. Walker must have explained."

"He did. Maybe this weekend," Danielle said. "Where are my cats?"

Oh, dear. She'd forgotten to tell Edgar to feed them.

"They're in the workshop. I'm afraid they'll have to stay there. Mother's allergic." She stepped away from the dresser. "Why don't you come by tomorrow afternoon after the men have eaten?"

Danielle entered the room and kicked off her shoes. "Sundays, I'm off at four."

Lee Ann bolted toward the hall. "See you then. And congratulations on your remarriage!"

23

A DIME-SIZE SPOT OF CHILE dripped off the ladle onto Lee Ann's skirt, just above the knee. She was out of Shout. Walt's charged double for that sort of item and she refused to pay his prices. She'd quit shopping at the Alibi Creek Store since the marquis that once announced the price of gas began advertising the cost of liquor. Plus, the combined smell of booze, cigarettes, and greasy pine floor was sickening. Mother would know a home remedy. She should've written down her household tips when she'd had the chance.

Perhaps Grace had stored some spot remover at Mother's. Crossing the yard, she heard voices, a woman and man talking and laughing. Light from inside Mother's living room window shone onto the porch. The talking and laughter stopped, replaced by footsteps shuffling through leaves. Eugene carried an armload of firewood from beneath the overhang at the end of Mother's house up the steps. He walked erect, chest puffed out, shoulders back. Danielle stood above him, lit from behind, her shoulder against the porch post. Beside the front door, Eugene bent from the waist, gallantly almost, and placed each log precisely, as if he alone had perfected the art of stacking wood, his posture the same as when he and Lee Ann first started seeing each other—that of a man aroused, a man redefined by a woman, proud of his appeal, smug in his ability to seduce. Big man helping little lady.

She backed up, breathless. For heaven's sake, calm down…nothing had happened…though it could…he'd never…Lord, he'd cheated with her, she with him…do it once…really now, he was trustworthy…

But Danielle…

He hadn't laughed like that since before Walker came home…was it the night Caroline and her husband came over to play Mexican Train…or on August 21st, when Dee gave him a tiny mustache brush to comb the long wiry hairs that had begun to sprout from his eyebrows for his birthday…or the night he played the rogue and she the innocent victim…

She slipped back to the house and ate four cookies, took a bite of another one and threw it across the room, covered her face with her hands and shook with all the energy stored up from bearing up—with Walker, with the commissioners, with Mother.

Mother, Mother, Mother! All the time and effort spent caring for her. Cooking, cajoling, feeding, dressing, laundering, cleaning. Tending to her bath and toilet needs. Talking softly when a scream would better voice her frustration. Now, the skin on Mother's legs had begun to blaze red, ooze, and stretch over swollen ankles. She'd soiled herself twice this last week. Got the hiccups after every meal. Did she have a headache, toothache, stomachache? Heartache?

Eugene, whose arms comforted, words encouraged, smile praised. Couldn't remember the last time they'd held hands, exchanged knowing looks or pet names—Doll, Jellybean, Ever Girl, Captain, Jujube, Gumdrop, Buttercup. Couldn't lose him. Had been losing him. He'd been slipping away since the moment Walker returned. Damn Walker, anyway. Damn him!

But now you must put them all away: anger, wrath, malice, slander and obscene talk from your mouth. Colossians 3:8.

The Bible. For solace. For wisdom. Read, search, understand, accept. Look to The Word to find The Way. She crossed the dining room to the round table with its perfect arrangement of Bible, bookmark, and portrait. Her pink gardening gloves had been left on the Bible and muddied the word *Holy*. Clumps of potting soil had fallen on Grandma Edna's handiwork, the tiny knots and loose spaces clogged with dirt.

Scott and Dee came in, tossed their hats on the buffet, and went to the bathroom to wash up.

"You'll have to wait for dinner tonight," she said, whisking the Bible, blowing on it, lifting the tablecloth and running her palm underneath. "I'm busy."

Scott turned back.

"Everything okay, Mom?"

She nodded, everything okay. She rubbed the Bible with her shirtsleeve and set it on the edge of the table. It teetered precariously and she pushed it closer to the center, dragging the tablecloth and Jesus with it. She ran outside without a jacket and hid in the trees, blowing on her fingers, pressing her knees together to prevent them from knocking.

Eugene swaggered down the steps like a teenage boy on his first date. Danielle waved. Halfway down the path he looked back and she tossed her hair, waved again.

24

WALKER DROVE BY VERA'S SEARCHING for Keith's white Suburban and not spotting it, accelerated past Owen's pickup parked in front of the Church of Christ. Rose Fletcher's flabby, bland face, contorted into exaggerated sympathy, would be advising Owen and Rita on Ross's funeral arrangements. Of course, a donation would be welcome if they chose to show their appreciation. Damn preachers and their suffering wives.

When he died, he'd be buried up the canyon under the stars between a pair of ponderosas he'd watched inch their way into the sky since he was a boy, no headstone summing up a man's life in a couple of brief sentences, no numbers dating his existence, no preacher embellishing his memory with a line of bullshit. He hadn't specifically defined his thoughts on life and death, but there had to be more to the great mystery than anyone figured. Before birth, his spirit had probably toured outer space and oops, got trapped on the physical plane and without being consulted, had been assigned a brief stint here on earth. Confined to a body too small to contain his exuberance, he'd bounce around this world as best he could until his organs wore out or a sudden accident set his essence free. Beyond that, it was anyone's guess where a soul might travel, what inconceivable realities were yet to be encountered. No sense mulling over the alternatives because no one, not Pastor Fletcher himself, could fathom or prove anything beyond the limitations of this here planet. So, hey, "be here now," as they say. Operate by your wits in any given situation. Play the game. On the moment of departure, the physical world and all its trappings vanish.

He zoomed along the highway, took the turn into Plank's Plot on two wheels, splashed through the creek and screeched to a halt in front of the trailer, choking on dust thick as fog. Keith came down the steps clearing the air with his hat.

Walker left the cab door open and motor running. This would only take a minute.

"Mornin'. Glad I caught you before you trekked off somewhere," he said, withering in front of the not-so-jolly green giant. The trailer provided some consolation, its tacky construction whispering, *You and I recognize each other. It's as uncomfortable for me having him living inside as it is for you dealing with him.*

"You're doing just fine, I see. I'm guessing this property has awakened your senses, excited a long lost part of yourself. The kid in you."

"It is pretty special."

"Damn right." He scratched the back of his neck. Might as well come right out and say it. This dude wasn't about to make conversation easy. "The price is $880,000.00."

Damn, he did look like a giant—feet planted, arms folded across his chest, biceps and forearms bulging.

"I'll consider that when I see proof of ownership."

Walker scurried to produce the envelope.

"Got a quitclaim deed from Ross Plank right here. It's legit. Signed and notarized."

Keith studied the form. "Drawn up just this week."

"And lucky, too. The old man died yesterday, in his sleep. As I said, I'm just checking to see if you need anything.

Otherwise I'll come by Monday after you've given it some thought and we can wind things up."

If Keith were any other man, Walker would offer to stick around, point out hidden trails, buy drinks at Art's, and treat him to a meal at Vera's. This iceberg wasn't going to melt, though. Let Danielle work him.

Keith handed back the deed.

"I'll have to see a clear title."

"No question about the title. This property's been in the Plank family for three generations, never a loan on it, no liens against it. Reason I know is my family's been here longer than that. Around here folks got nothing better to do than keep up on other folks' business. And believe me, I could tell you some things about Ross Plank, how he saw the world through a two inch pipe, blind to everything outside that scope. The man had no imagination, wrapped up what could have been a great story in a couple of sentences. Couldn't dance, didn't drink. Repetitive as 'Silent Night' at Christmas, so boring we'd yawn soon as he opened his mouth. But he was honest. George Washington didn't have anything on Ross in the never-told-a-lie department. If you asked how he was doing he'd tell you, 'My feet ache. This morning I had a bout of diarrhea after a week of constipation. I sprouted this darn wart here on my left cheek and wax is clogging my ears, making me deaf. My back tooth on the upper right side needs pulling because of a quarter inch cavity worrying the nerve.' He'd reveal down to the last penny how much he paid for his yearling calves and how much his taxes went up and the amount of Charlotte's inheritance. He'd tell you if you looked bad, and how bad. You'd about want to smack him in the mouth. No, there ain't no problem with the title to this place. Half the county would know about it if there was."

Keith said, "I'll pay you half now and the rest after the title search."

"Look man, investigating an honest man's record is a waste of time and money." Christ. "No, sir," Walker said. "It's all or nothin'. I got this quitclaim deed and if you don't want it, there'll be someone else eager to grab up the best bargain this side of the state line."

He slipped the paper back into its envelope and touched it to his hat brim.

"*Hasta* Monday," he said.

He spent the afternoon in Show Low filling a cart with a pair of beige Dockers, a sage green shirt, white socks, and a plastic belt—the outfit something a nine-to-five nerd would wear. And white fake-leather running shoes, size nines, with lightning bolts zigzagging along the sides. He twirled the sunglasses rack, settled on silver wire frames that weighed the least and looked the best and bought a brown baseball cap with a Dallas Cowboys logo. Christ, he'd sworn never to shield his brow with one of those bird beaks advertising a bunch of dumb jocks owned by a few rich guys in big cities. Big cities, small cities, they were all the same—monster machines chugging along, oiled by mortgage payments and car payments and credit card debt, young couples signing on the dotted line for a shot at the American Dream—a house they couldn't afford, a car they could afford, a day without shopping unimaginable. Green forests a memory, silence forgotten. While he was at it, might as well get one of those cell phones with prepaid minutes.

He left his truck in the Safeway/Hairs To You/Taco Bell parking lot and walked down West Deuce of Clubs and into the High Lonesome, an upscale joint compared to Art's. He straightened his collar and ordered a Dos Equis.

Late afternoon turned into early evening, conversation moving from the world going to hell to the best whiskey to the pathetic Diamondbacks to weather predictions. A couple of older gals plopped their soft behinds on stools beside him, ready for anything on a Saturday night. Didn't take much to get them giggling. He told them about driving twenty-five miles into the forest with a woman new to Alibi Creek to collect flat rocks for her walkway. The axle broke on his truck with nothing but a cooler of beer in the bed and a ten-foot rope behind the seat. Ordered that city girl to settle down, take a walk, and be patient, they weren't going to be stranded and die of starvation. Being a genius, he used the rope to tie the axle together and drove home *very* slowly. That woman chased him around Bud Berry's New Year's Eve party until he had to hide in the closet to get away from her. Apparently, rope tying impressed women. At nine o'clock he tucked the napkin with both gals' phone numbers in his vest pocket, tossed it in the first trashcan he passed and started the two-hour drive home.

At Mother's, he tiptoed down the hall, cracked Danielle's door. Empty.

Hell, might as well ride along with the roundup crew in the morning. The saddle called.

25

SUNDAY
OCTOBER 7, 2007

NOT THAT NIGHT DIDN'T HAVE certain advantages or bestow certain delights, but morning offered possibilities. A morning was like a newborn baby—full of potential. Some insignificant detail might align loose thoughts that hadn't quite jelled into a plan, bring certain energies into play, tickle some urge that had been lying dormant, like the day a little Cheerio in the breakfast bowl triggered the desire to buy Jo a pair of hoop earrings and he'd taken off for the Albuquerque Flea Market where row after row of folding tables offered hot bargains at cheap prices. He'd struck up a conversation with a long-hair selling genuine merchandise and ended up at a party in a second story apartment where a maniac came at him with a knife and he'd dropped to the floor, crawled under the coffee table, scrambled to his feet, shot out the glass doors to the patio, jumped the railing on one hand, dropped like a circus act onto a kid's trampoline, hit the air a few times, and bounced off without a scratch.

From the chicken house Sir Galahad sounded off, claiming his territory before sunup. Walker considered drifting back into dreamland, but nature's alarm clock wouldn't quit. He threw off the covers, rose up on one elbow and crowed along. "Sit up. Stand up. Roundup."

He met Scott and Dee at the barn loading the horses into the stock trailer, ready to drive the rutted roads across the range to Turkey Mesa. Dee latched the bolt and they climbed into the pickup.

"Let me tell you about these two gals I met in Show Low..."

"Jesus." Scott slammed the door, put her in reverse, then drive. "Later, okay?"

So he quit talking, slumped down in the seat and leaned against the door, watched the stars burn out one by one. Jo hadn't looked so good in the morning. No sir. Still, he'd rolled her over, spooned her, and buried his nose in her hair, cupped her breasts and asked if she'd like to postpone breakfast. She made a noise between a sigh and a groan and wiggled her butt against him. Thankful for curtains blocking direct sunlight, he'd tried to recreate the magic. Didn't work. "Abracadabra" didn't bring the bunny out of the hat. His palms went clammy, so did his feet. The head of his penis dropped and his half-hard hard-on lost its hard.

"Right back where we started," Jo said.

"I got a lot on my mind."

"Sometimes I think your mind is like a vegetable strainer, full of holes."

"Well, that's good. Nothin' gets stale."

"Nothing sticks."

She sat up and threw her legs over the edge of the mattress.

Although he couldn't see her face, her bowed head and drooped shoulders signaled tears brimming. He stepped into his jeans and took both her hands and circled them around his waist. She rested her head against his pelvis. She wouldn't hold on too long. He let her say good-bye.

As they crested Turkey Mesa, milky blue light seeped into the sky. The sun spilled its rays over far-off mountains, striking tumbleweed branches with gold. Round chamisa bushes stood alone and apart—companions, not lovers—looking ready to roll across dirt that appeared light as dust. But Walker's boot treaded on sand and clay, hard as the rocks imbedded in it. A windmill groaned beside the metal stock tank. Jackrabbits had been busy the last couple of months, producing babies with long, translucent ears darting, stopping, hopping between anthills and gopher mounds. They unloaded the horses and waited for Eugene to arrive with the second trailer.

Scott scoured the ground and knelt to inspect a handful of earth, snapped tumbleweed and Apache plume branches, and compared their growth patterns. Dee blinked with heavy lids and fiddled with the horses' reins and readjusted their saddles. Walker followed his shadow off a ways and nudged stones with his boot heel, kicked a few, did a little dance, took a deep breath. Morning!

The clank and rumble sounded long before Eugene's pickup bumped to a stop, Manuel and Rudy filling out the cab. They led the horses out of the trailer, mounted, and looked to Eugene to set the day in motion. No one questioned Eugene's authority. When he stepped into the stirrup, Walker and the boys did the same.

They paired off and fanned out, Walker on the gray with Dee on the buckskin, riding south toward distant ponderosas that looked like a manicured hedge trimming the horizon, jackets zipped, breath misting the air, the horses high-stepping in the brisk morning. Butch, Dee's red heeler, dashed ahead, detoured down shallow arroyos and returned with his nose to the ground, tail straight, tracking a scent, chasing another.

He'd been home eight days and already the light had changed, the sun's distance coloring land and sky in cooler tones. Crazed elk had begun bugling until mid-morning.

Animal patterns had shifted; bears seeking havens in which to hibernate, birds heading south, squirrels hoarding acorns, rodents wintering in, everyone putting on a warm coat. Bruja Mountain, her craggy, pockmarked face more visible out here, warned of ominous, unpredictable events—flash floods, wind storms, blizzards, hail in July, forest fires. He snubbed the witch, flipping his fingers off his chin. This glorious day would not fall under her spell. As a matter of fact, old woman, life had taken a turn for the better. Tomorrow, he'd be rich. Bruja's enemy, Lady Luck, was on his side.

"One hundred bottles of beer on the wall, one hundred bottles of beer…"

"Oh, no you don't." Dee gave Sonny a light jab with his heels and took off.

"…if one of those bottles should happen to fall, ninety-nine bottles of beer on the wall. Ninety-nine bottles of beer on the wall…"

At eighty-two bottles, Dee returned and directed him to a grassy area just this side of the forest. The tall pines were sparse and evenly spaced, decades of dropped pine needles creating dense groundcover at the base of their trunks. In front of the trees, where the grass ended, eight cows stared at them, as if they'd held those exact poses all season. Walker split off to one side, Dee to the other. The cows got nervous and started to shift their weight and lift their feet.

"Well, hello to you, too, good lookin'. Now, take it easy," Walker said. "Nobody's going to hurt your little one. We're just fixing to move you toward the tank."

He veered off after a calf.

"Come on, little fella'. Your mama will be missing you. Time's a-wastin'." The exact moment a calf changed from a lively, frolicking midget into a heavy, lumbering giant was a mystery. Seemed to happen mighty quick. "Come on now. We ain't got all day. You know the routine."

Cows weren't stupid. They babysat each other's calves, recognized their owner's truck, and ambled over to say good afternoon. They bleated and bawled if upset. Each one had a personality, buried, but there, this big red one obstinate as hell.

"Hi ya! Get a move on, gal. Eighty-one bottles of beer on the wall, eighty-one bottles of beer…"

Damn cows moved slower than jail time. The mamas' heads bobbed up and down, up and down, little ones dallying along. Low mooing. The sound of plodding hooves. Dee's horse sneezing. Tails flicking. Not a cloud.

A dozen young ravens cruised overhead, wings pumping air, powerful and steady as a heartbeat, flapping over the trees. As their caws grew weaker, their message grew stronger: "Join us! Join us!" And Walker raised his hat to salute them and yelled, "Tomorrow!" The birds got smaller, the swoosh of their wings faded to a hush, black specks dwindled to no specks and dissolved into the blue.

The men brought the cattle to the tank, Manuel and Rudy arriving last, having gathered the largest group. Eugene took a head count.

Walker squirmed in the saddle. He said, "Look, man, let's take a shortcut along the highway instead of traveling the usual route through the hills. Save about two hours."

"I don't think so," Eugene said.

Walker kept on. "We'll get to lunch quicker, reserve our energy for the afternoon's work. One mile along the road will save three miles up one mesa and down another, through two canyons and up the valley. Hell, we don't have to stick to the same routine year after year, do we, huh? Do we?"

Eugene glared at him. Walker stared back. The others sat in the saddle smoking, tucking plugs of chew behind their lips.

Eugene said, "You and Dee do what you want with a quarter of the herd. The rest of us will go the regular way."

There were sixty pairs of mothers and calves in all. Walker winked at Dee.

"Think you can handle fifteen pair of sleep-walkin' cows?"

Dee chuckled, sure. With Butch running drag in the rear they separated their share of cows from the herd and with hats lowered against the sun, headed across the mesa toward Thatcher Canyon.

"Thought I missed this work, but my ass is kinda' sore," Walker said, sipping from his flask.

"You're out of shape is all."

"That's why I picked Howard here." He bent forward and stroked the gray's neck. "Old Howard was born with horse sense, ain't that right, Howard? Between you and Butch, we'll deliver this whole gang to the Walker Ranch in record time. If the hammock ain't full of holes, I'll lay my sorry ass in it and light up a smoke while we wait for the others to show up for lunch. I guarantee before the first bite's swallowed Eugene will commence with the afternoon schedule. He's your step-dad and he's been good to you, but he's what's known as a benevolent dictator."

"I don't mind. Most often he's within reason. Now you, you don't like taking orders."

"Don't like giving them, either."

By late morning they'd crossed the mesa and stopped to rest above the rim rock overlooking the highway. Walker pinpointed Lee Ann's house, its shape suggesting a tiny white rectangle snipped out of the landscape rather than an object situated on it. They rode south until they found an elk trail and made their way single-file down the rocky slope, unlocked the forest road gate, and turned the cows onto Highway 34 north of the Alibi Creek Store, a mile from the Walker Ranch.

About six cars an hour used this road, less on weekends. The speed limit was fifty-five, but folks drove slower. No hurry, no worries, no deadlines. Walker felt Howard anxious to get home and told him, "Be patient, old boy." They approached the top of the last hill, the cattle tromping through tall, dry grama grass, thistle, and cota along the shoulder, Walker between the cattle and fence, Dee riding Sonny on the edge of the road, his hat's shadow just touching the asphalt. Butch nipped ankles and darted out on the highway, keeping his charges in line. The day had warmed and a gentle south breeze pushed against their backs. The cows maintained a steady pace, as if they too anticipated the journey's end.

A car topped the hill, a silver sedan, speeding straight at them as if the wheels were locked in a track. The highway in front of the vehicle sloped downhill, clear of traffic for two miles, the cattle and riders clearly visible. The car came on, first in silence, then wheels humming, silver paint flashing, sunlight reflecting off the grill, zooming down the hill at eighty miles an hour. Walker yelled to Dee, "Maniac!" and Dee gave Sonny a sharp tug away from the pavement. The horse jerked his head high, stopped mid-step, ears back. Walker yelled, "The car! The car!" Dee tugged again. Sonny reared and twisted, came down on his front legs, lowered his head and kicked his hind legs in the air. Dee lost control of the reins, grabbed for the saddle horn too late, sailed into the air and landed among the cattle. Brakes screeched. In the passenger seat, a woman spread her fingers in front of her face as the vehicle swerved into Sonny's forelimb. Glass smashed, the windshield crazing into an opaque maze of blinding cracks, and the left headlight jammed up under the hood. The man wrestled with the wheel, but the car spun a circle and dove nose first into the ditch, stinking rubber streaking the road.

The cows had scattered. Butch dashed here and there after them. Dee sat up wincing, clutching his upper arm, his hat ten feet off in the weeds. Sonny lay on the road, his nostrils expanding and contracting, snorting short gusts of wind.

Walker jerked his leg over Howard's back, slid down his side and rushed to Sonny, knelt and ran his fingers over the humerus. The skin hadn't broken, but he felt the fracture. End-of-life fracture. An eight-inch gash had slit Sonny's golden chest. Blood pooled on the asphalt, red on black. Walker laid his hand on Sonny's neck. A rock—or was it his heart?—sank to the bottom of his stomach.

"I know you want to get up," he said. "But, don't. Rest easy."

The man and woman sat behind the shattered windshield. The passenger door was crushed. The man helped the woman crawl over the seat and climb out his side. They spewed apologies and worries over the injured horse. Walker paid them no mind. He mounted Howard and slapped his rump, said, "Git on! Make it quick!" The couple asked Dee what they could do. They had no idea horses and cows on the road presented a danger. They were from Cleveland.

26

PLACEMATS WERE ARRANGED ON THE dining room table, silverware laid out, napkins folded. Lee Ann re-counted chairs and took glasses from the buffet. Despite attempts to decorate, the house lacked frilly touches. Men lived here and she catered to their interests and needs. A narrow print of a southwestern landscape with a too-bright sunset ran the length of the buffet. Hunting magazines, work gloves, and equipment manuals formed sloppy piles between vases of dried, dusty flowers. A canning jar ring Dee had tossed when he was twelve was looped on a pair of elk antlers hanging over the doorway to the kitchen.

She laid her palm on the carrot cake and mixed softened butter and cream cheese, adding two cups of confectioner's sugar and a splash of vanilla. As a girl she'd balanced on a stool in an oversized apron sprinkling chocolate chips and pecans into a batch of cookie dough in this same turquoise Bauer bowl. Chocolate chips had been her favorite, but Walker had once thrown up from gorging himself and couldn't stomach the sight of them. Since then, Mother had limited her repertoire to oatmeal crinkles, brownies, and lemon bars.

She licked her finger and spread the icing, raising her head to activity outside. Between the binoculars and geranium above the sink, Walker galloped up the road past the house. Lee Ann put down the spatula, wiped her hands, and rushed outside. Before she got fifty yards, the tick-tick-tick of the big Kubota tractor sounded from behind the barn, Walker driving at full speed.

She waved both arms from the middle of the road. Leaving the engine running, Walker dashed into the gun-room. She chased after him, but before reaching the house, he was back, stuffing Eugene's .45 ACP revolver into his belt.

"There's been an accident," he said, jumping back in the seat, shifting gears.

"Wait. What?" she said.

"Out on 34. You'll want to get Dee to the hospital. He's broken his arm or dislocated his shoulder. Take the Blazer. I'll lead Howard back."

"I'll be right there," she said. Dear Jesus, let him be okay.

Dee held his right elbow to his waist. Sonny raised his head and stretched his neck and lowered it again. She crouched beside Dee, her eyes darting from the horse to her son, her body as immobile as theirs. Toby Utley, in a green Forest Service truck, and Emilia Holguin in her white Malibu, had pulled over. Toby took hold of Howard's reins and led him down the road, talking low. Emilia reached for the sobbing woman's arm and guided her and the man away from the horse and faced them toward Solitaire Peak, as though the mountain would offer consolation. The tractor ticked. Walker bent over and pointed the gun between Sonny's left ear and inner canthus and pulled the trigger.

The shot stilled the leaves, silenced the birds. Lee Ann lost touch with where she was, where the house was, that Dee was injured, that Sonny had died. When she came back, Toby was tying Howard to the fence. Cows wandered down the road, the calves roaming from side to side. Worn out,

Butch nipped at the ones that drifted too far. Emilia asked Toby if she should drive to the store and call the sheriff.

Walker yelled, "No!"

Lee Ann picked at a loose piece of skin on her ring finger with her thumbnail. One thing at a time.

She asked Dee, "Where's Eugene?"

"Coming down Salida Canyon with the rest," he said.

"If you can get up, we can make it to Silver City by 3:30." The clinic in Brand wouldn't be open today and even if it was, she didn't trust the staff. She reached under Dee's good arm and helped him to his feet.

Walker lifted Sonny in the tractor's bucket and steered to the side of the road, as solemn as she'd ever seen him, face and neck shiny with sweat, his shirt soaked. He took off his hat, wiped his brow with a forearm and said, "Toby, I'd sure appreciate it if you'd stick around and help me with these cows."

Lee Ann sent Emilia on, asking her to call Lyle when she got home. She settled Dee into the Blazer and adjusted the seat. Forget the seat belt. She pulled onto the road. In the rear view mirror, Toby was untying Howard from the fence. The woman stood beside the SUV while the man got inside. The tractor inched along the highway, turned, and crossed the cattle guard to the ranch.

An hour later, the sun fell behind the pines on Saliz Pass as she maneuvered the sharp hairpin curves through short stretches of shadow and sunlight.

Dee shivered in spells that shook his legs and head.

"Are you cold?" she asked.

He didn't answer.

The ponderosas closed in, the road narrowed to a ribbon. The twinge that preceded a migraine traveled from her shoulder to behind her left eye. Sonny had been Dee's horse since childhood—a strong, proud animal whose soft color belied an energetic temperament. His suffering was as real as if she'd been injured herself, the gash in his chest a slice in her own. His blood mixed with hers, swirled and surged, concocting a vile substance, and she pulled to the side of the road and vomited between two clumps of bear grass and slumped to the ground. She wiped the bitter taste off her tongue with the back of her hand. Get up. No time to cry.

The road descended into the Gila Wilderness and the land opened with prickly pear and yucca growing out of soft sand against purple mountains. She stopped in Los Olmos to fill up and use the restroom, where she wet her face and rinsed her mouth. Goodness, her apron was still on.

Dee's eyes stayed closed when she got behind the wheel. "Walker is an asshole," she said. God forgive me.

27

Fuck. When Eugene got back, he'd fall into a rage, madder than a bull elk defending his harem. If he settled down, it would be into a self-righteous, close-mouthed snit, pretending to ignore the disaster while tallying every detail. Without Dee, the crew would be short a man and without Lee Ann, lunch (if they got to it at all) would drag into a wordless ordeal, mouths chewing and swallowing, slurping lemonade, hiding their disgust for The Screw-up, The Loser, The Clown—Eugene the quietest, stiffest of all.

Walker drove the tractor across the cattle guard, Sonny's legs sticking out at odd angles like a broken carousel horse. When they reached soft ground behind the barn, Walker lowered the bucket and stepped down from the tractor, reached for the flask in his back pocket and took a long drink. Liquor and sorrow loosened his joints and his knees buckled. He leaned against the tractor wheel, tilted his head back, and emptied the flask into his throat.

"You been a good horse," he said.

Butch would be thirsty. He walked to the barn and ran water from the hose into an empty coffee can, snapped on the lid, and strapped it to the ATV under a bungee cord. The cows wouldn't appreciate the noise and he would despise the image of himself herding cows on wheels, but roundup had already turned into a day from hell, so what the hell.

Toby helped him move the cows onto the property before Eugene and the others got back.

"I owe you one," Walker said.

He drove to the store and convinced Shelly to pour off a quarter of that special bottle and took his cup into the storeroom. The old men came for their papers and sat on the porch and went on about the same useless shit they always jawed about and he didn't go outside to join them. When they asked Shelly why Walker's truck was parked out back, she said he'd met someone and taken off, she didn't know where. Atta girl, Shelly.

That night he buried the horse alone in the beams of the Kubota's headlights, using the old Yanmar utility tractor to dig the grave. He drank, fortifying his nerves against the thud of Sonny dropping into the hole, a deep abyss blacker than night shadows. Stars that usually winked at him looked elsewhere. Even the dogs left him to himself. In the end, he had no words for Sonny.

He parked the equipment back at the barn, checked their exact positions and angles twice. Had to. Eugene was P-I-S-S-E-D. Silent guys were the scariest, but not for long, because in the end men like Eugene, intent on holding onto what they bottled up, couldn't think fast, couldn't come up with creative moves, invent stories to mesmerize, tantalize, hypnotize. The quiet ones couldn't talk long enough or fast enough to convince an opponent to abandon reason and act against his better interests. Being slippery, sly, smart, and sassy compensated for a whole hell of a lot. Quick thinking bull-shitters provided the fun in life, the pizazz, the icing on the cake, and admit it—a cake is nothing without icing.

He stripped and lay on the bed. A shower would feel fine, water pelting his back and shoulders, running through his hair. Too tired to get up. Too drunk to care how he smelled or that the crew would be a day late branding and inoculating, or that Danielle hadn't been home for two nights, or that Dee's shoulder would put him out of commission for who knew how long.

Lee Ann's Blazer pulled in, or maybe he imagined that. He waived a finger in the air making a mental note to get Mother dressed and fed in the morning if they didn't get back from the hospital tonight. He needed to find his duffle bag, ought to get up and pack, raid the cookie jar… vamoose…let loose…don't forget a toothbrush. Nah. Pick one up on the road.

28

S IR GALAHAD ANNOUNCED THE NEW day well before sun up. Walker went outside, took a leak, and wandered over to Lee Ann's. The Blazer was there, the hood cold. The dogs romped around him, jostling against his legs, and he patted their heads and said, "Git," and when they disobeyed and snuck back to Mother's, he growled, "G'wan!"

With one sweep, he emptied the cookie jar, running his knuckles around the bottom to corral any change. Danielle's room remained unoccupied. Mother snored softly. He groped around the top shelf of his closet and yanked down the old duffle bag, spread it apart, and opened his bureau drawer. Tee shirts were neatly stacked beside socks folded toe-to-toe and heel-to-heel in neat pairs. He shoved the drawer shut and stuffed the duffle bag back on the shelf. Early light struck the Anasazi bowls and ladles, bone tools, *metates,* and grandfather's spittoon on the bookshelves, and a dull sheen reflected off his breakaway roping trophy. The delicate black and white Mimbres pot with the narrow neck, the one the posthole digger had brought up while replacing a rotten fence post, would make a nice souvenir. It had clinked when he'd cleaned it off and four obsidian bird points had fallen into his palm. He shook out the contents now, picked out an arrowhead, polished it against his shirt, and slipped it in his vest pocket. He reached for the 9mm Glock 26 subcompact and shoulder holster in the drawer, wrapped his fingers around cool metal, shut out the memories, and walked out.

The pickup slowed and his pulse raced as he rounded the knoll at Plank's Plot and pulled up beside Danielle's Jeep. He cut the engine, stretched his legs under the steering wheel and sipped from the flask. The cinderblocks had settled, sending the southwest corner of the trailer into a nosedive. Ought to put a rock under it. A couple of rusted fifty-five-gallon drums had overflowed with garbage, some of it finding a home under the crawl space. The back of Keith's SUV was open, a canvas overnight bag and paper grocery sack stuffed with dirty clothes inside. All right. They were both ready to deal, wind things up, and split. He squinted against the sun's reflection bouncing off a small metal strip running along the edge of the roof. The go-ahead light. Poor now, rich by night. Offer the bait, let him bite. Close the deal, take flight.

Quitclaim deed in hand, he sprinted toward the steps and came to a full stop. Whoa, boy. Don't kill the transaction with enthusiasm. Keep the zipper shut. Don't slap the dude's shoulder. Hold off on that handshake until the money's delivered and stowed in the truck. Tonight there'll be plenty of time to let loose, order a shot of Johnnie Walker Gold, and celebrate. Hell, buy the whole bottle and pass it around the bar in some unknown town. The world didn't lack watering holes, no matter where he'd bed down. Hey, he might use the big bucks to purchase a dive in the UP, with padded leather trim along a shiny bar, low lights, high stools, red and black décor, nothin' fancy, a hangout for the common man. Pat said folks drank a lot up there, to get through the winters and all. The place would have a jukebox, if they still made those things, and a rock fireplace, a dartboard, and pool table. And to hell with what the law said about cigarette smoking in closed quarters, because those would be *his* quarters, his and Pat's, and he'd do what he damn well pleased. Don't like smoke? Go elsewhere. Music too loud? Bring earplugs.

Keith opened the door, the living room darkened by heavy curtains. Down the hall the bathroom door closed.

Walker slipped inside, the deed against his thigh.

"Beautiful day," he said. "My bones tell me the weather's about to change, though. We'll be getting some rain in a day or two."

"No need for small talk," Keith said. "I have your money."

Sunlight broke through dusty kitchen blinds, shooting pinstripes across the floor. Keith reached into the cabinet under the sink, pulled out a black suitcase.

"Open it," he said, shoving it across the table.

Walker's mouth watered, as if he just got a whiff of strong coffee with a big splash of Bailey's.

"Okay, then."

He flipped the clasps and exactly like in a B-grade movie, tightly packed stacks of hundred dollar bills filled a suitcase that seemed custom-made for that purpose.

"I'll take the deed," Keith said. "Sign this receipt for the cash."

Walker shoved the deed next to the money. Keith placed his index finger on it and slowly drew it across the table. Walker picked up the pen. Wait a minute. In the long run, land was worth more than any amount of money. But the short run won out and he signed. The Handsome Man side of Keith's face turned ugly. Cold air seemed to come off him, cold beyond a freezer on the highest setting. The hairs rose on the back of Walker's neck and arms. He lifted the suitcase and with his free elbow nudged his jacket. The

Glock peeked out. With a brief salute he backed into the living room, and keeping his eyes on the motherfucker, fumbled behind his back for the doorknob.

Out of here quick, down the steps, suitcase on the seat, ass behind the wheel. A shot rang out. Walker turned the ignition, put her in reverse. Another shot. He slouched down in the seat, his foot to the pedal. A hissing sound leaked from the tires.

Grab the suitcase! Run! He zigzagged across the field to the barn. Two bullets whizzed by. Walker jumped into overdrive, his legs bounding on invisible springs. A regular kangaroo. Run! Think! Take cover in the barn until nightfall, then cross the clearing to the mesa, hike through dense piñon and cedar to the road a few miles north and hitch a ride.

He squinted through a crack in the barn's siding. Keith drove his SUV behind a crinkled metal shed and faced it toward Walker's get-away route to the mesa. The automatic window opened and the engine cut off. Dust tickled Walker's nose and he squeezed his nostrils against a sneeze. Crouching low, and using the barn as cover, he retraced his steps to the trailer. Danielle kept the key to the Jeep under the seat and sure enough, there it was, gas tank half full.

He drove away slowly, letting Keith assume Danielle had left for work. When he reached the highway, he gunned the engine and headed north. Let's see how fast this red crate'll go! Five miles up the road he took off his hat and laid it on the suitcase and laughed and laughed and laughed.

29

SCRAMBLED EGGS STEAMED ON A platter. Bacon, sausage, and leftover cornbread were already on the table, coffee had been poured. Odd how men grew silent after a catastrophe, whereas women rushed to bake a cake, utter assurances, dress a wound, and send condolence cards. Eugene broke open a biscuit and asked for the jam. A stranger might think his soft-spoken manner and no-tell expression conveyed an easy-going man, an uncomplicated man. Anyone who knew him understood that long ago boundaries had been set, codes of conduct established.

"Scott will have to postpone college," he said.

She passed the eggs to Dee's left hand. Across the table, Manuel and Rudy said nothing as they loaded sausage and bacon onto their plates, feigning disinterest. Conversation uttered at this table would be common knowledge throughout the county within twenty-four hours.

She said, "This is not the time."

"It's okay, Mom," Scott said.

She shook her head. Since childhood, the limp swing of his arm tossing a rope over a colt's head, his slow gait to the hen house to feed the chickens (detouring to chase a lizard, or inspect a spider weaving her web), and the lazy way he brushed the horses signaled boredom with ranch chores. Rural life was too small. By the time he was a teenager, he'd not only observed much of the local flora and fauna, he'd studied books about the unique species in the Galapagos, been captivated by South American parrots and poisonous snakes of Africa, banyan trees in India, creatures and plants of the sea and jungle, intrigued by information about the larger world.

Scott laid his knife across his plate and tapped his fist lightly on the table, left his food half-finished and went outside.

"He was counting on going," Lee Ann said. "We'll never know where this disappointment fits on the list of others he's experienced—number ten, twenty, forty. He mustn't be assigned an unfulfilled life."

Dee said, "Stuff in books is always there. There's work to do right here."

"You don't share his interests, Dee," she said. "Don't berate his passion. This isn't a question of one endeavor being superior to another."

"Right now, it's a question of what's practical," Eugene said.

He swallowed a final gulp of coffee and took his cup to the kitchen. The others cleared their places. Dishes clattered in the sink, the back door opened, footsteps crossed the porch and thumped down the steps.

She stayed at the table, folding and re-folding her napkin. Too much space. Too many men. But friendships with women had always seemed complicated by confidences and snide insinuations. At school, girls who'd shared romantic secrets and compared beauty tips had paired off around her and she'd treated them like another species. At work, betrayals and shifting loyalties warned against bonding with co-workers and subordinates. She trusted Mother. She trusted Grace.

"I'll be praying for a girl," Mother had said at the news of Lee Ann's first pregnancy, twenty-one years ago. "Boys grow up to find a woman of their own and leave their mother. A daughter stays forever."

Lee Ann had proved her right. They'd planted and harvested together, ran errands and shopped together, sewed, cooked, and attended church together. They lived together by choice and circumstance. Together because of a promise, because of obligation, because of loyalty, family ties, soul ties, and tradition. Together—side by side, eggs in a box, cards in a deck, bread in a toaster, cherries on a stem. Mother and daughter.

Mother had been mistaken about sons. Except for his marriage and periods in jail, Walker had stuck even closer to home than Lee Ann, his bedroom the base from where he came and went as he pleased, partly to play, partly to escape, accountable to no one. Mother collapsed like a wilted daffodil when he left, jumped for the phone the entire time he was gone, and perked up when he returned. When his inane exuberance, lies, and deceit beat Lee Ann down, she worked ugly thoughts out with her Lord, for Mother had made it clear—Walker was the one person Lee Ann must never criticize.

She found Danielle on a paint-splattered stool next to the workbench in the shop, boot heels hooked on the top rung, a black cat on her lap.

"I'm sorry we missed each other yesterday," Lee Ann said. "There was an accident."

Danielle stroked the cat's head.

"His name is Woolly. The other one's Mister."

Lee Ann leaned her hip against the table saw.

"I assume they're fixed," she said.

Actually, she was surprised Eugene hadn't "mistakenly" let them loose. But, of course he wouldn't—they belonged to Danielle. Every hair in place, gold earrings twirling even when her head didn't move, bright red lipstick, flimsy, semi-transparent tee shirt that looked like something to wear to bed. A fallen angel, or one about to fall. No bigger threat than the magic or wizardry of a gorgeous woman, and nothing more unfair.

Jesus stood behind Lee Ann's shoulder. *But I say to you that hear, love your enemies, do good to those who hate you, bless—*

She moved away from the table, away from Him.

"Please ask Walker to stack wood for you."

Danielle lowered Woolly to the floor and whisked cat hair off her jeans.

"He wasn't around. And I didn't ask. Eugene offered."

Several milk jugs filled with water lined the back edge of the table. Danielle unscrewed one of the caps. "It wasn't a big deal."

"Walker can do that for you."

"Tell him that. Tell them both." She retrieved the cats' water bowl and filled it, splashing water on the legal pad beside the chop saw. "I don't want to be here any more than you want me around," she said. "As far as Eugene is concerned, you need to take the matter up with him."

Before the crew returned for lunch, Lee Ann stacked plates by the stove and set out pitchers of lemonade and iced tea. She left a note telling the men to help themselves, retrieved her Bible, and called the dogs, who sensed her destination and shot past Mother's toward the mesa. Walker's truck was gone. Typical. Bungle things and disappear.

Up the canyon, they added paw and footprints to fresh elk and coyote tracks. Often, she'd dally along this route and admire lichen or pick up interesting rocks. This morning she trudged, leaning forward as if fighting a swift wind, one arm swinging free, the other holding the Bible like a school book. Cedar branches, stripped and mangled by bull elk in mating frenzies, hung from maimed trees, droppings everywhere, the musky odor of fresh urine pungent in the stagnant air. The trail crossed an arroyo, flattened out some, and continued climbing at a steep angle, flanked by rocky walls.

Danielle, curvaceous and coy, with skin like silk and heavy lashes, was there for the asking. Eugene was unhappy. Wordless messages passed between men and women. *I'm married, but it doesn't mean anything.* I'm married, too, but looking elsewhere. *I have erotic secrets to share.* I want to experience them. *I'll keep things light.* I'll appreciate that. *I can make you feel good in ways you can't imagine.* You already do.

The narrow passage ended at a weak spring seeping from porous rock, a destination they called "the dribble." The pebbled conglomerate oozed water into soggy muck beneath it. Panting, she turned to Proverbs 27:4. Alternating waves of dizziness and heat left her light-headed and she swayed, struggling to keep her balance. She reached to wet her palm and cool her forehead. The Bible weighed nothing, no more than a leaf, and slipped from her hand into the mud. A single note escaped from her throat and she held her ears against the sound of her own anguish. *Wrath is cruel, anger is overwhelming, but who can stand before jealousy?*

30

TUESDAY
OCTOBER 9, 2007

NEWSPAPER REPORTERS FROM ALBUQUERQUE, SANTA Fe and Las Cruces appeared at the courthouse first thing in the morning. Lee Ann flattened the collar of her blouse over a fitted navy blue suit jacket and invited the two men and one woman to take seats in front of her desk. Caroline served coffee and left the pot, sugar, and powdered creamer on the bookshelves.

Bill Joffe of the *Albuquerque Journal* started off the session by congratulating Dax County on receiving the biggest windfall in the nation.

"Actually," Lee Ann said, "the financial analysis by the Associated Press is misleading because so much of the money will end up going into the state funding formula for schools. Basically, the money will take care of essential needs that we have not been able to fund for years." Remembering Harley's instructions, she added, "So, you see, it's not a windfall."

She explained that with the founding of the U.S. Forest Service in 1908, Congress approved a revenue-sharing program to placate rural counties, allotting them twenty-five percent of the funds generated by commercial activity on the new forest. Local governments appeared satisfied until the 1980s when logging declined due to court-ordered enforcement of the Endangered Species Act. As a result, by the 90s, county payments fell seventy percent nationwide.

She defended the "windfall," saying, "This fiscal allotment seems likely to be a one-time deal. Congress is promising to change the funding formula in 2012, once again lowering the amounts the counties would receive."

The reporters scribbled on their pads.

"In New Mexico," Lee Ann continued, "logging on the five national forests plummeted to a quarter of the usual amount and by 2003 three major sawmills closed around the state, Brand one of them. We're a very depressed area. Our population is declining. Young people leave the county after high school and don't return. We haven't had a school bond issue pass here since 1989."

The Santa Fe reporter, Melanie Coulter, said, "Controversy has been voiced over the handout. Adversaries claim the money undermines local governments from promoting economic diversity and encouraging new business."

Lee Ann crossed her legs. Her low heels, worn only for special occasions, pinched her toes.

"How would you suggest we promote economic development when the federal government owns four fifths of our county's land? It isn't possible to convince a population subsisting on welfare to support a shopping center. Low-income families, who for generations have cooked almost every meal at home, don't dine out. Brand can support one restaurant, Vera's Cafe. The only time the Brand New Motel turns off the Vacancy sign is during hunting season."

She rose to refill her coffee cup. These people hadn't a clue what living in the wilderness meant. News from this part of the state pertained to environmental issues and crime, the most recent articles addressing the relocation of the Mexican gray wolf and the shooting of Geraldine Pierce by her "mentally challenged" grandson.

Las Cruces reporter Jim Kraft flipped a page of his notebook.

"Several New Mexico counties have voted to use the money for large, one-time purchases. Do the Dax County commissioners have a plan in effect for the money?"

Harley, Saul, and Ed had coached her—be congenial, fend them off, tell them nothing. Sweat trickled between her breasts. If the useless window opened, she'd jump out and catch a ride on that cloud floating over the Dax County Bank.

"Considering the sizable sum of money, and the fact that this might be a short-lived allocation program, the Dax County commissioners will not act quickly, but intend to evaluate the settlement with the utmost thought and consideration."

31

WALKER PASSED THROUGH THE LAST town in Dax County—five deserted houses and a gas station, half the weathered boards fallen off half the broken windows, old washing machines and rusted cars trapped in tangled weeds. Poor suckers, thinking they could build a house and root cellar, store homegrown vegetables, raise a few cows and sheep, open a Phillips 66 service station, and survive. Must have been sweet until traffic detoured north to join the mainstream speeding along the interstate. Those sorry folks must have rocked on the porch trying to ignore the hungry ache in their bellies wondering what the hell happened. That was always the way, people lacking the flexibility or foresight to see what was coming next. The guy who invented McDonalds sure predicted the American future. Drive-thru. Smart man. Genius.

Just outside the Colorado border, he registered as Ross Plank at a Motel 6 and sat behind the wheel outside his room. Take the money inside, or leave it in the trunk. Take it in. The car might get stolen. He slept with his arm draped over the suitcase, waking several times in case a shady night manager tried to sneak in, lift his arm ever so gently, and slide it from his side.

Dax County law would still be trying to locate Danielle's Jeep. A mechanic in Grants had given him a name and he'd followed the kid from behind the counter at Dairy Queen to his uncle's doublewide west of town. A couple of cars in various stages of body repair were for sale under a metal carport. He'd paid too much for a just-waxed, '97 silver Honda, considering he'd thrown in the Jeep, but there hadn't been time to haggle over a couple hundred bucks. He paid an extra hundred for a Nevada license plate that dangled among others at the end of a wire from the roof. After filling out the bill of sale, he sent the kid into the house for a glass of water and transferred the suitcase to the Honda's trunk. When the kid returned Walker handed him the key to the Jeep and wrote down the uncle's address, promising to send the title in two days. The boy would get a lecture when the title never arrived. *Never buy or trade a car without transfer of title—at least write down the name of the buyer, his address, blah blah blah.* Ah, the pains of growing up. All the mistakes Dad had promised would make him smarter had never amounted to a scrap of sense. Useless logic, believing man learns from his screw-ups. Maybe the kid would learn you couldn't learn a thing. If so, he might stand a chance of having some fun.

In the morning, frost coated the windshield. He drove to the nearest restaurant and ordered a breakfast burrito. His gut swirled and churned, the way it always did close to the border. Soon he'd be operating outside his playground. *Huevos* with red or green chile might not appear on a menu for a long time, if ever again.

He zoomed across back roads and passed the *Welcome to Kansas* sign. The sky was almost as big as New Mexico's and the late afternoon sun shone down on flat fields, but mesas no longer defined the horizon and the air had lost the smell of piñon and sage. He took a quick look at the map and lit a smoke. This trip was going to be l-o-n-g.

The country was tidy, all right. Huge, tight hay bales seemed to have rolled randomly and stopped like a fleet of abandoned highway leveling equipment. Every last blade of wheat, hay, and sorghum had its use. No waste here. No lazy farmer here. No goofing off here. Kansas and Nebraska were serious about hog and cattle farming, and grand-scale grain production. He smelled dollars. Damn them, though, he'd never met a farmer or rancher who claimed to make a profit. No sir. Weather did them in. Disease did them in. Government did them in. Banks did them in. Yet, somehow they earned enough to build big sturdy farmhouses and enormous barns, moaning all the while about the price of feed, seed, and greed. Did anyone chuckle around here?

He rolled down the window.

"Ha ha!"

The wind tickled his ear.

Forget industrious farmers, silos, and feedlots. Focus on recent events. He popped a Tecate. Hell, it was a drag dwelling on the past, but Pat Merker's intentions had to be addressed. Was the con in cahoots with the vet? Had they both intended to kill him, keep the land *and* the money, or had that been Keith's independent plan all along? Here he was, driving to God-knows-where to partake in early retirement intrigues with Pat Merker, whose commitments and promises suddenly appeared more than dubious. Son-of-a-bitch. He ought to slam on the brakes, change direction and split for Montana. Uh-uh, hold on a second. If Pat hadn't been in on the plan to cut his life short, he'd surely resort to murder upon arriving in the UP and discovering no Walker and no loot.

Any adventure, imagined or real, packed more zing with an accomplice along to plot tactics, share the hilarity, count the winnings, and revel in their wits. In prison, he and Pat had sat side by side on Pat's cot memorizing each other's social security numbers and practicing each other's signatures over and over, until Walker didn't even have to think about how to sign Pat's name, how the slash missed the "t" and the "k" bled into the "er" and eased off into a scrawl at the end. Sworn to secrecy, as dedicated as teens in a backyard clubhouse, they'd declared loyalty their number one priority. Shit. Could have been a set up.

32

For two days clouds blocked the sun, not a sliver of light poking through solid gray. In prison, although the sun's rays remained aloof, the big yellow ball did its thing. Its beams were so bright even indirect light sent the message that the planet's bigger-than-you-can-imagine candle was burning, and because of that all was right with the world.

Back home, the sun was a constant fixture, a sidekick. It brought freezing days to a bearable temperature and relieved the winter blues. Outdoor chores were postponed until late morning when the sun helped out simply by being out. During the rainy season, only a day or two passed before great shafts of sunlight broke through parting clouds. This midwestern darkness was gloomy and constant. A pervasive dread worked its way into his playful mind and stiffness settled into his neck and joints and the wheels of the car rolled on, covering mile after mile, delivering him into what felt like a prison of a different sort. A pain popped up in the middle of his chest under the breastbone. Rolaids wouldn't relieve it, nor Pepcid AC. He sipped from the flask. Like a little kid, he grew impatient. Mom, are we there yet?

The situation called for hunkering down out of sight for a couple of weeks. At the next gas station he opened the map. After a night in Holdrege, he'd travel on to Lincoln for a week's stay at some cushy place. Hell, he had the money. Those clothes he'd bought in Show Low—time to put them on. Now that he was rich, a certain amount of class and a degree of cleanliness were in order. In a grand suite at the Lincoln Marriott Residence Inn, he peered inside kitchen cabinets, flopped into the over-stuffed chair, and crossed his boots on the puffy ottoman, the décor meeting his new standards. After a couple of days, though, he went on a bender and could have been anywhere. A swimming pool was useless if it was cold and anyway, he didn't care for swimming. His arms were too skinny. Water might appeal to a fish, but to a man raised in the desert water was too wet. Fish never took a breath of air. Aquariums gave him the willies. Not only could the fish not breathe, they couldn't get out. And he might as well be a fish right now, confined to a suite that to a person living in Tokyo would appear a mansion, but to someone raised in Alibi Creek was teensy weensy. Harvest gold and sage green walls couldn't compare with the southwestern winter sky. Plush upholstery felt fine, but nothing like lying in a field of grama grass that whispered in the wind. Ornate bathroom fixtures didn't improve the quality of water flowing through the pipes.

PART
TWO

33

Two weeks after roundup, drifting smoke from a new neighbor's fireplace announced the beginning of winter. Eugene wouldn't fend off chilly mornings this early in the season, even though temperatures on the thermometer outside the kitchen window read well below freezing. The afternoons still warmed into the high sixties and like most locals, he insisted on waiting until the last day of October before striking a match.

Lee Ann buttoned her good wool coat, tucked her soiled, water-stained Bible under her arm and joined the boys in Scott's pickup. When the Bible had fallen into the mud, it had landed on its backside. She'd carried it home splayed over her arm and let it dry over a rolling pin. The dirt had flaked off easily, but the edges of the pages remained brown.

Although Ed Moody arrived at the church an hour early to light the stove, the vaulted ceiling did nothing to hold the heat and the room had risen to only a few degrees warmer than the temperature outside. Lee Ann took her usual seat in the third row, Scott and Dee on either side, the chill from the cold chair seeping through to her thighs. Muffled sounds of women setting out baked goods alongside the chugging fifty-cup percolator came from behind the kitchen door. Folks filed in and exchanged greetings, mothers telling their children to hush and behave.

Since Dee's accident, Lee Ann took special notice of the way he combed a wave away from his forehead and stooped to check his image in the mirror while setting his hat. She paused to listen to Scott's gentle voice coming from Mother's room, reading Willa Cather's *O Pioneers!* Despite bickering and teasing, affection prevailed between her sons. And for this she felt blessed, and felt them blessed. The best intentions, strictest instruction, and good examples couldn't foster compatibility if siblings didn't prioritize congeniality. A coarse, bombastic boy would not cherish a gentle, sensitive brother, and vice versa, unless directed by God. And although she interpreted the word "brother" in the Bible to refer to any man, she had taught her sons: *That in this manner no one should wrong his brother or take advantage of him. The Lord will punish men for all such sins, as we have already told you and warned you.* 1 Thessalonians 4:6.

Wayne had been softer on Scott because he'd caused less trouble. Dee had been too busy with his red wagon to care. When Wayne moved to Texas for good, without so much as a Christmas card to the boys, they'd warmed to Eugene, who'd treated them equally, until Dee's enthusiasm for ranching established a bond that soon ranked him favorite child in Eugene's estimation. Scott must have known he would one day leave Alibi Creek and this secret allowed him to cede *first* place for what he deemed would be a *better* place.

She jumped at the hand on her shoulder.

"Good morning," Lyle said.

"I must have been daydreaming. Good morning. Lovely sweater, Denise."

Lyle winked. "No sleeping until the sermon starts." He nodded at Dee. "How's the shoulder?"

"There, but not bad."

"Those tourists have been investigating the legality of moving cattle along the highway. That wasn't too smart of Walker."

"It wasn't his fault. We've all done it for short stretches plenty of times. That car was speeding."

Walker. He'd missed Ross Plank's funeral. The boys hadn't seen him all week. His truck hadn't been parked in front of Mother's, or at Art's. Danielle hadn't seen him either—her Jeep was missing and she'd had to borrow Art's second pickup with the passenger side window missing. On Friday, she'd barged into Lee Ann's office demanding to know Walker's whereabouts, throwing her arms in the air at Lee Ann's shrug.

"It's time to call Lyle and organize a search."

"He'll show up soon enough," Lee Ann said, inserting papers into a folder.

"If you won't call, I will."

"We'll wait until Monday. There's no sense bothering Lyle over the weekend."

One thing struck her as odd, though. Walker hadn't called Mother. Every week, in prison or out, in Dax County or half way across the state, whether Mother recognized his voice or not, he'd insist Lee Ann hold the phone to her ear so he could holler hello, ask how she was, say he was fine, he loved her, take good care, he'd call next week.

Pastor Fletcher said, "Please rise."

Ed struck a chord on the piano.

The congregation sang:

> *Still, still with Thee, when purple morning breaketh,*
> *When the bird waketh, and the shadows flee;*
> *Fairer than morning, lovelier than daylight,*
> *Dawns the sweet consciousness, I am with Thee…*

Saul Duran's charcoal gray suit was sprinkled with dandruff. A Kleenex fell out of Fran Scully's sleeve. Mary Womack dropped her purse and when she bent to pick it up, a run in one of her stockings ran from her ankle up her calf. Ed Richter moved his lips without knowing the words. Pastor Fletcher's shirt was frayed at the collar. Cal Zimmer forgot to take his hat off and Anna, his wife, jabbed him in the side and pointed to his head.

The congregation remained standing for a moment of silence and Lee Ann reached for the boys' hands. Dear Lord, mend Dee's shoulder quickly. Open the door for Scott to attend university next semester. Bring Mother comfort in her final days and when the time comes, provide a peaceful passing. Quiet Walker's mind so that he finds purpose in positive endeavors. Bring him home a changed man. Forgive me for abetting the indiscriminate transfer of money. I have sinned as much as the commissioners. This weighs on me, Lord. I've always claimed moral superiority where Walker's concerned, but honestly, part of my hesitation to criticize him stems from the fact that I've committed similar offenses, mine veiled under a veneer of respectability. And most important, Lord, please end Eugene's period of discontent.

34

S HE ATE HER SANDWICH IN the courthouse common room and folded the plastic baggie into the pocket of her pants. A three-page request from the Brand volunteer fire department for funds to upgrade their equipment had been placed on her desk. The commissioners' excuses would cause the fire chief to lose his temper and yell insults, which would further ruin his chances of getting what the fire department needed. She set the request aside.

At two o'clock, Lyle made a rare visit to the office and invited Lee Ann to take a walk. Caroline was tallying payroll, Roxanne was entering county statistics into the computer, and Maggie was working in conjunction with the clerk's office to recruit census takers over the phone. Everything seemed in order.

"Let's head toward the fairgrounds," Lyle said, pushing open the glass doors.

They crossed the street toward Leo's Garage, all the doors open, Leo out to lunch. Yvonne and Sally waved from their windows at the bank, no customers in line. One pedestrian crossed the street to the post office without looking right or left. Larry Corkin's trailer marked the end of town and Lyle took Lee Ann's elbow, quickening his step past three barking dogs straining at their chains behind the fence.

The fairgrounds consisted of a rodeo arena, bleachers, and a long, metal building situated on a thin strip of land between the highway and mountains. They walked under the Dax County Fairgrounds sign toward two rows of picnic tables under a metal roof. A month ago, vehicles had been parked bumper to bumper clear to the highway. Lamb, cattle, poultry, and rabbits added their aromas and sounds to the noise of excited children. Folks waited in an endless line for hot dogs slathered with mustard and hamburgers smothered with chile, while dust billowed from the arena during the barrel racing and roping competitions.

She took a seat on a picnic bench, in a patch of sun sneaking under the roof. Lyle sat in the shade, fingers folded loosely on the table.

"Lee Ann," he said, preoccupied with the length of his fingernails.

She said, "I take it you have something to tell me."

"This is difficult," he said. "Last Thursday, Owen came into my office complaining that a man named Keith Lampert owns Ross Plank's ranch. Owen is pretty upset, believing he's the rightful heir to his family's property. Keith Lampert claims he paid $880,000.00 cash to Walker for the place and has a quitclaim deed to prove Ross had transferred ownership."

"Walker?"

"Of course, I checked with Eileen right away and she verified that Keith filed the deed at the courthouse last Tuesday. It's signed by Ross and notarized. I visited with Ted Bowles to check the legality of the signatures and he assured me the deed is legitimate."

"Explain what this means, exactly."

"It means Walker pulled a fast one. It means the signatures on the deed are binding, signed by both parties of their own volition, in their right minds, in front of a witness. It means Walker sold Owen's inheritance out from under him. I found Keith camped out there in the same trailer Walker had parked on the highway. He showed me the receipt for $880,000.00."

She leaned forward on her elbows and stuck her fingers in her ears. Don't hear. She closed her eyes and pressed her fingers against them so hard they hurt. Don't look.

"Now, I need to ask you where Walker is."

She shook her head.

"Lee Ann, look at me. I need you to remember the last time you saw him, the last time anyone in your family saw him."

Walker. Bigger and badder than ever. Congratulations! Laugh, or cry, or scream. Hit something, throw something, kick something. Punch something. Choke something. And she, a fool. To assume. To trust. Eugene was right. A criminal. He'd said, "Admit it! He's one step away from a hardcore criminal!" And now, Lord, he's taken that step.

She stomped across the field, searching for the appropriate Bible quote on rage. On trickery. On deceit. On disappointment. On shame. Damn Walker. Damn him! *A quick-tempered man does foolish things, and a crafty man is hated.* Proverbs 14:17. Oh, she did hate him. Blood flooded her eardrums, pounded against her temples. A scream stuck in her throat, her jaw too tight to open.

Lyle caught her arm and turned her around, holding steady as she stamped her feet and beat his chest and fell against his sheepskin vest. Tension drained from her neck down her back through her limbs, the ground a sponge, drawing poison.

Lyle said, "Tell me."

"I last saw him the day of the accident. Two weeks ago Sunday."

Back at the office, she unlocked the top drawer of her desk and spread out three bids for the construction of a youth center on Main Street. The commissioners had adjusted the figures to ensure the contract would go to Saul Duran's first cousin. The material and labor costs bled together, impossible to tally and compare. Lord, have You heard me? Do You see me? Do You ignore me intentionally? Have I not been faithful? Why have You allowed Walker to fall into his old pattern? Her hands shook. Mother mustn't find out. She jostled the papers, returned them to the drawer and turned the key.

At five o'clock she walked down the street to Art's, pushed open the door, hit a wall of cigarette smoke, yellow haze, and rank odor and moved down the length of the bar.

Jo tilted her head and raised one eyebrow, flicked her ashes as Art set down an amber-colored cocktail on a small square napkin.

"We need to talk," Lee Ann said.

Jo drew the napkin closer. "Shoot."

Lee Ann turned her back to Art.

"Lyle came to see me today. Walker's in trouble."

"What's new?"

"Real trouble."

"What's new?"

"He's sold Ross Plank's land to some stranger from Arizona. For $880,000.00."

The smoke Jo exhaled clouded her face.

"Walker's not smart enough to do that."

Lee Ann fumbled for a Kleenex in her purse. She wiped her eyes.

"You're serious," Jo said. "Oh, honey, I had no idea. No idea."

"Don't protect him."

Jo insisted she knew nothing. He'd been absent from Art's for over a week. She'd figured he was up to something, but didn't know what. Since he got out of prison, he'd borrowed a couple hundred bucks and took her to supper in Show Low. Sure, she'd heard about the accident with Sonny and Dee, the whole town knew. Maybe he'd simply decided to side-step Eugene for a while. She couldn't imagine what he'd do with the money. A bundle that big would be hard to hide, too obvious to squander. Lee Ann left her sitting there, cigarette turning to ash, drink untouched.

The cookie jar was empty, Walker's bed unmade. She fed Mother supper and wheeled her in front of the TV with food still on her chin.

"Mother, God doesn't acknowledge me. I search for reasons why, find none, and still trust in Him. I'm a fool. You would tell me, 'do not falter, keep the faith,' but I *am* faltering. I *am* in doubt. I need proof, just once."

Psalms, Proverbs, Song of Solomon. She flipped quickly through Matthew, Luke, Romans. Faster: Galatians, Timothy, 1 Peter, James. Faster, every passage offering advice, counsel, instruction, the promise of deliverance and salvation, faster, faster. A page tore at the binding. She gasped and ran to the kitchen, rummaged through the junk drawer for the Scotch tape. With shaking fingers, she aligned the tear perfectly and attached both sides, but when the Bible was closed, the page stuck out a sixteenth of an inch.

Chicken thighs frying in a cast iron skillet spattered the stove with oil. Eugene, Scott, and Dee dipped chips into salsa and sipped Dos Equis, discussing when to take the pigs off high protein feed and start them on regular. At the first lull in the conversation Lee Ann turned the chicken and set the tongs on a paper towel. As calmly as possible, she reported Lyle's news about Walker.

Eugene finished his beer and turned the bottle, as if looking for flaws in the glass.

Scott said, "I've never heard of a guy named Keith Lampert. I wonder how Walker got Ross to sign the deed." He took over cooking the chicken while Lee Ann drained the potatoes. "How did Owen find out? If everything is legal, can Lyle do anything about it?"

She added butter, salt, pepper, and milk to the potatoes and mashed them.

"Those are good questions," she said. "I don't have the answers."

Dee laughed. "Uncle Walker! Did it again! You can bet Keith isn't likely to give up property he's paid $880,000.00 for."

"Quit laughing," Scott said. "The whole thing speaks to the lawlessness in Dax County. You're just as bad, if you think your uncle ripping off a sick old man and his naive son is funny."

Eugene got up and pointed his beer bottle at Lee Ann from across the table.

"This is your fault," he said. "Not a damn person in your family has ever put that son-of-a-bitch in his place." He glared at Scott and Dee. "You boys included."

Scott transferred the chicken onto a serving dish.

"Please," Lee Ann said.

"Don't defend Scott and Dee. And don't preach."

She lowered her head.

Eugene waved the bottle. "Sure, act humble." He came around the table. "For once, instead of thinking you're immune to problems because God's on your side, own up to your part in allowing this disaster to happen."

"I had no idea," she said.

"Because you refuse to look. You think God takes responsibility for everything you don't have the guts to deal with. You've given your *self* away. And the worst part is, you don't see it."

"We're not discussing God," she said. "We're talking about Walker."

"We shouldn't be discussing either."

He dropped the bottle in the trash, walked into the dining room and opened the buffet, took out the whiskey saved for weddings and wakes, and clutching the bottle by the neck, slammed the door on his way out.

Lee Ann slumped into a chair and wiped her eyes with a napkin.

Dee stood behind her and held her shoulders. "Those were pretty harsh words. No one can control Walker—God, or any of us." He touched his chin to the top of her head. "I'll go close up the hen house."

Scott knelt and rested his hands on her knees. "I know how hard you try, Mom."

No, no one knew how hard she tried, how she believed in a God who ignored her, how she reached out to a man who didn't touch her, how she defended a brother who didn't regard her, how she obeyed commissioners who used her. She hung her apron. Time to put Mother to bed.

She stayed long after Mother fell asleep and returned to find the fireplace cold, the chicken and potatoes in the fridge, the pots and pans washed and stacked in the rack. Eugene's pickup was parked out front, but he wasn't in the house. She got into bed and clasped her hands under her chin. Lord, what has happened to Eugene and me? Gestures and words at bedtime reveal the condition of a marriage.

Mine is disintegrating. Asking Eugene for an explanation feels like a confrontation. I don't want to hear his excuses. Dutiful kisses goodnight, avoidance of being in the same room together, talk of tasks instead of emotions are signs of declining love. I know your advice on marriage—*Above all, love each other deeply, for love covers a multitude of sins.* 1 Peter 4:8. And yet You teach that Yours is the only love I need. Why then, despite my faith, does the loss of Eugene threaten my sense of wellbeing? Why, now that Walker has shamed me completely, do I seek Eugene's support rather than Yours? Forgive the weakness of longing for a hand in mine, a body beside me at night, a smile to sweeten my day, a husband to receive the tenderness I offer. Forgive me for needing Eugene's approval that Walker's crimes do not reflect on me, that I am good, decent, and honorable.

Sometime after midnight his bare feet crossed the floor. He lowered himself on the bed and carefully pulled the covers over his shoulder, lying as far from her as a body could get. She lay perfectly still until his breathing deepened and he began to snore gently. Only then did she sleep.

35

TUESDAY
OCTOBER 23, 2007

Sнe waited for her morning cup of coffee. Even though the house was quiet, she propped her pillow and stayed under the quilt and waited. The room brightened and the clock ticked past the time she usually showered. She would continue to wait, for hours, until noon, into the night. Waiting was her specialty. At seven o'clock, she threw off the covers. Mother would be needing the bathroom.

He'd left a note on the kitchen table. *I've gone to the cattle auction in Belen. Don't hold dinner.* Odd. He'd attended the auction three weeks ago. He didn't like eating in restaurants and always looked forward to a hearty meal after a day away and the two-hour drive home.

On the way to work, leafless cottonwoods with smooth, gray bark spread their limbs like giant feather dusters against a pale blue sky. One of Pete Herrington's cows was out, grazing on the shoulder of the highway. She'd call him from the office. Lyle had likely informed the deputies of Walker's latest "activities" and by now, Lewis would have confided in his new bride, Loretta. Jeremy would have passed along the information to Leo at the garage and Melba, the dispatcher, would have called her twenty best friends and four sisters. Every table at Vera's would be occupied with folks exaggerating details, exchanging opinions, saying, "I told you so."

At nine o'clock, she called the second floor clerks into the commissioners' conference room and gathered them next to the green chalkboard. There were chairs, but everyone stood.

"I want to tell you the facts about my brother as I understand them from Lyle."

Blank faces stared at her. The latecomers unbuttoned their coats.

"Ross Plank signed a quitclaim deed, giving Walker ownership of his ranch. Walker sold the property to a man from Arizona for a large sum of money. Naturally, Owen is upset, as am I. Since the deed is legal, unless Owen brings charges, nothing can be done. Lyle and I have no idea where Walker is or what Owen intends to do." Beth Ramirez blew her nose and dabbed her eyes, but it had nothing to do with sympathy. She'd had a cold for a week. "Now, I would like you to return to work. Caroline, please call the commissioners." She pushed back her shoulders. "Tell them I'll be out of the office today."

Pastor Fletcher agreed to open the church if she used the side security door upon leaving. When asked if he might offer consolation, she said, "Thank you, I'd like to be alone."

Along the side aisle, a lopsided poster of Christ had been thumbtacked next to the haphazard collection of donated crosses on the south wall. The chairs formed sloppy lines, some shoved sideways. She knelt on her knees in front of the pulpit and breathed deeply, opening her palms and bowing her head until her chin touched her chest. Oh, God. Help me endure this. Show me what Walker is meant to teach me. I have tried to understand. I have believed You would guide me, as well as him. Has my patience not been tested, my compassion, my trust in You?

She raised her head. The room was cold, the pulpit nothing more than a rectangular box. The cross, two sticks of wood nailed together. The light harsh. The pine floor scuffed and dull, the white walls in need of paint, the piano dusty. The place that once promised miracles: spiritless. Depleted of pleas, questions, promises or bargains, she turned from the cross and exited through the side door.

At the motel, she asked for Danielle.

Suzette looked up from behind the counter.

"She didn't come in today. She called in sick."

She found the shovel in the garden and dragged it out front and rammed the blade into the row of red hot pokers, scooped up a clump and heaved it aside. Stabbed the dirt again. Auction in Belen! Danielle sick! Her foot drove the blade, slicing the roots. She dug deeper. *But now you must put them all away; anger, wrath, malice, slander and obscene talk from your mouth.* Colossians 3:8. No longer! Red. *Jeep.* Hot. *Sexy.* Poker. *Well!* She plunged the blade. Red. *Heart.* Hot. *Furious.* Poker. *Cattle prod.* Red. *Blood.* Hot. *Boiling.* Poker. *Stud.* Red. *Alert.* Hot. *Wire.* Poker. *One pair.* She stopped and wiped her neck and face. If one crude, bold flower shot up, she'd gouge it out of the ground. Give her pansies, columbine, and Shasta daisies. The door opened and Grace placed a jug of water and a glass on the step, muttering something about wearing gloves, nothing harder on the skin than dirt.

She finished mid-afternoon, the yard a disaster, and wiped her blistered, cracked hands on her pants and walked into the field, through dried *gaillardia*, sunflowers, and mallow, around gopher mounds and prickly pear cacti turned purple from cold nights. Thistle burrs stuck to her pants. Coneflowers and grama grass supported seed heads on long, graceful stems, cottonwood leaves matted between them. The trees from which the leaves had fallen stood tall, their bare branches cracking the sky. Mullein stalks and prickly poppy filled bare patches of ground. Beyond the golden-brown foliage a strand of diamonds shimmered—sunlight reflecting off the creek. The trees, weeds, and wildflowers ended at a two-foot drop where floodwaters had eroded the bank. On the other side the land flattened into a rough, sandy beach with tufts of sedge grass sprouting between sand, rock, and boulders. The creek was shallow, its current barely discernable. A fallen cottonwood trunk spanned the water and she crossed, one foot in front of the other, arms outstretched, and plopped down on sun-warmed sand and rested back on her palms. The air was still, everything so quiet silence was almost a sound.

To her right, two arm lengths away, a long and lean snake, perhaps seven feet, stretched out in a sloppy *S*, rubbing its head on a rock. Snake: the lowest of creatures, physically and spiritually the embodiment of Satan. The Bible told us so. *And the Lord said unto the serpent, Because thou has done this thou art cursed above all cattle, and above every beast of the field; upon thy belly shalt thou go, and dust shalt thou eat all the days of thy life.* Genesis 3:14.

Scott would not panic. Don't move. In autumn, or before shedding, a snake can become cranky and aggressive. Breathe.

Its tail was ringed and smooth—a bull snake. The chocolate brown, diamond shaped markings were dull, its eyes cloudy and dark. The snake rubbed its head under the rock and against the sand, occasionally tucking its head to work the area on top of its mouth. Semi-opaque skin had already come loose on the underside of its jaw. Its tongue flicked in and out.

The skin came off the head and collected in a collar below the jaw and the snake opened its mouth wide, as if to yawn. Slowly and effortlessly it crawled out of its skin, leaving it inside out like a dirty sock, and moved off in the direction of the rocks, its new scales vibrant and lubricated.

She sat for half an hour beside proof of the snake's transformation. Its body would have been warm to the touch and firm, its line elegant as a master artist's stroke, its movement fluid as flowing water, a creature that approached quietly, without footsteps, its only sound a hiss to fend off predators.

From the opposite bank the cottonwoods' shadows reached across the water onto the sand. The creek ran dark, its jewels invisible. Walking back, her feet crunched branches woven into haphazard, thatched designs along the bank. Swallows swooped as swiftly as darts into the grasses, their wings and forked tails silhouetted against the cloudless sky. In the center of the field she threw open her arms and spread her fingers. Open, open, heart! Attach to every living thing, every color, scent, shape, taste, and sound. Stop believing in the Great Mystery. Become part of it.

Grace's car was gone. While Mother dozed in her chair, Lee Ann entered Danielle's room, stepped over slippers and toppled cowboy boots and opened the bureau drawers. She rifled through underwear and nightgowns, filtered through the closet, turned skirt and pant pockets inside out, opened a jewelry box and dumped the contents. Several handbags hung on a peg and she unhooked them and searched every compartment, pricking her finger on a toothpick at the bottom of a shiny black one with a chain strap. A year-old monthly planner stuck out of a side pocket and she leaned against the wall and scanned it, tossed it aside, got on her hands and knees and ran her hand under the bed. More shoes. Still kneeling, she opened the night table drawer. A key lay on top of a slip of paper with a local telephone number on it. She took the note into the kitchen and dialed.

A recorded voice answered. "This is Keith. I'm in Phoenix. Anyone needing to reach me knows the number."

Mother still slept. Leave her alone, or wait until she wakes? She was done waiting.

It had been years since she'd been to Ross's place, the last time to deliver a casserole after his wife died. Less than a month after Charlotte's passing, he'd suggested Mother might make a good second wife. Lee Ann had never returned.

She climbed the trailer steps, unlocked the door and opened the curtains. Bedroom first. Two shirts, a pair of jeans. A poncho. Empty dresser drawers. In the bathroom, two toothbrushes, a razor, shaving lotion on the sink, an assortment of shampoos and conditioners in the shower. Paper plates and plastic utensils in the kitchen, a small paring knife, a few pots and pans, a spatula and ladle. The phone hung on the kitchen wall above an address book. Her finger trailed the entries, starting with the As. All the listings were in Arizona. Then, under the Ms, a name with a New Mexico address—Pat Merker, Central New Mexico Correctional Facility, Los Lunas.

36

S HE MOVED THE BIBLE ASIDE and ran her hands over the nubby surface of the tatted cloth and peered at Jesus. The gilded gold frame isolated Him, boxed in His aura that until now had saturated every atom of her world. Flaxen hair that suggested perfect ears beneath shoulder length locks, sweet, pink lips that never pouted or grimaced, evenly proportioned facial features, and a soft, manicured beard had offered a lifetime of direction and solace. On closer inspection, He never spoke, never blinked or met her gaze directly, never inhaled, was but an image created for the likes of her, a blind believer in a personal God. Since childhood He'd perceived her as weak, a sinner. Alone she would falter, without Him she would fail. She held the frame up close, and at a distance, and turned His picture face-down on the table.

The bookmark slipped out of 1 Corinthians and she carried the Bible to the living room bookshelves and tucked it between *The Red Pony* and *Lonesome Dove*. She folded the tablecloth and put it on the washing machine. The little table was easy to dismantle and she picked it up, along with Jesus' portrait, and took them out to the shed. The table fit behind the folding step stool, and the portrait found a home in a plastic storage box with the boys' report cards and old taxes.

She walked back to the house and stood at the kitchen sink. The red geranium petals on the windowsill looked as vibrant, the silver cottonwoods as stark, the roast in the oven smelled as savory. She found Scott's journals and sat on his bed leafing through them, while a cottontail he'd adopted hopped around the bedroom. He claimed rabbits could be housebroken, and in the corner, on layers of newspaper, was proof. In this sanctuary, his mini-museum, samples of bark and feathers were pinned to corkboard and birds' nests were tucked in tree limbs propped against the wall. He'd built shallow boxes divided into compartments for rocks and roots and dead insects, displayed above his desk. On the first page of one of his journals he'd written, "Nature is not bestowed upon us, but is an evolutionary process of which we are a part."

"It's me, Mother. How are you today? I recognize Cary Grant's accent."

Mother's head tilted back and her eyes stared down as if scrutinizing a newspaper from a distance.

"Mother? Mother!"

She bent over Mother's mouth. No air kissed her cheek. She pressed her ear against Mother's chest and felt her wrist. No heartbeat, no pulse. Her hands and feet were still warm. Grace must have left less than an hour ago. In a dark suit on a cruise ship, Cary Grant repeated the word "darling." She reached for the remote and shut him off, sank to the floor and wrapped her arms around Mother's swollen calves and rested her temple on her knee. The end. Darling.

She took Mother's hand and whispered, "Thank you, Lord." But Jesus had been banished to the shed to live among report cards and taxes. Who would she be without Mother, without Jesus? Mother couldn't abide in paradise without God having created such a place. If Lee Ann ceased believing, and Mother still believed, did "*a place for her*" exist?

Jesus, her Truth, her Savior. Perhaps God had ordered her dwindling faith, so that after straying she would return to the Lord with greater fervor, for a world unorchestrated by God had always seemed inconceivable. Yet without asking, a snake had triggered an alternate way of viewing life, and death. A wire in her spine had tightened, straightened her up, opened her eyes, and sharpened her senses. An inner voice directed, *be alert. You're on your own. Don't you see? Abandoning to a higher power and appealing to your higher self amount to the same thing.*

She called the dispatcher and sat with Mother as daylight faded, stroking her ankles. The boys rushed over when the EMTs arrived. Scott made a pot of tea and Dee cleared the furniture out of the way and propped the door. The medics lifted Mother, shoved the gurney into the ambulance, shut the doors, and pulled away.

"I'll call Pastor Fletcher," Dee said.

"Pastor Fletcher, yes," Lee Ann said. "And Grace."

She and Scott sat on the sofa with Mother's polar fleece blanket between them. The house smelled of old person, sick person, furniture polish, and overly scented bathroom. Scott folded the blanket and scooted closer, the agnostic, the curious one, who questioned and probed and wondered.

"Where's Dad?" she asked.

"I don't know."

Dee returned from the kitchen. "Pastor Fletcher is on his way."

"Have you seen Dad?"

Dee shook his head.

She sent the pastor and the boys home. Mother had said night was special, a time for contemplation, darkness protective as a velvet cloak. Her passing didn't seem real, then seemed real. It didn't seem possible, then possible. There would be time to indulge in memories forgotten or minimized by the demands of illness, time to feel the loss and honor her life, but for now, relief. The house would be empty, unless Walker showed up. Walker. He would have no idea. Thank God Mother hadn't lived to weather the current scandal. Lee Ann clenched her fist. Do not thank God, or any entity. Life begins, irrespective of one's hopes, and ends independently of one's wishes.

She crossed the hall to her old room, still a girl's room with the white and pink gingham comforter on the white bed and matching night table. She shoved Danielle's bracelets and necklaces to one end of the bureau and straightened Grandma Edna's antique hairbrush set and sat on the edge of the unmade bed. Twenty-two years had passed since she'd inhabited this room, eight with Wayne and fourteen with Eugene. Aside from Mother, men had dominated her thoughts—Dad, Walker, Scott, Dee, Edgar, Wayne, Eugene, and the county's commissioners. Only one man's name had come up more frequently than any of theirs. Jesus.

Just after nine o'clock the front door opened. The kitchen faucet ran and a glass knocked against the sink. The bathroom door closed and the toilet flushed. Danielle entered the bedroom and gasped, tripped over a stray boot.

Lee Ann stood up. "You are to leave these premises within twenty-four hours. Any belongings left after that time will be thrown in the yard and hauled to the dump."

She raised a hand, blocking Danielle's face, and strode out.

Eugene emptied his pockets and put the contents on his night table. Lee Ann closed the door.

"It's time for an explanation," she said.

He sighed and unbuttoned his shirt.

"Is it Walker?" she asked.

"Partly," he said, draping the shirt over the back of the chair. "It's a lot of things."

"You've fallen in love."

He sat on the bed and leaned on his elbows, his head bent toward his knees.

She held onto the doorknob behind her back.

"I don't know if I can rightly explain it," he said. "This is not my place, never has been, never will be. It's the Walker Ranch and I've been the manager."

She let go of the doorknob. "Eugene…"

"I know you think that's nonsense. That's part of the problem—I already know your response to whatever I say. I've quit speaking what's on my mind because things have always been a certain way. You expect them to continue that way. Putting up with Walker is only one example. Your damn job is another. That place eats you up. You accept it. I've suggested a dozen times that we send Edgar to his sister's, but you can't imagine the place without him. He'll demand as much attention as your mother before long."

"Mother's dead."

"I know. Dee told me." He lifted his head. "I'm sorry. But I see Edgar taking her place—another soul to care for, wear you out…"

"Steal attention from you."

"I'm not jealous, Lee Ann. You don't seem to understand the energy you put into people and hopeless situations brings you down and has stalled us."

"Walker's gone, probably for good," she said.

"It doesn't matter. Your attitude is the same whether he's here or not. I need to feel you'd throw him out if he shows up again. See, I would, but my hands are tied. Like I said, this is not my place. Never has been, never will be." He hadn't shaved. His jaw, usually firmly set, hung open, and he said, "You seek God from a book. The worse things get, the more you search the pages. Your lips move in private conversations like a crazy person's." He touched his pillow. "More than two people share this bed. You consult your God more than me, take his advice more than mine."

"You used to respect my beliefs, even though they weren't your own."

"That was before I realized how much they undermined my efforts."

"I've begun to see…"

"Please." He held up his hand. "You're blind as a new-born kitten."

She charged across the room and jerked the bureau drawer open, threw his socks and shorts into the air, and slammed it shut with her hip.

"I've ordered Danielle off the property. I've not been blind to that. Take your things and join her."

She left him to gather his clothes like bits of trash and stumbled to Mother's, felt her way down the hall and climbed into Mother's bed, enfolded herself in her blankets, her smell, and smooth sheets. The stars packed a moon-less sky, so many she couldn't pick one. She floated through the window and merged with the unknown, a mere speck connecting to an unimaginable number of other specks, in-tricately linking her life to the greater whole—apart, yet a part—and wept.

37

IN THE MORNING, THE DIESEL's tire tracks imprinted an inch of snow out to the highway, clear as two chalk marks on slate. She walked in the tracks for a while and returned to her house and made coffee. Enough hay had been stored for the winter. The boys would drain the water from Mother's house and help empty it of her belongings. Eventually, Dee might live there when Scott went to college. She turned from the window and paced the floor in Mother's coat, checking the clock, listening for sounds of the boys. When she heard cupboards opening, she joined them at the table.

"Dad has left," she said, rolling the corner of a placemat, fearing she might cry. But she was cried out. "I don't know if or when he'll be back."

The boys ate with their shoulders hunched, spoons scraping their bowls, as if she'd just reported the weather. She'd fooled no one, blind to what everyone else had seen.

"Well, that leaves us in a mess," Scott said. "Walker's taken off, the Yanmar is leaking fluid and the fence adjoining Herrington's is torn up. We need hay for the winter."

"We'll manage," Dee said. "If you keep your mind on the job instead of catching butterflies."

"And you quit chasing Ginny all over the county."

"Dad'll be back before you know it," Dee said, refilling his coffee. "He'll miss me."

"He should be missing Mom."

195

She said, "We'll have to assign Edgar some chores. He can take care of the chickens and feed the pigs. I won't plant the garden. We'll simplify."

"I'll see if Lyle will send Manuel or Rudy over once a week," Dee said. "My shoulder will be okay in a couple of months." He socked Scott in the arm. "Until then, you're in charge. I don't know why that doesn't give me confidence."

Up the canyon, wet snow fattened oak and pine branches into smooth, soft shapes. Hugged by towering walls, she plodded toward "the dribble." Only a few elk, javelina, and coyote prints marked the snow. The dogs shot off, a whiz of black against white, and when she turned to whistle for them, her foot hit an icy patch and she slipped. As if shaken loose, tears flowed. She searched her empty pockets for a Kleenex and wiped her nose with her coat sleeve, touched her eyes. Puffy. A dull pain throbbed in their sockets.

Had she abandoned Jesus, or had He abandoned her? Had she forced Eugene out, or had he fled? Did she miss Mother's companionship, or did she need someone to care for to justify her life?

When the weather was beautiful, it was foolish to think God made it so, that He created snowflakes and raindrops, that He'd written the past and prescribed the future. Blind belief had deadened her curiosity, robbed her of skepticism. Now, her mind might wander, ponder, and wonder. Intuition might prove to be the only truth. This seemed backwards. When all was lost, that was the point at which people *found* faith, trusted God, turned to Jesus. She'd done the opposite—stepped out of God's protective palm, discarded skin that no longer fit.

She shook her head and said, "Crap."

Snowmelt dripped from tree limbs. The dogs poked her sides with their noses, come on, let's go. They didn't question whether God put a rabbit behind that bush for them to sniff out, didn't justify the chase or the kill or near escape. Instinct drove them toward a single goal. Her instinct dictated that she be good. She could work toward that goal without Jesus telling her how. She could flounder, err, and try again without His judgment or His insipid acceptance of her weaknesses and His unrelenting forgiveness of her mistakes.

"Okay," she said. "Okay, let's go."

That stupid ceramic pig. Wherever Walker had gone, he'd taken every last penny. Never again. She took the cookie jar outside and smashed it with a hammer, swept up, dumped the pieces in the trash and set Mother's recipe box in its place. The curtainless window in the living room let in the subdued tones of winter. In due time, spring, summer, and fall, each with their changing skies and foliage, would be invited in also. There would be no new drapes.

From her pocket, she unfolded a slip of paper and dialed the office of the state auditor in Santa Fe.

"I am the county manager of Dax County. I'm calling to inquire about the procedure for reporting fraud. Yes, I'll hold."

Gerald Murray took her call. As public investigator, he would be assigned to the case. When asked if she would like to remain anonymous, she replied, "Only for the moment. I'll be away next week and can assist with the process when I return. At that point I'll be willing to attach my name to the investigation and provide any information you need."

The Central New Mexico Correctional Facility provided Pat Merker's full mailing address. On a sheet of Mother's plain white stationery, she wrote:

Dear Mr. Merker,

An urgent matter has come up regarding my brother, Walker. I would value your input— confidentially, of course. Please include my name on your visitor's list. I will be there late Saturday morning.

Sincerely,

Lee Ann Walker

She drove to the mailbox. It was either too cold or too early for the men to have gathered on the store porch. A couple of numbers had fallen off the marquis, or someone had picked them off with a stick, and the six-pack special was now selling for $ .99! Even so, the place was deserted.

38

W ALKER HIT THE ROAD FRIDAY morning and arrived in Des Moines three hours later. Done with fancy-shmancy, he checked into the Holiday Inn Express west of the city. He called Jimmy Zebrowski and scribbled directions to a six o'clock dinner at Applebee's. In the motel lobby he found a map of the city and went sightseeing, not in the regular sense of taking in the main attractions, but rather a slow drive through the suburbs and downtown, across the river and back.

Up and down the blocks and around the corners, he passed two-story, brick or wood-sided houses on tended yards with evergreen and deciduous trimmed hedges and paved driveways. Sidewalks with proper curbs lined the streets. Cement steps led up to porches with solid, square posts, the overhanging roofs pitched and layered with proper shingles. The people who built these homes were good, sturdy stock, descended from ancestors in northern Europe or Scandinavia, tradesmen who brought their masonry and carpentry skills across the ocean. Street after street of solidarity, security, and conformity. Ah, the predictability of it all. In New Mexico sidewalks were a rarity and streets bled into yards, loose gravel served as a driveway, if you had one at all, and a mansion might fill an acre right next to a shack. Houses were made from the dirt they sat on, with flat roofs that leaked. Front yards crowded with cosmos thrived happily next to vacant dirt lots littered with trash and rampant weeds.

He drove past insurance companies, banking establishments, and high-rises with meager bits of landscape at their feet, no space wider than a horse stall between them. Man, no air. Reflections of obtrusive rectangular structures bounced off glass windows, distorting the sky and blocking the horizon. Inside, people worked nine to five, scurrying down hallways into rooms with no natural light—a death sentence. High-heeled shoes. Suits and ties. Damn, cowboys lucked out being spared such a fate.

Jimmy hadn't changed since prison, fat and sloppy, the same high, nervous laugh, and up to the same old dealings that got him in jail in the first place. He'd held onto a job at a 7-Eleven, augmenting his minimum wage income by selling pot to his wife's relatives and abetting their slimy activities. Walker accused him of being the personification of yet another rehabilitation hope failed.

Jimmy said, "Look who's talking." He looked Walker up and down. "You look like a fucking mega dweeb."

The steak on the menu looked good, but when it was placed before him, whatever appetite Walker had left the premises. He missed Vera's, the hands that waved, even the heads that turned away, the air foggy with cigarette smoke, the chile so hot it burned his nostrils and made his eyes water. He missed the grimy bric-a-brac and the smudged glass case behind the counter filled with day-old, maybe week-old pies, and the ancient register from the fifties with the numbers worn off, and the drawer that stuck.

Jimmy sliced into his meat, sending juice oozing around his plate. Walker looked away. Bloody food was for savages. Seasonings, sautéed vegetables, salad dressing, rolls, and butter tightened his throat. The only thing able to slide down easily might be liquid, alcoholic liquid.

"I need a driver's license," Walker said.

"I'll need a photo."

Jimmy held up his phone.

"Okay, then. Finish up and let's do it."

Back at the motel Walker stood against the white wall while Jimmy moved close and stepped back, getting it just right.

"Let's see." Walker took the camera. "Good. I want the name to read Ross Plank." He tore a slip from a Holiday Inn notepad. "Here, I'll spell it out."

"Give me a day or two," Jimmy said. "I'll meet you here at noon Sunday."

A lot of people had screwed on this mattress, consumed umpteen bottles of beer, wine, or champagne, quarreled, promised eternal love, and betrayed their one and only. He crossed his feet on the maroon, yellow, and green floral bedspread, and turned on the TV. An excited weatherman warned of an early snow blizzard coming down from Canada. Treacherous conditions. Stay indoors. Do not travel unless absolutely necessary.

He stocked up at a liquor store and stopped at TD's Sports Bar. Fair-haired, well-fed twenty-year-olds in sweat-shirts and jeans filled the place. Ponytails and rosy cheeks. On TV, the Colts were ahead of the Jets seventeen to ten. TD's rambunctious patrons cheered and booed. For the first time in his life Walker sat alone, this crowd, the game, and this establishment of no interest whatsoever.

Right about now, Jo would be perched on her stool at Art's, sliding a Manhattan across the slick, wood counter. She'd light up and postpone taking the first sip until she took the first drag and after a while she'd cross her legs. Smoke would come out her nostrils and linger around the impenetrable helmet of red hair. Art would know better than to say, "Any word?" His expression would remain unchanged, his voice would stay low, as if a relative had died, and they'd drift into familiar small talk until the crowd picked up. At seven o'clock, she'd drive home, heat a Lean Cuisine and watch one of those lawyer shows.

The first snowflakes blew in from the northwest, hit the windshield, and stuck. A fierce wind picked up, and when he shut the motel room door, the wail and chill came through the walls. He cranked up the heat. Out the window snow blew at a horizontal angle, already collecting against the brick wall.

39

THE SIGN ALONGSIDE THE FREEWAY read PRISON FACILITY. DO NOT PICK UP HITCHHIKERS. Lee Ann turned off at the next exit and parked in the area assigned to visitors, checked her hair in the rearview mirror, and collected her purse and notebook.

Saturdays and Sundays, Level 1 admitted visitors to a large, yellow common room crammed with long Formica tables, metal chairs, and a few vending machines lined up on gray linoleum, everything jammed together and smelling of Pine-Sol. A chain link fence enclosed an outdoor area with a few concrete tables and benches.

Lee Ann passed through security and took a seat at one of the indoor tables between a family of four and a young couple tattooed all the way up to their chins. A month ago, she'd have forgiven their sins and offered compassion. Today they were questionable characters—sad and crude, smelling bad, and talking too loud.

Pat Merker walked through the double doors, taking only a second to spot her. He might have been Walker's twin—slight build, light step, twinkling blue eyes, long nose, and ready smile. He looked like he'd been washed in warm, all the colors having bled into a faded, neutral tone, and yet a hot, orange flame burned inside. He winked and made his way across the room. Two warm hands captured her cold one and she blushed when he said, "I've seen your picture, but let me tell you, you're a hell of a lot better look-ing in person!"

The same Walker con. A carbon copy.

"Thank you," she said, retrieving her hand. "Let's talk outside."

"You'll be cold."

"I'll put up with the chill to have some privacy."

"All right then," he said.

They stood next to the cinderblock wall, benches and tables empty, shadows of two leafless locust trees spreading veins across the concrete.

"I'll come right to the point," she said. "I need to find my brother."

His lips stayed set in a smile and his eyes held hers.

"An urgent matter has come up regarding a large sum of money he's inherited."

"I wish I could help, ma'am, but I wouldn't know where he is."

"The money is from our mother. She died."

Pat's smile vanished, as if swiped by a damp cloth.

"Where is your mother?" she said.

"She died when I was twelve."

"I'm sorry."

Two young boys burst into the yard and chased each other around the tables.

"Walker doesn't know." She bowed her head. "He was very close to Mother."

The boys aimed their index fingers and shot at each other, yelling, taking cover behind the benches.

"The money was left by our grandfather, who was a gambling man. I believe it comes to about twice the amount of what Walker got from Keith Lampert for Ross Plank's property."

"Bam! Bam!"

Pat leaned in, hands in his back pockets.

"Walker has to sign the appropriate papers in order to claim his half of our ranch, either in person or by mail. And of course, half of the large sum of grandfather's money is his due, as well. I need an address."

Pat's eyes darted back and forth across the pavement.

"He's in Des Moines," he said, finally. "You can find him through Jimmy Zebrowski."

"Bam!"

He held the door.

"Wait inside, I'll get Jimmy's number for you."

She stopped at the Los Lunas Walmart and washed her face and hands in the bathroom, then washed her hands a second time. On a pre-paid cellphone, she called home from the parking lot. Scott reported everything under control.

"Be careful, Mom. They're expecting blizzard conditions in the Dakotas, Iowa, across Michigan, and Illinois. I wish you'd let me come with you."

"I'll be fine," she said. "See you in a few days."

A fat man struggled with his shopping cart, maneuvering it between two trucks and letting it roll into the back of his car, and she got out to help.

"Stocking up before the storm," he said.

During the blizzard of '88, when she and Wayne were building the house, the power had gone out for four days. Snow piled on itself, half burying the stacked lumber, sheetrock, and vehicles, covering the fences. The first night she cooked hamburgers in the wood stove. The second night she roasted hot dogs in the fireplace and made popcorn by candlelight. The snow was supposed to stop by morning, but it kept on. Wayne grew irritable and resisted her attempt at a romantic interlude, grumbling about the lousy electric co-op's inability to fix the power lines, how it'd take days to get the vehicles out, how he despised kicking the dreaded muck off his boots. She had the first inkling of her mistake then, and as time passed, the premonition proved true. She would have continued, had Eugene not appeared and persisted and won. He'd been patient, offering her time to work it out with the first man in her life, the Lord. When she broke her promise to love, cherish, and obey her husband, Eugene stood by her, sympathizing with her inner turmoil, respecting her faith without engaging in spiritual dogma, for Jesus was not his savior. Eugene asked for nothing more than taking life a day at a time, acceptance of man and nature at his core. He'd married a woman who prioritized virtue at the expense of everything else and sought guidance from a phantom god—a wife who, from the start, had relegated him to second place. A man couldn't help resent that rank, feel diminished compared to perfection.

The storm might strand her in a cheap motel, eating packaged muffins with weak coffee for who knew how many days. She took the exit to the Albuquerque airport and found the long-term parking lot. A shuttle delivered her to American Airlines, where she booked a flight at 10:35 the following morning. After a stop in Dallas, the plane would land in Des Moines at 4:50. She caught another shuttle to La Quinta Motel, left her suitcase in the room, tucked the key in her purse, and walked over to Denny's. A baked potato and a cup of hot tea were all she could stomach. As a girl, she and Mother had flown to a cousin's wedding in Phoenix. The wind had blown that plane around like a tissue.

40

BY MIDNIGHT SNOWPLOWS HAD STARTED piling long, white berms along the city's main roads. Walker sat on the edge of the bed and checked the time, his arms and legs aching, as well as his lower back. Traveling screwed up his internal clock. Without Sir Galahad's wake-up call, he slept late. To break up the drive, he'd stopped at rest areas for naps, a habit that kept him staring at the ceiling half the night. He hauled the suitcase out from way under the bed and took out a bundle of bills and inhaled. Nothin' like the smell of money. A pizza might taste good right about now, but the promise of a hundred dollar tip couldn't get one delivered on a night like this.

The way to the ice machine was carpeted and he let the door click behind him and walked down the hall in his socks. If number 107, 109 or 113 would open, some fun-loving *mature* person might poke his head out and invite him in for a drink. Hell, he'd supply the booze. 110 seemed to have some fun going on behind it, the TV and laughter seeping into the hall, but the door stayed shut. He returned to his room, put on his boots, filled his insulated coffee mug with scotch and ice and carried his drink to the lobby. A chubby brunette in a green Holiday Inn jacket smiled at him from behind the reception counter.

"Evenin'," he said. "Quiet night."

"I'm loving it."

"I guess there might be some advantages. Tell me about them."

She closed a window on her computer screen.

"Well, for one, I get to talk to you. Where you from? Where you going?"

"I'm from New Mexico. Going to the UP."

"You'll find it a heck of a lot colder and snowier up there."

"I'm starting to worry about that," he said.

"Worrying will kill you."

"I got medicine." He held up the mug. "I can get some for you."

She giggled. "Maybe just one."

He bounded back to the room and tore the wrapping off two plastic cups, fit one over the bottle and filled the other with ice.

She wouldn't let him smoke and he launched into how you could do anything you damn well pleased where he lived. Everybody in Dax County made personal choice top priority. There was plenty of room for everybody's individual idiosyncrasies because folks lived and let live. Sometimes, when idiosyncrasies crossed the line to infractions, people resorted to the use of firearms. Didn't make much sense to call the sheriff. He'd just tell you to solve the dispute yourself.

"I wouldn't like that," she said. "I'd feel lost without boundaries and convention."

"Sweetheart, we call it freedom. Supposedly what this country was founded upon."

Two hours later they were silly. He dragged a chair behind the counter and drew a detailed picture of Mother's ranch with the creek running through it, the mesa, the canyons and all the animals that lived there—the horses, Sir Galahad and his harem, Patch and Blue, Butch out with the cattle, Scott and Dee with mama pig and her piglets. He added his sister, carefully illustrating her widow's peak, Mother in a wheel chair, and his brother-in-law with a frowny face.

"And where are you?" she said.

"Passed out on the couch. Ha ha!" He drew himself stretched out with one leg hanging over the edge, hat covering his face, bottle in hand, glass tipped over on the floor.

"No. No. Wait." He erased the figure. "I'm gone."

He stopped laughing. His house was a thousand miles away. A huge, black walnut tree played drums on the roof in the fall and a graceful weeping willow shaded it in summer. Existing in a cold, gray city seemed crazy when you could live where eyes needed sunglasses every day and black bears swiped juniper berries off trees right outside the back door, where double rainbows began and ended in between creases in the mountains, where the Milky Way streaked the sky, where sleep was interrupted by bugling elk instead of sirens.

"It's been swell," he said.

The security chain refused to slip through the lock. His head swirled. He stumbled to the bathroom and fumbled with his fly, his stream missing the toilet, and staggered sideways. The edge of the sink bonked his forehead. The tile floor was cold as a sheet of ice and he crawled on all fours to the bed, pulled himself up, and swung forward and back. The flowered bedspread blurred into rocks, hills, and mountains where he'd discovered the pottery sherds, arrowheads, *metates*, bone tools, and fetishes of the ancient ones who'd built stone houses and hollowed kivas out of the southern slopes of mesas. He flopped on the bed and tucked his arms under his head. On the ceiling, wispy clouds moved in circles around Solitaire Peak. From the very top, he scanned a hundred miles—the plains to the east, the lower mountain ranges to the north, the Rio Risa to the south, around and around and around....

In the morning, the bathroom mirror reflected a pale face with a quarter-size purple bump on his forehead. Ooh. Tender. He adjusted his baseball cap carefully.

A young man had replaced last night's receptionist.

"Tell the maids not to clean room 106."

"Yes, sir."

"What's the latest weather report?"

"Should pass through by evening, sir."

"Is this the army?"

"No, sir."

"Just checking."

He flipped through ESPN, CNN, Discovery Channel, Preachers, PBS, Turner Classic Movies. Right now, Mother might be staring at Bogie in *The Caine Mutiny*. Let's see, she'd have been in her late twenties when that movie came out, wearing a denim skirt and plaid blouse, telling him to hold that chicken tight while she put a leg ring around its ankle. That was how they were going to tell the age of that hen after they got more and forgot all about this one. This one had shiny feathers and was about to lay her first egg, but like all God's creatures her looks would fade and eventually they'd come to think of her as a workhorse, or workchicken. You could tell a chicken's age by her feet, just like people; and like people, some aged quicker than others. Mother kept track of her chickens on a chart in the mudroom, where she also marked the first frost, first snowfall, and last freeze. The chart hung over a cabinet with forty long, narrow drawers full of seeds. On top, Mother's gardening gloves, a trowel, and pruners were laid out beside an old Apache basket that overflowed with vegetables and fruit in the summer.

Bogart was ugly, stiff, and miserable looking, and spoke without moving his upper lip. Mr. Tough Guy. Walker put on his fleece-lined denim jacket and trudged down the block to the Chevron Station Redimart. Snow blew in his face. In order to survive these winters, he'd have to give in and buy one of those down-filled jackets that made a man look like a marshmallow.

He kicked the snow off his damned running shoes and whacked his sleeves. Hunger nagged at him and he scanned the aisles. Just the thought of food left a lingering, greasy film on the roof of his mouth. Come on man, try *something*. A package of cheese crackers stuffed with peanut butter. A loaf of bread and a can of tuna. He bought a bag of Fritos, a ham sandwich and two packs of Winstons.

His feet were soaked and Bogie was still slurring his S's when he got back. He put his shoes and socks on the heater, ripped open the sandwich and took a couple of bites, checked his watch. Twenty-four hours until Jimmy showed up.

41

"Jimmy Zebrowski, please."

"You're talking to him."

"Hello, Jimmy. My name is Lee Ann Walker," she said, her voice breathy. "Walker's sister. I'm calling from the Des Moines airport. An emergency has come up in our family. Pat Merker gave me your number and said you can help me find Walker."

A man asked for a pack of Marlborough Lights at the other end of the line.

"You don't know me, but we could meet," she said. "I'll take a cab to wherever you suggest, and will pay you one thousand dollars for this information, if you agree not to tell Walker I'm here."

"Cash?"

"Of course."

A cash register closed. The man said, "See ya."

"I've got business with him at noon tomorrow," Jimmy said. "If you can hold off seeing him until after we're done, okay. I'll need the money up front."

"That won't be a problem."

"I get off at seven o'clock. Meet me at Farley's at seven-thirty. Any cabbie will know where it is."

She ordered a quarter pounder and fries, settled herself at an empty gate rapidly filling with whining children and crying babies, and called home. The answering machine picked up.

"It's Mom," she said. "I took a plane and just arrived. Tomorrow is Grace's birthday. You might take her some eggs."

At seven o'clock she hailed a cab. The snow had stopped and the main streets were being salted. The city must resemble San Francisco, Boston, or New York, with its streetlights, malls and theaters, art museums, and cinemas showing the top ten rated movies. Green neon letters advertised Farley's, a bar in an old downtown hotel.

From brass fixtures, dim, orange light warmed a cozy room with high-backed wooden booths and dark green walls. She ventured toward a barstool and scooted her suitcase close in, hoisted her rear onto the leather seat, and rested her feet on the long brass footrest. Eugene might have fancied bringing her to a place like this. She would have resisted. Sinners frequented bars and the virtuous attended church. If someone in Brand considered patronizing both, Art's clientele reduced them to the lowest level in no time. But in this elegant establishment, no one would punch their buddy in the face over an insult, unintentional or otherwise. The patrons wore clean clothes and polished shoes, and the bartender had on a black vest with gold buttons over an ironed shirt, a red bow tie propping his chin. She ordered a Coke and waited for a tap on the shoulder.

So, the Urbandale Holiday Inn Express, room 106. Lee Ann scribbled the address on a cocktail napkin.

"Yeah, Walker and Pat," Jimmy said. "Quite the pair."

"I take it you know them well."

"Well enough to know they look alike but are mighty different. Walker's a lightweight con artist. Pat's a heavy-weight felon. Only reason Pat's serving time in minimum security is because of a minor misdemeanor. In his youth he served fourteen years for armed robbery. Shot a jewelry store clerk in both legs, crippled him for life."

Lee Ann's palms itched and she rubbed them on her thighs. From her purse she took ten one-hundred-dollar bills and handed them to Jimmy. He finished his drink in one gulp, laid a ten next to her Coke and said something like "good deal," or "good luck," and "so long." She placed another five on top of Jimmy's ten, hesitated, added three more dollars and asked the bartender to call a taxi.

The clerk at the Urbandale Holiday Inn gave her a room on the second floor overlooking the parking lot. A silver Honda was parked in front of 106. She placed her suitcase on the dresser, took out her toiletries, and splashed warm water on her face, drying off with white towels that wouldn't last a day at home, no matter how much bleach. She set out her comb and squeezed toothpaste onto her toothbrush. In the mirror her hand went back and forth and up and down, spreading toothpaste over her teeth and gums, over and over, so tired, too tired to rinse, but she did. The heater was noisy and blew a draft around the room. Her sweater pulled off without a struggle. So many pillows. She tossed the extras aside. The decorator pillows on their bed at home had ended up teetering on an overloaded chair or tossed on the floor at night and were soon stored in the closet, and eventually donated to the thrift store. Lorraine Connely bought them for her guest room. Lee Ann's eyes closed and the journey's purpose faded to a remote notion.

She said, "Eugene."

Eugene unhitching the horse trailer, Eugene pouring maple syrup over a stack of pancakes, Eugene hooking his belt buckle, zipping his jacket, teaching Dee how to shoot, nodding *okay* when Scott refused to handle a weapon, taking her hand in the evening and strolling down the rows of vegetables, snapping a green bean in two, half for her, half for him, picking a squash blossom and tucking it behind her ear. He'd be finished in the bathroom in a minute and collapse into the empty spot beside her and sigh, rest his arm over her waist. It would grow heavy as his breathing deepened and she would turn on her side. They would sleep with their legs touching.

42

SUNDAY
OCTOBER 28, 2007

IN THE MORNING SHE BREWED coffee, showered, and put on a fresh pair of pants with a beige turtleneck and re-packed her suitcase. She straightened the covers, hung the Do Not Disturb sign on the door, and pulled a chair next to the window. On TV, overly enthusiastic news anchors reported depressing events in between annoying commercials. She'd forgotten to bring food, but that was okay—she'd forgotten to be hungry. For three hours she sat, stood, peered between the drapes, and paced. At noon, she parted the curtains and remained stationed at the window.

Jimmy parked his truck beside the silver Honda in front of 106. He knocked twice.

Lee Ann grabbed her bag and purse and hurried down the outdoor staircase, past the three maroon doors and three windows of 100, 102, and 104. The temperature must have dropped below ten degrees. Her breath shot out of her mouth in gusts of steam which froze in tiny beads on her upper lip. Further down the sidewalk, a maid was layering fresh linens on her arm from a cart.

"Please, I've lost my card to room 106 and have forgotten my glasses. I'm late for an appointment. Can you let me in?"

A lamp hung over a round table, a plastic grocery bag stuffed with clothes, a black suitcase, and a six-pack of Bud huddled at its center—one in Walker's hand, of course.

Jimmy shot a glance at Walker and bolted outside, leaving him standing beside the table getting into his jacket.

"For Christ sake, Lannie, shut the door. It's freezing out there."

She took two steps toward him. What a get-up. Shiny shirt, polyester pants, new belt, and dirty white running shoes. And a Dallas Cowboys baseball cap!

"Jimmy told you I was here," she said.

"If you've come to take me home, forget it." He raised his arms above his head and dropped them by his sides. "Lannie, Lannie, marching through life with God's guidelines stamped like a badge on your chest. Trouble with you is, you believe in something too strong. Then you got to defend it."

"You believe in nothing, so think you can do anything."

"And you hate me for it."

That's right. He had it wrong, though, assuming himself to be the only target of her resentment. She kicked those polyester pants. For the rules. Again. For the guidelines. And he took it, like the eight-year-old brat in the bathroom when he'd stolen money from Mother's bureau. She stopped, out of breath. His eyes focused on the door, his fingers playing a tune on his thighs. The runt was thinking of running. If she had a lasso, she'd tighten it around his torso, drag him to the chair, shove him into it, and scream that she'd never let him out of her sight, or give up chasing him until justice was served.

She said, "Mother died."

Any twitching on his part stopped.

"I'm not giving you your half of the ranch unless you return Owen's money. He deserves his rightful inheritance."

His smirk had vanished.

"When?"

"Last Tuesday."

He paced a circle, rubbing the back of his neck.

"The service is Wednesday. You are going to fly home with me and be there. You are going to give Owen the money. I will deed you the northern half of the Walker Ranch and if you ever step one foot on my half, I will shoot you." She held up her cell phone. "I can call Lyle right now to inform the Iowa police where you are and have you apprehended."

"Was she alone?"

"Yes. Watching *An Affair to Remember*. Cary Grant. She seemed peaceful."

"Tear jerker," he said. "All those films…maybe she understood the words and actions, maybe not."

She said, "*Seven Year Itch….Rear Window….On the Waterfront….Hud….Bridge on the River Kwai….Guess Who's Coming to Dinner…*"

He added, "*Some Like it Hot….Lawrence of Arabia…. From Here to Eternity….For Whom the Bell Tolls….True Grit….To Have and Have Not….*"

"That's enough," she said.

A card on the dresser listed taxi services.

"Hopefully, we'll get to the airport early enough to catch a flight back today."

"I've got a car," he said.

"Not anymore."

43

Nabbed. Merk the Jerk turned Pat the Rat. A thousand bucks amounted to a nice piece of change for Jimmy, but Pat wouldn't have accepted such a puny bribe with almost a half million coming his way in a matter of weeks. She'd got to Pat some other way and he'd swallowed whatever she'd doled out. Screw you, buddy.

These damned, overcast days had turned his mind around, anyway. That receptionist had said the swarms of black flies and mosquitoes around Lake Superior were worse than in Alaska and he'd heard Alaska mosquitoes were big as ice cubes. She said fishermen slathered mud all over their arms and faces against getting bit. She said Lake Superior was so vast it seemed like an ocean and that gales blew up out of nowhere. In fact, they called it an inland sea. She said in parts of northern Michigan houses had doors on the second floor that seemed to open to nowhere, but folks had to use them to get outside in the winter, the snow could get that deep.

If he could just exit this goddamn plane and set his feet on solid ground he might come up with a plan. He unscrewed the tiny bottle of scotch. Lee Ann sipped coffee, her foot resting on the black leather suitcase stashed under the seat in front of her. He offered her his bag of peanuts.

"Nuts for the nutty," he said. She was anything but nutty.

He couldn't stretch his legs. A cramped body couldn't think. Clouds beneath a body didn't compute because the formula for daydreaming demanded lying face up looking into the great beyond, not being in it. Being propelled inside a speeding bullet at thirty-five thousand feet turned his stomach upside down. No sense talking to her. She'd made her mind up about things. He might slip away when they changed planes in Dallas, duck into the men's room, hang around there for a couple hours and take off on the next available flight to somewhere in Idaho, Montana, or Oregon. Did mosquitoes and black flies buzz around in those states?

He adjusted his seat as far back as it would go, which wasn't much, and downed the scotch in two gulps. They hardly used the northern half of the ranch. The valley narrowed quickly, as if cinched by a belt, and high mesas began their rise close to the creek. Mornings stayed darker longer and evenings arrived earlier. Bald eagles lived there. Willow thickets thrived on either side of the water, overtaking the grasses. From a source atop the east mesa, Widow Creek cut a route downward, carrying rocks that collected where it joined Alibi Creek. The combined flow spilled south where the land eventually leveled out, but even then, the area wasn't suitable for cattle. Dad had raised hogs there, once. There was a small, crude log cabin with a leaky roof, a good well, and a barn with more cracks than boards for walls. Across the north fence line the Rossmans had fixed up an old, rock house on thirty-five acres, then changed their minds and decided not to live there after all. Let's see. He might figure a way to get them to part with that piece of property. Hell, they lived in Albuquerque and only visited a few times a year. Had to rid the place of mice every time they showed up…the upkeep and taxes must be a burden… they might want a quick, easy way out…

In Dallas, Lee Ann marched toward their connecting flight at Gate 43. Walker tagged along at her heels, sniffing fast food, ignoring the bar on the left, eyes forward, away from the list of departing flights to places unknown. Children's voices and flight announcements faded. In his mind, hawks screeched and crows squabbled. Small ground animals—lizards, toads, gophers, squirrels, and snakes—called him back to Alibi Creek. And ants, army ants that built those graceful mounds he'd destroyed with his boot until Dad taught him to quit kicking and start looking. Over the years he'd discovered turquoise, coral, and stone beads in those piles of sand. Got bit more than a few times while poking around their houses, disturbing their work. One time he discovered two beads on the same hill.

The Albuquerque airport kiosks displayed chile products, New Mexican cookbooks, turquoise jewelry, Native American fetishes, weavings, and pottery. Folks waited for their flights on padded chairs from the 1950s. Walker's feet tread on tile floors laid like brick. He heard Spanish spoken.

"Come on, Lannie." He ran ahead and faced her, walking backwards. "Here we are! Give me a smile."

She continued straight toward him.

"Look," he said. "I've agreed to give Owen the money. So help me, I'll never step foot on your property. I won't bug the boys, ever. I swear. And I will wait until after the ranch is legally divided to divorce Danielle, so she won't have any claim to your half. I promise, every square inch of your share will be protected." Oh, she was done talking, he could see that. Maybe forever. For sure forever. He fell in step beside her. "I'm going to build me a one-room adobe house with a kitchen in the corner and a bathroom off to one side. I saw a picture of a house with a garden growing smack in the middle, lettuce and sunflowers and tomatoes all packed together reaching for a skylight. I'm going to try that. The plants might attract bugs, but they've got sprays." He cleared his throat. "Guess I'll pass on that. Just the thought's makin' me cough. But, there's other ideas for one-room living, like built-in storage under the bed and a table that folds out from the wall. See, when you're in the kitchen, the whole house is the kitchen, and when you're in bed, the whole house is the bedroom and when you're in the living room, the whole place is the living room. Get it?"

The three-hour drive from the airport took an extra hour at night, the half-moon creating crazy shadows between chamisa and Apache plume, fooling the eye into thinking coyotes, elk, and antelope were moving across the plains. He drank the rest of the six-pack and was half asleep when they drove past Highway 34 and on to Brand, arriving at Jo's at three a.m.

Referring to the suitcase on the back seat, she said, "I'll keep that. Find me at the courthouse tomorrow."

He stood on the road holding the plastic bag of dirty laundry and blinked at her taillights disappearing down the hill. Shit. He snuck around the side of the house to Jo's bedroom and pressed his ear against the cold windowpane. At the front door, he raised his hand, but didn't knock. She wouldn't hesitate to pop a hole in an intruder's chest with the Sig Sauer .380 in her nightstand. He carried his laundry down the hill and traipsed along Main Street. A couple of strays followed at a safe distance and worked up enough courage to close the gap. He stopped and opened his palms.

"Ain't got nothin' for you."

The only light in town shone from the courthouse entrance onto the gravel parking lot. They should've put the front door facing the street, like the state capitol building in Des Moines. This was the courthouse, in the county seat, with a conference room for legislating, where file cabinets and computers in the clerk's office, treasurer's office, assessor's office, and Department of Motor Vehicles stored important facts and figures. The jail windows were black. He quickened his step to Art's trailer and climbed the creaking steps onto the flimsy porch. That little yapping mutt of Art's barked and the strays retreated back down the street.

A lamp turned on. Art cracked the door.

"Hey, man, it's Walker. Put your gun down and your pants on."

44

Scott carried Lee Ann's overnight bag and the black suitcase inside.

"I don't think I can sleep," she said. "Let's put some coffee on."

She sat at the kitchen table in her coat, the weight of it bending her spine.

"Has Eugene been back, has he called?"

"No."

The machine gurgled and sputtered and coffee dripped into the pot. She shook her head at his offer to make toast and eggs.

"Your uncle is a criminal," she said. "There's a name for someone like him—a sociopath. He'll never be any different and it's up to us to distance ourselves. I'm dividing the ranch. He'll get the northern half. You and Dee are to have nothing more to do with him."

"After two days of obeying boundaries, he'll do whatever he wants."

"I'll shoot him if he sets foot on this half again. He knows I mean it. A surveyor will determine an accurate division of the property. Owen maybe, who will likely take great satisfaction in knowing the acreage is equal, but that Walker's half is useless."

"If you strand him on land where he can't earn a living, he'll get into more trouble."

"I don't care. He can go to…" If heaven didn't exist, hell didn't either. "…jail."

Scott filled two mugs, set them down and took a seat. He seemed twice his age.

"I heard at the store that Dad's taken a job at the Diamond T Dude Ranch, down south. The previous manager quit after an argument with one of the guests."

She held her forehead. A separation. Possibly, a divorce.

"Edgar's almost useless," Scott said. "Dee's stuck with the whole load. I mean, he can manage things, but it's hard without Dad and only one good arm. You know, he considers me hopeless when it comes to ranch work. I'm doing the best I can."

She said, "Please drive down there and talk to him."

He reached across the table.

"Give him some time, Mom."

She took his hand.

"I can't."

"Dee will have more influence. I'll ask him to go."

The courthouse hadn't collapsed without her. She stepped into stale air smelling faintly of ranchers' sweat, first time late in twenty years.

Lyle looked up from behind his desk.

"I've brought him back," she said.

He leaned back in his wooden chair.

"Doin' my job," he said. "Better'n I could myself."

"I have more reason," she said.

"Walker's agreed to give Owen the money." She set the suitcase on his desk. "Most of it's there."

Lyle got up slowly and walked her to the door.

"Owen would've sold the place in the end," he said. "You could say Walker did him a favor."

At the Brand New Motel, Danielle was updating reservations through Thanksgiving weekend on the computer.

"Walker's back," Lee Ann said.

"Whoop-dee-doo."

"I hear Eugene is working at the Diamond T."

"I have no idea."

The clock chimed ten. Danielle ran her tongue over her teeth.

"Look," she said. "There isn't, and never has been anything between Eugene and me. I flirt with anyone under sixty whose name isn't Walker. There's a big distance and a huge difference between flirting and fucking, pardon my English."

Lee Ann stepped back.

"I talk to men about some dumb thing like the weather while my eyes say, 'I want to sleep with you.' That leaves it up to the guy to make the move. Eugene gave me nothing more than a helping hand."

"The livestock auction in Belen…"

"I don't know what you're talking about."

"You met him there. Suzette said you'd called in sick."

"The only day I missed work was when Loretta and I drove to Albuquerque to catch the John Anderson concert at Sandia Casino. Loretta called in sick, too," she said. "If you're assuming I've been seeing Keith, you have good reason. Eugene? No."

The nasal twang and seductive pitch in Walker's voice had the women in the office tittering.

"I'll tell you the truth, ladies. I sold Ross's property so Owen wouldn't have to. Handled the details myself to save Owen a trip and Ross a lot of hassle. I had business up north, a little venture I couldn't postpone. Needed a few grand and figured I deserved a small commission for all I'd done. Owen will get his money this afternoon. Look at you beautiful things! Midwestern gals got nothin' on you." He swung his hands out and around his hips. "Broad asses and complexions white as Eugene's diesel, personalities bland as the diet they eat. Corn and more corn, ham and more ham. I stopped for breakfast in Colby, Kansas. The special was four eggs, four pieces of bacon or sausage, potatoes, biscuits and gravy. The men were so big their butts took up two chairs. I swear. Bigger than Harley's. Oops. That might be him now."

Lee Ann entered as he ducked under a desk. The girls covered their mouths.

Caroline said, "Good morning, Lee Ann."

"Get out from under there," Lee Ann said.

She jerked her head toward the door and left the room. Walker's boot heels clipped down the stairs after her. When he ran ahead to open the door, she scowled and disregarded his questions about where they were going.

At Heaven on Earth Realty, Sue Reedy happened to be in.

"The Walkers!" she said, extending her hand. "Have a seat."

"Good morning, Sue," Lee Ann said, shaking hands. "We're here to divide the family ranch. I need to have Owen do the survey and split the north and south acreage equally. Walker will get the northern portion and I will keep the southern half. I want you to make certain all the documentation is correct and legal. Ted Bowles is handling Mother's will and can provide additional legal information if needed. The assessor's office has the correct property description and records."

"I take it this is okay with you, Walker."

"It is," Lee Ann said.

45

WALKER WAVED AT LEE ANN's back as she hustled back to work. Adios, sister. Damn, he was developing a rash, probably fleabites from Scruffie's doggie bed next to Art's lumpy sofa. He kicked a golf ball sized rock back to the courthouse, scratching his armpits, and entered the county clerk's office with a sheepish look on his face.

Jo squealed.

"You skunk," she said.

He scratched under his arm.

"I itch, but I don't stink."

"I should never talk to you again."

"You will though." He jumped over the swinging gate and picked her up and kissed her cheek. "Darlin', I missed you. More than mourning doves, more than piñon nuts, more than…"

"Oh, shut up."

He held her hips, nibbled her earlobe, refusing to let go. She hugged his neck and threw her head back and he laughed because any other woman's hair would have fallen away in loose waves, but hers stayed put and he stuck his nose in it, at least as far in as he could get. He set her down and cupped her chin and took in her face, every freckle, every pore.

"I need a shower," he said.

"The house is open."

"Come with me."

"I can't just up and leave."

"Sure you can."

On second thought, he'd best deal with bug bites in private.

"Sweetheart, you're right. I'll get spruced up and meet you at Art's at five. In the meantime, see if your dad wants to get rid of that ugly brown pickup, if it's still running."

"He'd rather crush it," she said.

"Not if he thinks you're going to use it." He kissed her cheek and jumped back over the gate. "It's just a loan until I figure a way to get my car back from Des Moines." If it hadn't been impounded. Hell, might as well let that Honda go, talk to Leo about locating a four-wheel drive.

Scrubbing down in the shower, he ran through a list of potential names for the new ranch: *The W W.* No, spell it out. *The Double W.* Or *The Double Double U.* Too much like a cattle brand. *Elk Canyon Cabins, Rimrock Ranch, Bear's Tooth Canyon, Eagle's Nest.* Those names were kinda' catchy, but conjured up images of some big-time Alaskan lodge, not quite right. The valley north of what would be Lee Ann's border was like no other country, rugged and untamed, yet intimate.

North of the Border.

That's it! He could see it. Welded letters on a steel portal, willows on each side, the creek just beyond, pink clouds fading to purple over the west mesa.

He dried off and raised his arms in front of the mirror and inspected his armpits. Checked his crotch. In the medicine cabinet he found anti-itch cream and smeared a generous amount over his body. Strange item for Jo to keep. She'd itched somewhere. He took his shirt, socks, and pants outside and shook them, dressed, and tucked the tube in his jacket pocket.

"Well, well," Danielle said. "Two Walkers in one day. I thought you were dead."

"Great to see you, too."

"We can talk about whatever you're here to discuss after work."

"I don't think so, precious. Let's see. In case you think I have $880,000.00, I don't. Lee Ann has it and she's giving it to Owen. She's dividing the ranch and I get the northern half. I've promised not to get divorced until all that's legal, which will be pretty quick."

"What the hell are you talking about?"

"If you go after me while I'm still part owner of the entire ranch, Lee Ann stands to lose half of her part. After the property is divided, you can only get half of my half. But, the way I see it, after the divorce, you'll leave me alone. I don't have any money to buy you out and you can't do anything with any part of that land." Her fingernail made an annoying noise on the counter. He ought to squeeze her cheeks until those eyes aimed at the ceiling popped out of their sockets. "We don't want to be neighbors."

"I said I'd take my chances when we got married," she said. "I should have known... you always screw up. God, I can hardly look at you." She quit tapping and jabbed her finger in his chest. "You took off without paying me my share."

He scratched the underside of his left arm and avoided her eyes, which squinted as if the lids were holding back poison darts aimed directly at his forehead. He knelt down pretending to pick something up off the floor and rubbed his crotch.

She said, "I've been living with Keith. We get along. I can't wait to end any arrangement with you—marriage, divorce, whatever. Your death would have been the best of all possible outcomes, but you screwed that up, too."

He stood up and scratched his chest. "I don't see that you have much to complain about."

She opened her mouth to speak, then turned her back.

"I got work to do," she said.

Women!

He needed a drink. At Art's, he called for a double shot of whiskey on his way to the bathroom, where he tore open his shirt, dropped his pants, slathered cream over his body, buttoned up, and winked at himself in the mirror.

He downed the whiskey and tipped the glass at Art.

"That dog of yours has some serious bugs," he said.

When Jo showed just after five, he felt no itch. He ordered her a Manhattan and hung an arm over her shoulder.

"I charged a few shots to your tab. We'll settle up later. I been thinkin'… aren't you getting tired of the same old job in the same old town, year in and year out? What do you say you and me open a hunting lodge?" He leaned close and explained his inheritance of the northern half of the ranch. "When the Rossmans find out I'm their new neighbor, they'll want to sell out. It might take a dozen hound dogs that bark day and night, and goats that pay no attention to fences and chew up everything in sight, and a little muzzleloader target practice right about dinnertime to influence them, but eventually they'll get the message that country vacations ain't all they're cracked up to be."

She hadn't taken a sip of her drink, puffed on her cigarette, or moved a muscle.

"It's a good idea," she said. "But I'm not giving up job security, health benefits, and retirement income to play hostess in the woods."

"You'll love it. The clientele will change all the time. We'll sympathize when most of 'em whine about the elk they almost shot and celebrate with the ones that got one. It'll be like having friends that pay us. When we don't have customers, we'll sleep late. I'll bring you breakfast in bed."

"I'd like that," she said. "I know you, though. After two days you'll forget."

"That's my appeal, baby. Always up to something new."

"Too many surprises can wear a girl out."

Not her, though. Not Jo. She had a certain something that took life seriously, and didn't—a unique combination of abiding by the rules and delighting when they were broken. She'd mull over this latest scheme, debate whether they could live together, whether she could handle the operation alone in case he took off and blew all their earnings on a whim, whether he'd default on his share of the work, or tire of her.

Her freckles danced like little dots of light and he wanted to kiss each one, separately, just a peck, a hundred pecks, a thousand, until she pushed him away, laughing. He'd fill with pride, pleasing her so.

"Is *su casa, mi casa*?" he asked.

"For one week," she said. "That's all I can stand."

They went to Vera's for gristly burgers and greasy fries and back to the bar to finish the evening. Holding her hand, he tripped into her bedroom, aimed his body at the bed, and dove onto the mattress. Amazingly, alcohol and Jo had cured his rash.

"I've never shed theesh wordsh." He threw his arm over her hip and spoke into her arm. "I love you."

"Say, 'I love you, Jo.'"

Uh-oh, what was he getting into? Women change once you commit. They nag at mud on the rug, clothes on the floor, how the toothpaste is squeezed, the way a towel is hung. She'd be his partner all right, throw a noose around his neck and lead him around like a horse about to be broke. Once broke, he'd behave. Maybe even like it. Maybe.

"I love you, Jo." He kissed her shoulder. "Can I use your car?"

46

Harley McKenna stopped by the office unexpectedly, asking for a history of New Mexico's shared water rights with Arizona. The girls rolled their eyes.

"Caroline, please get the file," Lee Ann said.

Harley drawled on. "The state engineer has called a meeting to discuss the Arizona Water Settlement Act, to direct water from the Gila River system as part of an exchange with the Central Arizona Project. Four counties are involved, including…"

"Excuse me, Harley," Lee Ann said. "An independent inspector will be arriving any day to assess the courthouse books. His name is Gerald Murray."

Harley panted through parted lips, his chin disappearing into his fat neck, stomach rising and falling like a toad's.

"I've called for an audit," she said.

The clerks abandoned their computer screens and vanished. Lee Ann gathered her belongings from the bottom desk drawer while Harley used the phone, neck and ears turning bright red as he grumbled the news to Ed Richter, ordering him to call Saul Duran.

The inflated bid for the proposed youth center and the adjusted figures for Women, Infants, and Children remained locked in the top drawer of her desk. She dropped the key in her purse, reached for her jacket, and made it to the stairs just as Harley boomed, "You're fired!"

Once home, she mopped the kitchen and pantry floors and caught up on the laundry, dusted the living room, and baked a macaroni and ham casserole and the boys' favorite dessert—chocolate cream pie. She put the pie in the fridge, took out two boxes of the freshest eggs and drove to Grace's, arriving late in the afternoon.

Grace's sprawling adobe sat on ten acres she'd held onto after her husband died. Tumbleweed, rabbit bush, and sage crowded the road up to the house. The gate was open and blind Rosco, too old to muster the energy to bark a warning, raised his nose in the air as Lee Ann approached. She knocked, then raised her voice over the hum of a sewing machine and called Grace's name.

"Come in, come in," Grace said, appearing from a bedroom down the hall. "What a nice surprise! My goodness, I hadn't noticed how late it's getting. I'm catching up on unfinished projects." She led Lee Ann into the kitchen, turned on the light, and reached into the hutch for plates. "Of course, I would trade it all to be sitting quietly beside your mother. I believe we communicated until the end."

"Grace, please, I didn't come to eat, or for a cup of coffee. Your devotion to Mother meant so much to all of us." Lee Ann placed the eggs on the table. "I'm here to solicit your help again."

She spoke slowly, keeping things in order. First, she wanted to make sure someone kept an eye on Edgar, a compassionate eye. He wasn't one to complain, but his right hip was so painful he could barely hobble around. And the house needed to be overseen from a woman's perspective. Scott and Dee wouldn't notice dust balls if they grew big as thistle heads. They'd swish a dish under the tap and call it washed. Lee Ann would arrange with Carlinda to do the heavy cleaning every other week, but someone needed to check in every few days to organize the boys' clutter—work gloves, catalogs, tools, hats, and jackets. A hot dinner twice a week would be nice, nothing fancy, something Grace could prepare at home and deliver on the days she dropped by.

"You see," Lee Ann said, "I'll be away for awhile."

47

S HE MET GERALD MURRAY OUTSIDE the Alibi Creek Store, and in addition to her desk key, gave him a list of files and contracts to review, offering to be available for any questions. He nodded, more solemn than she, even though it was the day of Mother's funeral.

Celebrating Mother's life rather than mourning its loss called for a bit of color. The dresses, skirts, and blouses in Lee Ann's closet ranged from neutral to neutral, a shade darker or duller than the garment hanging next to it. A pale blue suit bought in a fit of spring fever was inappropriate for the season, but came closest to honoring Mother. She held it up in front of the mirror. It was the right color, but plain.

Danielle had left two boxes of discarded belongings on Mother's front porch, which Lee Ann had labeled *Thrift Store*. She rummaged through them and headed home with a silver and turquoise necklace, a deep red scarf with gold thread running through it, and a sparkly rhinestone pin. She was fiddling with the scarf, adjusting it looser and tighter, when Dee came in with the mail.

"There's something here from Dad."

The envelope was small, one used to mail checks. This, instead of his presence. This, instead of a phone call. Today, of all days.

"I need to be alone," she said.

Dear Lee Ann,
Dee has been here and told me the day of Kay's funeral.
I don't have to tell you your mother was a remarkable
woman. Duties prevent me from attending the service, but
I will be with you and the family in thought.
Eu

The handwriting was slightly slanted and neat, as if the sentences had been composed on a lined pad. He always signed his notes *Eu*. She wanted *Love, Eu*. She smelled the paper and the envelope. They smelled like paper and an envelope. Give me more. Give me a clue that you'll be back, that we'll talk, begin again. The boys report you're fine, busy, that you need time. How much?

Brand shut down for Mother's funeral. The crowd overflowed into the street and remained quiet while Pastor Fletcher performed the service. Lee Ann and Walker sat in the first row, Scott beside her, Dee next to Walker, Grace and Edgar directly behind them.

While the pastor spoke, Mother seemed close by, waving a broom at the pesky raven that stole clothespins off the line when she hung the wash, deftly braiding Lee Ann's hair with satin ribbon, straightening the hem of her skirt. There she was, commanding a new pup to stay within the fence line, nodding approval when Lee Ann delivered her first lamb, slicing a thick piece of banana bread and passing it to Walker. Be nice to your brother. Take care of your brother. Watch he doesn't wander down to the highway, ride along with him until he knows how to handle a horse, take care he doesn't trip on the ice, ignore his faults, indulge him, admire his enthusiasm. Don't call him a liar. Don't say you hate him. There, be friends. Family first, always.

Lee Ann turned her head in his direction. Walker blew his nose into his bandana and wiped his eyes. Cowboy criminal crying over his mother. Fitting.

48

WALKER SKIPPED THE COMMUNITY CENTER potluck after the funeral. He stopped at the Alibi Creek Store, charged a fifth of whiskey and drove to Mother's. Lee Ann couldn't be two places at once. She wasn't *that* spiritual.

Mother had worn jewelry occasionally, a ring or brooch, but he was after something special. He reached for her Bible and thought better of keeping such an item around. Old lady housedresses lined the closet. Her slippers were worn and kind of disgusting. From the nightstand he took her Bulova watch and Dad's old Hamilton and put them in his pocket. If only he could bottle her smell, capture the texture of her skin and hair. He picked up her pillow and hugged the limp down, brought the smooth cotton pillowcase to his face. In the pantry he found black plastic bags and stuffed the pillow in first, then went through his own dresser and closet and cleaned out his clothes. Dee could box up the rest and leave it at the store.

From Mother's porch, Lee Ann's house still shocked the landscape, rude as a white Post-it note. In a couple of hours the white stucco would darken to gray, but never quite dissolve into the night. He raised his hand in a salute and clicking his heels, paid homage to the four directions.

"Patch, Blue. Come here, you ugly mutts. Where's Butch? Out with the cows, no doubt. You tell him I said good-bye." He patted the dogs' sides and kneaded their ears, took one more look around, bent an arm over his waist, stretched the other arm wide, and bowed toward Lee Ann's house.

"It's all yours, Lannie."

He walked his land. Mother and Dad had always said this portion of the ranch was useless, but they looked at things through ranchers' eyes. There were plenty of other ways to earn a living—easier, more profitable ways, and assets beyond good pastureland. He slipped through the fence to the Rossmans' place. The rock house would make perfect hunters' lodging. If the small amount of money Mother left didn't cover the down payment, he'd offer the Rossmans a deal; from August through November he'd run the lodge and split the profits. They could use the house the rest of the time. He scrambled down to the creek. Here, he'd stack hay bales for archery and rifle practice. Over there, in that flat, open area he'd build a corral. He'd sell camo tee shirts with *North of the Border Hunting Lodge* printed in red letters in a little square left of center, over the heart. That might be too many words. Maybe just *N. B. H. L.* Shelly would display brochures. Jo would design a website.

He walked back to the cabin. Let's see, a cot over here, a table there. A car pulled in, and out of nowhere Danielle appeared at the doorway carrying a legal-size folder.

"I've got the divorce papers," she said.

"Efficient gal."

"You can't be serious about living here. I can see the entire east mesa between the logs."

He took the folder and laid two papers on the wood counter.

"Excuse me while I read every word."

The details seemed fair enough. He asked her for a pen and signed his name as her feet clipped along the floor, walking the perimeter of the room.

"A guy's been looking for you," she said. "He looks like you. Like a rat."

He gathered some rocks and built a fire pit by the creek, propped his boots near the flames, and drank his whiskey. Coyotes howled nearby and he howled back. "Ah–ooh. Ah–ooh. Yip, yip, yip." By midnight, the conversation had become repetitive and he drove to Jo's.

"Gallivanting already," she said. "You smell like smoke."

"I've been up to the land. Plotting the beautiful future."

He dropped his pants and got into bed.

"Pee-ew," she said.

"I'll sleep on the couch."

"No. Don't go." She reached for him. "The potluck was nice. Most everyone loved your mother."

"*Most* everyone?"

"Yeah. Some thought her stuck up."

"Jesus, Jo, she was the most down to earth woman who ever lived."

"Don't get upset. Get some sleep."

Tomorrow (if he remembered) he'd ask just who thought Mother stuck up, straighten them out. Tell them a thing or two. On his list for the week, he'd written a broom, a bed and a chair. And a dish, a fork, a spoon, and a good skillet. Oh yeah, and a fridge and a Coleman stove and a table. That ought to keep him busy for five days. Oh, and a cat. Or a litter of six. They'd get picked off fast up there.

49

THERE'D BEEN NO WORD FROM Gerald Murray. Lee Ann stayed close to the phone, but left the ranch Saturday for groceries. Pulling into the Round Valley Safeway parking lot, she changed her mind and drove on to Show Low where there'd be less chance of bumping into someone from Brand or Alibi Creek. No one from the courthouse had called, including Caroline, or Lyle.

She and the boys tackled items on the To Do list, small tasks put off for ten years that took ten minutes to complete. Scott screwed a new bulb in the porch socket. Dee replaced the screen in the mudroom door and secured the loose rafter in the barn. At Mother's, they emptied the fridge and drained the water lines and closed the house up for the winter.

"Dad must be pretty involved at his new job. He hasn't picked up the phone once to see how we're doing," Dee said, closing the main shut-off. "Talk about a disappointment."

"There's life beyond cattle," Scott said.

"He's just traded running cows for herding people. I don't know how he can stand catering to a bunch of tourists on a dude ranch. It's pathetic."

"Anything beyond ranching is meaningless to you," Scott said, handing Dee a case of Ensure.

"Especially researching pansies and caterpillars."

"You'd perk up if animal scientists bred a small heifer with a bigger uterus and wider birth canal."

"Now you're talking. Feed her less, make birthing easier."

"There you go, perked right up."

Lee Ann asked to be put through to Gerald Murray.

"I've been expecting to hear from you regarding charges against me for abetting illegal activities."

"Lee Ann, I assumed you understood," he said. "Those who report fraud are exempt from prosecution."

He went on to say he'd just begun his investigation, that it would take time and she needn't concern herself with the details. There would likely be calls, and perhaps a few meetings to verify certain information, but she was clear of any criminal charges. He wished her a good day.

The dial tone buzzed until the phone beeped. She replaced the receiver and walked twice around the table. This day! The kitchen seemed large, grand in fact. She opened the cupboards and took stock, reached for a gourmet cookbook Caroline had passed around the office, and searched the index for recipes requiring hours of preparation because there was all the time in the world to try something new, something to please the boys, please herself.

Goodness, everything called for fresh vegetables, fresh ginger, strange herbs, coconut milk, and unheard of spices. Exotic dishes required sour cream or crème fraîche, (what was that?), saffron, and Parmesan cheese, lemons for Hollandaise sauce, basil for pesto. For today, she'd use Dijon mustard, Swiss cheese, and fresh sage from the garden to fix Stuffed Tenderloin with Potatoes Gratin.

Scott said, "Good dinner, Mom."

Dee took seconds, thirds on potatoes.

Lee Ann said, "I'm going to Albuquerque the day after tomorrow to shop for Thanksgiving. Make a list of anything you need. Dee, you're welcome to ask Ginny. We'll eat at three."

"I'll go along," Scott said.

"We set a wedding date," Dee said. "June 14th."

She rose quickly, gathered the silverware, and stacked their dishes. Scott collected the glasses and napkins.

"Wow, you'd think I'd said I caught the swine flu."

When Lee Ann announced her intentions to marry Wayne, Mother's reaction had been mild, although she must have been distraught. Dee would have problems with this girl, not a doubt about it. Lee Ann sat next to him and touched his arm.

"I want you to be sure," she said. "I rushed into marrying your father. I can't say it was a complete failure, seeing as you and Scott are the results of that marriage, but you know what I mean. We were not compatible."

"She's got a great sense of humor," Dee said. "She's fun."

Perhaps those qualities kept a couple together, *if* generosity prevailed, *if* respect survived. She was certainly no expert on what kept a marriage intact. Chores and work and caring for Mother had killed any humor she might have possessed. Since the kids were little, she hadn't found many situations or jokes funny, really funny. Hilarity seemed childish, an indication of emotional instability.

Scott had never had a girlfriend and that had caused less concern than Dee's attachment to Ginny. Marriage was a gamble. Life's partner could stay the same, improve with time, or change for the worse. Eugene had stayed the same, or just about. He'd hardened some. Hard work had tightened his muscles; disappointment had lined his face.

Before bed, she inspected her face and neck in the bathroom mirror. Sun, dry air, worries, and work concocted a sure-fire formula for wrinkles—those around her eyes etched from gardening, the one on her forehead from the day of Mother's stroke, the ones around her mouth from Walker's last prison sentence. She touched the widening silver streak in her widow's peak, the gray sprouting at her temples, the slight change in her jaw line. Tired eyes looked back at her. Tension she'd assumed hidden had left its mark.

She pinched her cheeks, fluffed her hair, lowered her head, and squinted, catlike, lips parted. Eugene, if you come home now, there'll be fun to be had. Teasing and pleasing and laughter, apologies and sweet words of forgiveness. She hooked her finger in the elastic collar of her nightgown and pulled it into a V, exposing the crease between her breasts, let the neckline spring back and cupped her breasts as Eugene would, his working man's hands firm and rough, his stroking and petting gentle.

Propped against her pillow, she took a pad and pencil from her nightstand.

20 lb. Turkey (Dee liked dark meat, Scott, white.)

Sanchez Brothers' extra hot sausage (Edgar favored sausage stuffing.)

Celery. Onions. Parsley. Bread crumbs.

Brussels Sprouts (Eugene's favorite.)

Pumpkin. Evaporated milk.

Whipping cream (Mother's weakness. She'd cut a small slice of pie and smother it, sneak an extra spoonful when no one was looking.)

Cranberries.

Butternut squash and Granny Smith apples with Maple syrup (New recipe.)

50

A T SUNSET, WALKER LEANED ON a broom, a pile of mouse droppings and dust at his feet. Over the weekend he'd located a single bed (outgrown by Art's nephew), a set of silverware donated by Vera, and a card table and two chairs from the thrift store. He'd chinked the cracks between the logs with mud and straw. The cabin was taking shape. No hot water, but he'd shower at Jo's. No washing machine, but hers could handle an extra load once in a while. He'd buy a small fridge that fit under the counter in Show Low this week. He swept the dirt onto a piece of cardboard and opened the door to toss it, just as a tan Pathfinder splashed across the creek. Company already.

"Merk!"

A blast of cold wind blew his cellmate inside.

They hugged, slapped backs, tap danced, stepped back and came together, poked ribs.

"You got any glasses?" Pat said, waving a bottle of Jim Beam.

Walker set out two jelly jars and Pat poured. They clinked rims. Walker threw a log into the wood stove and they huddled next to the heat, warming their bellies and backs, and caught up, Pat reporting prison gossip, Walker filling Pat in on his deal with Keith.

"About the money," Walker said. "It just didn't work out, man."

Pat stepped over to the north-facing window. "Nice view."

"Bastard tried to kill me," Walker said. He closed the damper, glanced sideways at Pat and nice and slow, said to his back, "I figure you and him might have pre-planned that."

Pat faced him. "You and me are partners, buddy."

"How many partners you got?"

"Only one. Only you."

The cabin was as tight as their jail cell, with one dif-ference—the entire free world waited outside an unbarred door. Pat poked the bottle under his armpit and they took off for the bar.

Jo was on her perch, talking to a man Walker hadn't seen before, an administrative type wearing a suit. She borrowed his pen and wrote something on a napkin. The man slipped the information between the pages of a thin, black notebook.

Owen bought everyone a drink.

"Except for him," he said, pointing at Walker.

Walker winked at Jo, who didn't notice, and ordered a couple of beers.

"Don't pay Owen no mind," Walker said, steering Pat to a table. "It was his ranch I sold to Keith."

Owen came over, already drunk, told Pat he was keep-ing company with the biggest thief in the county, maybe the entire state, called Walker a slimy bastard, and drifted back to the bar.

"I hear you gave him all the money," Pat said. He raised his beer, took a drink. "I figure you owe me something."

"Like hell."

"I set us up. You fucked up."

"You gave me a name."

"That led to $880,000.00."

Jo laughed with the stranger.

"I happen to know your mother left you a shitload of money," Pat said.

"Whoa," Walker said. "Not true. Twenty grand, that's it."

He took out his wallet and opened it just enough to show one end of a cashier's check for $20,216.00.

"Bullshit," Pat said. "Your sister told me about your gambling granddad, about the money he'd socked away, and that your mother never told a soul."

Gambling granddad? Mother's father was a preacher, so poor he couldn't replace his coat buttons. Dad's father was a lean, mean rancher, raised on pinto beans and stringy beef. If there'd been any money in the family, Mother would have put up bail the last time he got arrested, bought back the two sections of the ranch he'd sold just north of the store, and made sure he drove a spiffy truck.

Owen yelled across the room. "I surveyed your property today. You'll get what you deserve! Serves you right for taking advantage of a helpless old man!"

"Let's go," Walker said, shoving his chair back. "Los Olmos is an hour south. The Hole in the Wall is open until two. They got a band."

He stopped by Jo's stool and squeezed in between her and the man, laid a hand on her shoulder.

"I'll be late tonight," he said. "Introduce me."

"Walker, this is Gerald. Gerald Murray."

Driving south, Walker filled Pat in on the hunters' lodge. They didn't have zoning laws in Alibi Creek and he could build what he wanted any way he wanted. He didn't know how to cook, but he could flip burgers and tell the difference between medium and rare, and Jo could roast a leg of lamb and whip up a few cakes and pies. The season would run from late August through November. Over the winter they'd kick back in their recliners and rest up. Out-of-state hunters had the big bucks. The only bad part would be waking up at three a.m. to get 'em fed and out the door long before sun-up. Hell, he'd stay up all night. Breakfast would be served in a big kitchen with men dishing bacon and eggs on their plates, drinking OJ. Bowls of energy bars, candy bars, and cheese crackers would be available to stuff into their camo vest pockets. There'd be a separate refrigerator just for beer.

Pat grunted. Must be the adjustment of getting out. Walker asked about his plans and Pat said, "We had plans. You fucked them up."

"Hey, I tried. You go on up to the UP and live up there. That part of the country ain't for me."

Pat stared straight ahead.

"Look," Walker said. "I'd take you in as a partner on the hunting lodge if you want to stick around. What's wrong, man? Your mouth usually runs looser than a woman's at the beauty shop."

At the Hole in the Wall, the three-man band played classic country. During the break Walker bought the musicians a beer. Pat loosened up some, but not enough to launch into the bullshit he'd told in prison that got Walker laughing so hard his stomach ached. Walker tapped his foot to the music. Two gals at the next table smiled.

"I'm serious, man, about going partners," Walker said. "That little brunette sitting across from the blond has her eye on you. Ask her to dance."

"I'll think about it."

"The girl or lodge?"

"Both."

The blond met up with her date and Walker sat back as Pat and the brunette danced to a Patsy Cline song. The lead singer played the guitar like a pro and sang with his eyes closed, dragging a tune out longer than a string of TV commercials. After a couple more dances, the girl led Pat outside.

Walker wandered over to the pool tables and listened to the balls clink, sink, and rebound to the cheers and moans of the players. He knew some of the guys, but games were a drag and he sat down again, put his feet up on Pat's chair and emptied his beer. Life was good—twenty grand in his wallet, a plan, a woman—*his* woman, Jo. He was as close to peaceful as he'd known. A little buzz vibrated in his right ear. He tilted his head. When everything seemed perfect, except for one little thing, that little thing usually turned out to be a big problem. He listened closely. The problem was Pat. Pat the Rat.

The rodent showed up at closing time, just before last call, all cocky, and said, "Let's split."

Walker stuffed a ten in the band's tip can and followed the rat outside.

51

Exotic spices and cooking ingredients from the Asian Market, Whole Foods, and the Mediterranean Specialty Shop took up a corner of the kitchen counter, and now, the day before Thanksgiving, Lee Ann stored them in the cupboard. Tradition called for plain old salt, pepper, and sage.

She picked through the cranberries, extra red and fresh this year, added sugar, and set them to boil. Mid-afternoon she poured a cup of the morning's coffee and leafed through a copy of *Bon Appetite* that she'd picked up in Albuquerque. Developing skills as a gourmet cook was pointless. Soon Scott would move, Dee would marry and get used to Ginny's cooking, and Edgar would die. Eugene would eat with the Bidwells, owners of the dude ranch. Between shots of whiskey and chugs of beer, Walker picked at a meal with taste buds that didn't discriminate. As for Grace, eighty years of meals prepared according to her particular tastes would resist change, and deep down, Lee Ann liked plain old-fashioned cooking, too. She closed the magazine as the phone rang.

Jo asked if Walker had been around. He'd borrowed her car and she needed it. She'd last seen him two nights ago at Art's, drinking with some guy that looked just like him. Owen had been shouting rude remarks and Walker and his buddy had left. He'd been busy fixing up the cabin. Would

Lee Ann mind driving up the creek to see if the car was there?

The north end of the ranch hadn't been used since Dad quit raising hogs, the failed endeavor having left the property with the reputation of being good for nothing. In winter, dense thickets of matted willows and bare, young cottonwoods clustered along the creek. Deep green pines shot up between massive boulders where it seemed unlikely any seed could take root, lending a chilling enchantment to the place.

Already the sun had dropped behind the mesa. Jo's car was parked with the key in it. Lee Ann expected Walker's head to pop out the door and when it didn't, she called his name and knocked, listened for creaking floorboards, and went inside. Dad had once stored slop buckets and garbage cans of ground corn and bean meal, extra fence wire, and sheets of corrugated tin, every inch of space stuffed with something or other. All that had been cleaned out and the cabin was lovely in a rustic way. As a girl, she'd despised pigs' swollen bodies and dirty noses. Funny, Scott and Dee's litter didn't bother her at all, perhaps because they hadn't grown to full size, or because the threat of Walker shoving her into the pen had long passed.

She picked Jo up that evening in front of Art's.

"Thanks for making a special trip," Jo said.

"It's the least I can do. He should have returned your car."

"Maybe he's off looking for a truck with Leo, or hauling supplies," Jo said, latching her seat belt. "He's got big plans."

Lee Ann's fingers tightened around the steering wheel. No prayer could save him. Prayers didn't save anything. All they were good for was pinpointing problems to solve and goals to achieve and dreams to actualize.

Boxelder and scrub oak lined the road, disappearing as they passed the turnoff to the dump. The smell of cigarette smoke came off Jo's clothes and hair. Lee Ann didn't mind. Jo did a good job. She was one of those people who could swear without being offensive and smoke and drink as if it were as harmless as popping gum and sipping ginger ale. She minded her own business while managing to know everybody else's and what she knew she kept to herself.

Jo said, "Gerald Murray told me all three commissioners could serve jail terms. You should run for office."

Lee Ann laughed.

"You know as well as I do, a woman would never be elected county commissioner in Dax County."

"Be the first."

They drove in silence for a mile or so.

"You should stay clear of Walker's schemes," Lee Ann said.

"You should take my advice and I should take yours. We've both got points."

Alibi Creek had iced over and they broke through it, Jo saying she wished she could see the land. In the dark, the closeness of the mesas blocked chunks of starlit sky and the willow thickets seemed like bodies crowding around. Lee Ann handed Jo her car key.

"I assume Walker has told you I want nothing else to do with him."

Jo got out.

"I understand," she said. "Thanks for the ride."

52

S HE WOKE EARLY AND STUFFED the turkey while the pumpkin pie baked. The boys left to help Edgar feed and water the chickens and hogs.

"Bring in extra firewood, and remind Edgar we're eating at three."

The table was set for five, with Mother's ceramic cornucopia the centerpiece. She placed an extra plate and silverware on the buffet, brought in a folding chair from the shed and leaned it against the wall and hung her apron. In the bedroom, she fussed with her hair, tried on the navy sweater, then the off-white. The pants with the side zipper were the most flattering. She fluffed the couch pillows, straightened the painting above the buffet, and plucked the dry leaves off the geranium. When the pie came out, the turkey went in and by one o'clock the entire house smelled of juices running and skin browning. Time to whip the cream. She opened the front door and listened, and set the beaters to whirring.

She greeted Edgar with a brief hug and spoke loudly into his better ear and he nodded as if he'd heard and understood. Ginny helped carry the platters and bowls to the table, setting the stuffing in front of Dee. Scott carved. At the last minute Lee Ann remembered the cranberry sauce still in the fridge, and holding it in both hands, paused in the doorway before returning to the dining room. Scott pulled back her chair.

He said, "Let's skip grace."

"No," Dee said. "I'll say it." He bowed his head and Ginny did the same.

"Lord, on this day of thanksgiving, we wish to express our gratitude for this meal. We send our thoughts and prayers to those who aren't with us today. Amen."

Scott forked turkey onto plates, dishes were passed and compliments offered, with a toast to the chef.

Before dessert, Lee Ann excused herself to take the dogs some scraps, which they lapped up with two licks of their tongues. They accompanied her along the well-worn garden path and stopped at the fence, at which point they were not permitted entrance. Clouds thin as gauze passed in front of the moon. She fumbled with the gate and walked southward, away from the house, between the hard, dry rows. He did not miss her, did not miss home, could celebrate Thanksgiving elsewhere, eat some other woman's food, sleep in a strange bed, alone, did not care if she got chilled at night, or stressed during the day, if the place fell apart, if she fell apart.

At the end of the row, she turned. The dining room and kitchen lights shone yellow-white. The muted dirt road dipped to the creek and the tin roof of the barn, reflecting moonlight, seeming to float like a giant raft in space. Mother's house and the weeping willow were barely visible. She turned south again, humming. "You have stolen my heart, now don't go 'way, as we sang love's old sweet song on Moonlight Bay." Scott's arm hugged her shoulder and guided her back to the house.

PART
THREE

53

TUESDAY
DECEMBER 25, 2007

Jesus' birthday. Scott and Dee had argued about cutting a tree, Scott claiming every living thing should be left to complete its growth cycle, Dee saying the forests were overcrowded and thinning them for a once-a-year holiday maintained their health, as well as upheld tradition.

He said, "City people buy their trees from Christmas tree farms. Country folk don't make a dent in the forest."

"That's the problem with the environment today. People like you don't have a conscience," Scott said.

"If butchering hogs and cows and hunting elk is acceptable, so is sacrificing a tree. What's this family coming to?" Dee swung his chain saw into the truck. "Ginny's family will appreciate it."

Lee Ann hadn't gone to church for over a month. Last week, when Pastor Fletcher came to call regarding her lack of attendance, she admitted having given up her faith, and when he wiped his brow with the dirty handkerchief from his suit pocket, sputtering about losing a lamb from the flock, his distress did not move her.

As a compromise to Dee, they'd exchanged small gifts at dinner the night before, and in the morning he left early to spend Christmas day with Ginny's family. Lee Ann left Edgar a tin of oatmeal cookies, half a ham, and a box of Leona Webb's peanut brittle. He still used an outhouse and would find them soon enough. She helped Scott break up the ice on the stock tank and feed the pigs. His new work gloves fit perfectly.

He'd given her two books: *The Agnostic's Bible* and *Women in Government.* At lunch, he pressed the point of her running for commissioner.

"You and Jo," she said. "I'd be the laughing stock, maybe get half a dozen votes."

She counted on her fingers those who might mark an X by her name.

Scott said, "James Catlett is going to run. You could end up working with him. He's a good man. You're the one with experience, though."

"I'm also the one who condoned what they did."

"Don't underestimate folks. They know the spot you were in. They'd have done the same to hold onto a job with benefits." He swallowed the last bite of his sandwich with a swig of tea. "Corruption has been accepted here for so long. Accountability in local government is going to be something different. Give them a chance to elect decent people. I bet they will."

"While we're on the subject of decent people, help me think of who I can hire as a permanent hand."

"I'm staying, Mom." He put his cap on backwards. "Edgar can barely make it to the chicken yard and Dee can't manage alone. My mind's made up. As Uncle Walker might say,

> *I'm resigned*
> *to toeing the line*
> *and being confined*
> *within the county line."*

She shrugged and offered a weak smile. Too much had been lost in too short a time.

"I know you don't want to hear anything about Walker," Scott said. "But he hasn't been seen for weeks."

"You're right. I don't want to hear."

In the days following, she wept into her pillow, touched the backs of chairs where Eugene had sat, the mug he'd used, and door handles he'd turned. She'd heard of heartache, but she hadn't known it referred to a specific gnawing pain under the breastbone, there at night, in the morning, and throughout the day, the only cure Eugene's return. She wore down the path to Mother's, back and forth, her coat wrapped tightly around her body, childhood memories drawing her into each room. The walls were cold, the sofa, closets, and beds odorless. She opened the kitchen cupboard and held one of Mother's china plates to her chest, held the cotton dishcloth to her cheek, took her slippers home to walk in her shoes.

And Walker. Where had he gone and what was he up to this time?

54

O N THE FIRST DAY OF the new year she made pancakes and announced that two or more emotions could exist simultaneously. Each day presented an array of sentiments —sadness and gratitude, anger and peace, regret and hope. There was time for rest, but also for duty. Taking action while grieving was possible. She would run for office.

Scott raised his orange juice.

"Good job. Way to go, Mom."

Dee said, "Are you crazy? You just got out of there."

"I'm going to go back and do it right, if they'll have me."

"Half the county will hate you," Dee said. "That's the nature of a commissioner's job. It's worse than sheriff."

"That's because they've all been unethical bastards," Scott said.

"She's a woman."

"No kidding."

"They'll eat her alive. Don't do it, Mom. It's not worth it."

"I've worked there long enough to anticipate the pitfalls. Someone's got to improve things."

Scott clapped. "Spoken like a true politician."

"Better get used to it, Dee," she said. "I've got a call in to Jo to help me run my campaign."

"Dad won't like it," Dee said.

"Dad isn't here. And if he should come back, I think he'd approve. He's criticized my attitude about my job."

"Ginny's cousin Derek has quit the rodeo circuit and is looking for work. He's coming over this afternoon."

"What's the condition of his body?" Scott asked.

"Probably better than someone whose nose is stuck in a book all day. It's a toss-up, though. Man with crushed spine, cracked ribs, and busted nose versus a cowhand who's only half here." He grabbed the beak of Scott's hat and pulled it down over his eyes. "Hope it works out, bro, so you can get on with figuring out how to breed that small heifer with a bigger uterus and wider birth canal."

55

THURSDAY
JANUARY 3, 2008

A MEETING HAD BEEN POSTED for seven p.m. at the Brand Community Center to inform county residents of Walker's disappearance and ask for help locating him. Under the stark glare of overhead lighting, the dingy cedar paneling and beige linoleum floor looked the same, day or night.

Lee Ann joined twenty others seated in front of Lyle, Jeremy, and Lewis, who addressed the group from either side of a county map propped on an easel. Owen sat front center, and Art, who'd been missing his best customer, had taken a chair directly behind him. Dee pulled up a chair for Sherry from the Alibi Creek Store. Henry Gillman, who had a small plane and used any excuse to fly it, motioned to Danielle, who strutted in wearing tight jeans and a fake fur jacket, to sit next to him. Jo and Gerald Murray arrived together. Lee Ann stood in the back.

Lyle held up a calendar and pointed to November 21st, the last night anyone had seen Walker. The man he'd been with, Pat Merker, hadn't been seen since, either. Foul play was not out of the question, since Walker had recently been issued a cashier's check for approximately twenty thousand dollars, which had not been withdrawn from the Dax County State Bank.

Lee Ann gripped Caroline's chair. The paneling melted into a brown haze, as if the whole room and everyone in it had been dipped in a mud puddle. The fool! Only an idiot would walk around with a check for that amount of money in his wallet. She should have taken him by the hand, like a little boy, and insist he deposit the money. Then again, it was his to squander, save, or lose.

"We're not coming to any conclusions here," Lyle said. "We're asking for clues regarding Walker's whereabouts and volunteers to search for him. The pair left the Hole in the Wall at closing time, driving a tan Pathfinder, an Avis rental. They weren't fighting. No one noticed what direction they headed. If they went south, they didn't make it to the border. If they went north, they didn't come back to Brand. I've checked motels and gas stations east and west. So far, the vehicle hasn't turned up, leading me to believe the car is still somewhere in the county."

"I hate to be a pessimist," Art said, "but you got a hell of a job covering seven thousand square miles of wilderness with deep canyons, rugged mountains, and unlimited places to hide a vehicle, and a body, or both."

"I'll fly over the region tomorrow, as many times as you want," Henry said.

"Jeff and I will hike Saliz Pass and cover the ground from Brand to Los Olmos," Terry said.

James Catlett, a member of Search and Rescue, said they were ready to help.

They talked as though Walker was dead. Lee Ann thought so too, although hadn't known it until this moment, when it suddenly seemed as if she'd read Walker's life story and his journey couldn't end any other way. His antics danced before her eyes. Walker scrambling over the fence as a three-year-old, hiding in a tree watching the whole family wonder if he'd drowned, delighting in hearing his name screamed, snickering while they searched up and down the creek until way past dark; conning Edgar into driving to the store to buy him cigarettes and beer before he was twelve; using valuable pre-historic Indian pottery for target practice; selling grandmother's precious wedding ring with the little diamond flanked by two sapphires and looking high and low for it, telling Mother it must have gotten lost. But the movie was a re-run and she lost interest. She remembered washing her hands in the Walmart bathroom after visiting Pat Merker, whose squinty eyes hinted at some dark aspect of his nature, perhaps more dangerous than what Walker could handle on the outside. Jimmy Zebrowski had said he'd shot a man in both legs. Walker might have not fully understood the depth of his dark side.

Caroline asked what, if anything, the commissioners' office could do and Lyle suggested the clerk write a letter asking county residents to stay alert for signs of the men and report anything unusual to the sheriff's department. He thanked everyone for attending, apologized for the lack of any new information, and closed the meeting.

Lee Ann joined Caroline on the way out.

"I'm so sorry about this," Caroline said. "We miss you at the office. What a mess this audit has been—Gerald Murray has the entire courthouse turned upside down. The commissioners haven't been around since he showed up. A hundred times a day I wish you were there."

"I'll be back."

Outside, snow sugared the ground. Everyone had left except for the sheriff and deputies, who were locking the building. As Scott walked Lee Ann across the parking lot, a small pickup turned on its headlights and swerved in close. Danielle lowered her window.

"He signed the divorce papers," she said. "But I'm not filing." She lowered her voice. "If he never comes back, that property is mine."

Lee Ann said, "That land is no longer of any interest to me. Good luck."

56

SATURDAY
JANUARY 5, 2008

Acalendar hung above a row of hats in the mudroom with Wednesday, January 16th circled in red. Dee's shoulder had been pronounced healed at his last orthopedic appointment, with no follow-up required. He and Ginny were planning an engagement party to be held at Mother's house on February 9th. Edgar wasn't due at the optometrist until March. Lee Ann straightened the line of boots under the hat rack and took another look at the date. Must have been a mistake. She collected the bulkier jackets and carried them to the hall closet before Jo arrived, and there she was, right on time.

They took chairs next to each other at the kitchen table and divided the list of registered Republicans. Walt's son, Terry McIntyre, would soon be instructing his wife and daughter to do the same in his taxidermy shop. Leo's cousin, Nestor Rodriguez, had also thrown in his name for county commissioner and Harley's nephew, Ralph Ellison, was hoping there'd be enough of Harley's loyal-to-the-end cronies to ensure him enough votes. James Catlett, the sheriff's son-in-law, was the only Democrat, but only twenty-seven percent of the county voted liberal, three percent Independent.

Registration was May 8th. Jo had insisted they start early, get folks used to the idea of a woman running for something other than county clerk or county treasurer. She suggested Lee Ann attend every friggin' county event (she slapped her hand on the table) and get back to church! They laughed at that, since Jo was no churchgoer.

"And I have no intention of pretending," Lee Ann said. "Look at us, presuming to elect a woman as county commissioner! Using a woman's kitchen as campaign headquarters!"

They laughed at the odds, at the chance. They laughed until they cried, until they had no breath, until their sides ached.

Lee Ann handed out paper towels and they dabbed their eyes and noses.

"Can I confide in you?" Jo asked.

Lee Ann's smile vanished. Friendships required trust. Throw up a roadblock, close that avenue. Or make a friend.

"Go ahead," she said.

"I'm seeing Gerald Murray."

A friend would express her feelings, comment, or add an opinion.

"I'm glad, Jo. He seems like a nice man."

"About the nicest thing with three legs that's ever come into my life," Jo said.

They giggled at that.

Lee Ann divided the list in half and straightened the envelopes. She tapped the stacks and took one off the top and put the envelope down.

"Jo, do you think Walker is…"

Jo laid her pen down and fingered the roll of stamps.

"Dead? I'd hoped not. But yes, I do. And I'm so sorry."

They lowered their eyes and gave Walker a moment of silence.

Lee Ann handed her half of the list.

"You start with the As and I'll start with the Ms. Would you like something to drink?"

"Not unless it's ninety-proof."

"Sorry, I don't have any hard liquor. But, there's beer in the fridge."

"Join me."

Lee Ann eyes twinkled like a kid who just got permission to stay up late.

"All right."

They addressed envelopes, telling tales and reminiscing about incidents associated with names that came up, Jo stopping from time to time to jot down points to include in Lee Ann's introductory letter.

"We want to mention education."

"I don't think so, not yet," Lee Ann said. "The topic makes people uncomfortable."

Education. The circled date on the calendar. The final day for late registration at the University of New Mexico.

"Excuse me," Lee Ann said, knocking her chair back.

She grabbed her jacket and ran to the pigpen. Scott wasn't there. She called out. Louder. The barn was empty. She found him behind the workshop changing the oil in his pickup.

"There you are! I've been looking high and low. Scott, the deadline for late registration is a week from Wednesday. You must go."

"We already talked about this, Mom."

"I know. Look, Dee and I can manage."

"I doubt it."

"He thinks Derek might work out. He's starting part-time next week. You can come home once a month, and for roundup and butchering."

He closed the hood and she leaned both elbows on top.

"I expect to see you packing tomorrow."

57

L EE ANN AND JO ARRANGED meetings at community and senior centers where only a handful of folks showed up, most to complain. The winter had been wet, but mild, so that not one session had been canceled and by spring, word spread and folks ventured out and began attending the rallies. With each opportunity, Lee Ann presented a new vision for county government and shared policies she'd long wished to see put in place. She proposed appointing a panel to review and record all federal and state funds awarded to the county. A check system would oversee all contract bids. An independent human resources department would be established to regulate hiring practices. Conciliatory meetings would be set up with the US Forest Service. The volunteer fire department would receive the money they needed to maintain and purchase new equipment.

Fat purple buds popped out on cottonwood limbs and baby cottontails bounced among the junipers. Robins poked the earth, elk started dropping antlers, and red-tailed hawks circled the field. The creek ran high and wide from snowmelt. On the equinox, she filled her pockets with roasted almonds and led the dogs up an elk trail on the west mesa to the rim rock. By noon, she'd worked up a sweat and she unzipped her jacket and loosened her scarf. The view encompassed all of the Walker Ranch and six miles of the valley from the northern plains at the base of Big Mountain, down the cliffs and along the creek to the store, a mere speck of the county. If six miles comprised a speck, a human body would amount to little more than an atom. Walker might be anywhere, inside or outside Dax County, inside or outside the US, but wherever he was the planet seemed minus his vibration. Even a windy day felt calm.

She hiked through pines and came to flat ledge and sat down, a dog on either side, and wrapped her arms around their necks until they broke free and shot off pursuing imaginary prey, leaving her with the opportunity to dream and plan. She'd resisted expressing excitement over running for office. The odds of winning were slim and even if she succeeded, skepticism and long-held attitudes towards women would test her resolve. Now she got on her knees and spread her arms, perched for flight. Of course, dream! Of course, plan!

The dogs returned and she took two nuts from her pocket and closed one nut in each fist. Their cold noses sniffed her knuckles until she opened her palms. Silly things, they ate them! She took Patch's head in her hands and touched her nose to his, did the same with Blue.

"Okay, have another nut."

Instead of returning along the elk trail, she forged her way straight down, carefully picking her way through juniper, prickly pear, and scrub oak, squeezing between boulders and scrambling over broken tree limbs, descending diagonally across a steep, sandy arroyo. Fine rock rolled underfoot and halfway down the slope she fell hard on her behind and slid before coming to a stop.

She caught her breath and leaned to push herself up. As if raising a hand, a weed not three inches tall cried *wait*. All alone, supporting one yellow flower the size of a baby fingernail, it claimed its right to thrive where no other plant survived. She reached to pluck it, to carry it home and identify it in one of Scott's record books, but stopped. A seed had sprouted from ground dry and rough as sandpaper, softened by just the right amount of rain seeping between perfectly spaced grains of sand at exactly the right moment. She retreated to a place far beyond the sky and saw herself so small—a complex organism with its own destiny, containing a fate separate from her desires, to be nurtured or not by the intention of the universe. She touched the leaves and stem and stood, leaving the flower to its fate.

Below, a vehicle appeared, a dot at first, approaching from the southwest. A white truck slowed down and turned north at the store. She quickened her step, not so careful now, thinking she heard, did hear, the faint, distinct growl of the diesel.

EPILOGUE

On June 27th, 2010, a memorial service and potluck dinner was held for Gaylan Walker at the Alibi Creek Community Campgrounds, two and a half years after his disappearance. The sum of $20,216.00 has not been withdrawn from the Dax County State Bank.

ACKNOWLEDGEMENTS

I WISH TO EXPRESS MY gratitude to the Iowa Writers' Workshop Summer Graduate Class, PEN Center USA, the UCLA Writers' Extension Program, the Norman Mailer Center, and the following mentors from these institutions and fellowships who offered crucial and constructive criticism that has stayed with me: Lan Samantha Chang, Steve Heller, Ellen Slezak, Ian Randall Wilson, and Jeffery Renard Allen.

Thank you to my agent, Susan Schulman, who read my work without insisting on the usual professional platform, and for believing in a story set in a remote area of the southwest.

At Torrey House Press, thanks to Mark Bailey and Kirsten Allen, co-publishers with a mission for preserving western lands and honoring the literary works of authors who live there; and Anne Terashima, enthusiastic public relations and marketing whiz. Special thanks to Kirsten Allen for her attention, editing skills, and suggestions during the revision process.

And a deep bow to friends and readers for their ongoing encouragement: Anne Cooper, Lorene Garrett, Sheila Blake, Audrie Clifford, Patsy Catlett, and Two Moons.

ABOUT BEV MAGENNIS

BEV MAGENNIS WAS BORN IN Toronto, Canada, and immigrated to the United States in 1964. She received her MA in Art from the Claremont Graduate School, Claremont, California. After a thirty-five-year career as an artist, she started writing, inspired by the land and people in the New Mexico wilderness where she lived for seventeen years. In 2009 she was accepted to the Iowa Writers' Workshop Summer Graduate Class and in 2010 was awarded an eight-month Pen USA Emerging Voices Fellowship. In 2011 she received a Norman Mailer Writers Colony Fiction Fellowship. She lives in New Mexico.

TORREY HOUSE PRESS

The economy is a wholly owned subsidiary of the environment, not the other way around.
—Senator Gaylord Nelson, founder of Earth Day

Torrey House Press is an independent nonprofit publisher promoting environmental conservation through literature. We believe that culture is changed through conversation and that lively, contemporary literature is the cutting edge of social change. We strive to identify exceptional writers, nurture their work, and engage the widest possible audience; to publish diverse voices with transformative stories that illuminate important facets of our ever-changing planet; to develop literary resources for the conservation movement, educating and entertaining readers, inspiring action.

Visit **www.torreyhouse.com** for reading group discussion guides, author interviews, and more.